Who are the Violets Now?

Also by Auberon Waugh
and published by Robin Clark Ltd

The Foxglove Saga
Path of Dalliance
Consider the Lilies
A Bed of Flowers

Auberon Waugh

Who are the Violets Now?

Robin Clark Ltd
London

Published by Robin Clark Ltd 1985
A member of the Namara Group
27/29 Goodge Street, London W1P 1FD

First published in Great Britain by
Chapman and Hall, London 1965

British Library Cataloguing in Publication Data

Waugh, Auberon
    Who are the violets now?
    I. Title
    823′.914[F]   PR6073.A9

    ISBN 086072 091 8

Printed and bound in Great Britain
by Nene Litho and Woolnough Bookbinding
both of Wellingborough, Northants

FOR MY PARENTS

PART ONE

October 1963

Chapter One

MRS QUORN'S DINING ROOM WAS NOT A PLACE WHERE THE men were encouraged to hold general discussion groups after breakfast.

"It looks like war," said Mr Dent. He paid six pounds ten weekly for the first-floor front room, and his opinions were generally treated with some respect. The prospect of war evidently pleased him.

"Christ, how boring," said Ferdie Jacques. At twenty-two he plainly felt that he had just finished fighting two world wars.

Nobody wanted to know what he thought. For three guineas a week in the top-floor back room, Mrs Quorn felt he should be seen but not heard.

"It's ten to nine," she said significantly.

"I suppose we shall all be blown up," said Jacques moodily.

Mr Dent grunted. He might have thought it would do the flower of the nation's youth quite a bit of good to be blown up.

They both looked at the third lodger, who was racing through his fried eggs. Martin Starter was a Captain in the Army Intelligence Corps. If anybody could shed some light on the morning's news, it was he.

"I must dash," he said. Captain Starter, the only lodger at Albany Chambers, Ebury Street, who went to work in a bowler hat, had to be at Whitehall by nine.

"What do you think about this Berlin business?" said Mr Dent.

"Berlin isn't really my province," said Captain Starter. "I'm in S.E. Asia. But if you want to know what I think." He suddenly looked serious, mature and very reasonable. "I think the Ruskies are a bit peeved with us for refusing to sell them those aeroplanes.

9

They're not such bad chaps, when you get to know them. Can't say I blame them."

Mrs Quorn decided that everyone had now had his say.

"You men and your politics," she said. "It's past nine o'clock."

They all knew it wasn't.

"Why can't we sell them their filthy aeroplanes, that's what I would like to know," said young Ferdie Jacques peevishly. He was immediately discounted.

"I must say," said Mr Dent – for six pounds ten a week, he was always allowed the last word – "it would make old Davy Crockett upstairs look silly if they started exploding atom bombs under his pants." The notion appealed to him so much that he broke into a loud cackle.

Mrs Quorn smiled indulgently. "Poor Mr Friendship. He's staying upstairs because he didn't finish his article yesterday, and today's his delivery. He's a much better man than any of you, I dare say." Her manner suggested that if that was the case, she was on the side of the unholy.

Mr Dent agreed. "The man's mad. He spends two days writing a couple of lines of book reviews which don't come out most weeks. Then he spends his evenings listening to a lot of bores talking about the modern world and how important it is that we should all like each other." Mr Dent knew quite well that his landlady loved the bluff, manly sort who paid six pounds ten a week.

She followed him to the front door, where they watched Ferdie Jacques taking his nasty, young Socialist ideas and his enigmatical beard to the advertising offices where he worked.

"Things have come to a pretty pass, Mrs Quorn. Between old Davy Crockett upstairs and young Jacques, I'm surprised that Captain Starter finds there's anything left worth defending." Musing in this vein, he limped to his grey Ford Cortina and drove off to the first address on his list as Area Representative for Three Aces Furniture Limited, of Mangotsfield.

In the front room, top floor of Albany Chambers, Arthur Friendship was writing:

When Mrs B. came into the consulting room, it was clear she had something on her mind. She needed a bit of drawing out, but I was soon able to discover that she was worried because she no longer enjoyed her housework, was listless, and felt tingling in her finger-tips in the early morning.

All the tests showed the normal responses. Her periods were regular. When I had finished my examination, I looked at her steadily for a short time.

"It is a good thing you came to see me, Mrs B." I said. "You have an incipient cardio-vascular aneurism. Now there is no need to be frightened by all those words. 'Incipient' means it is in its early stages. Luckily, you have come in time. It will mean a few days in hospital, and then a week or so of complete rest. No operation is involved."

I saw a look of relief. Obviously, I thought, she is one of those who do not like operations.

After she had gone, I reflected that if all women were as sensible as Mrs B. we doctors would be saved a lot of work – and a lot of families would be spared heartbreak.

Dr Dorkins regrets that he cannot enter into correspondence on individual cases.

Arthur did not enjoy the indignity of having to earn his own living, but the aspect he disliked most was his weekly visit to the offices of *Woman's Dream*. Ronald Carpenter, the editor, had been to school with him, at Bloxham. Neither had excelled as a school-boy. The only difference between them was that Carpenter had gone up in the world, whereas Friendship, as he was prepared to admit himself, had stayed at much the same level. There was no jealousy in their relationship. Carpenter had assumed the import-ance and prestige of being Editor of one of Britain's biggest women's magazines as if born to it. His attitude to Friendship was one of magnanimous bonhomie. Arthur, for his part, loathed and despised Carpenter.

Before he started on the familiar journey, by underground to Temple, then by foot to the *Woman's Dream* offices in Great Turnstile Street, he stood in front of the mirror where he brushed his teeth in the morning, and practised a little speech.

"Here's your copy, Ronald. I hope you enjoy reading it. If it is really good, it might add to your importance and prestige as Editor of *Woman's Dream*. There would be no need to pass on any of the credit to me, of course. I am your superior in every way – intellectually, socially and morally. The reason I could never hold your job is that I did not start with your advantages. For instance, I would not be prepared to put blue rinse in my hair, nor cut it short and brush it forward like a monkey. I was not called Farter at school. That must have been a great help with all the big tycoons. I do not seek any of the importance and prestige of an editor. I am quite happy to earn sixteen pounds a week by writing half the magazine for you."

Arthur Friendship was not an old man, as Mr Dent suggested. He was thirty-two, a particularly sensitive age.

"Mr Carpenter won't keep you a moment, Mr Friendship. Would you like to take a seat."

The gentle, pleading voice of the pretty receptionist was familiar. To begin with, Arthur thought the girl was in love with him, and became most excited. But it was the tone she used for everything, even explaining to a voice on the telephone that it had dialled the wrong number.

He sat down and scanned the current number of *Woman's Dream*. His own contributions were there, so lucid and beautifully written that they seemed to stand out from the paper. Every euphonious syllable contained the essence of poetry, without actually being constructed in verse-form. Beside them, the pull-out knitting supplement and cooking hints appeared shoddy in the extreme. He found he remembered every word of his criticism, and read it anxiously to see what had been cut out. All editorial matter was delivered to the offices nine weeks before it appeared on the book-stalls, but words which are born from the agony of creative travail are not quickly forgotten. Sure enough, a sub-editor had cut out the last sentence.

"Critic's Column" was the only one of Arthur's contributions which appeared under his own name, and the only one in which he took a personal pride. Industry, artifice and all the learning to be derived from an expensive education had been behind his elbow when he wrote his account of an Englishwoman's life with her kangaroo in the South of France, as described in "Jacquetta and I" by Elsie Peartree. The punch had been saved for the end, when Arthur revealed that Jacquetta was, in fact, a kangaroo. But the sub-editor knew better. Whether for reasons of good taste, libel or shortage of space, there was to be no mention of kangaroos.

"Mr Carpenter will see you now, Mr Friendship."

Loathsome Carpenter's office was the only comfortable room in the building.

"What's the Padre got for me this morning?"

"Hello Ronald, you're looking very well." For a moment, the editor seemed uncomfortable, and Arthur rejoiced. He's wondering if I've spotted the blue rinse in his hair, he thought.

"Let's take 'Padre's Hour' first. What's the theme?"

"Christian happiness."

"Go on."

"How Christianity should not always be associated with pro-hibitions – don't do this and don't do that."

"We had that last week."

"It is *the* Christian message of the second half of the twentieth century," said Arthur simply.

"What are we to associate it all with, then?"

"Love."

"Oh, all right."

"I get in a piece about Christians making themselves felt in the modern world and mention the series of lectures sponsored by Education for Peace and run by my colleague Arthur Friendship."

13

"All right, all right," said the appalling Carpenter. "You know, Arthur . . ." there was a sadistic gleam in his eye which Arthur did not like, "I think we may be sacking the Reverend Cliff Roebuck from 'Padre's Hour' soon and getting a newer man."

"Why?" Eight pounds a week was more than he could afford to lose.

"Keep your hair on. You can do the writing. It's just that the male model we used for the photograph of the Reverend Roebuck in his study on top of the column, also appeared in last week's *Woman's Dream* in shortie pyjamas as the Lucky Daddy whose wife ailows him to eat Oxo in Bed."

"There's no reason why Roebuck should not be the lucky Daddy."

"It confuses the image," said Carpenter. There was no answering that. Carpenter knew all about images, and Friendship didn't. That was why Carpenter, with his bright blue hair, had all the importance and prestige. . . .

"There's been some trouble about one of your book reviews," said Carpenter. He started reading.

"The story of a beautiful friendship between two youthful old women, Elsie Peartree, who is sixty-three, and Jacquetta, who would be getting on for seventy. Both are a little eccentric. For instance, Jacquetta calls Elsie every morning by bounding into her bed with yelps of joy. For a toilet Jacquetta prefers to use the coal scuttle in the living room. Why is Elsie eccentric? Well, even she would admit, I expect, that it is a tiny bit eccentric to live at such close quarters with Jacquetta."

"Yes, I know," said Arthur.

"If it's one of your intellectual things, Arthur, I'm afraid that's the end."

"The last sentence was cut out. It should have read: 'For Jacquetta, you see, is a kangaroo'."

"Luckily, not many people read 'Critic's Column'. I'm thinking of giving it up. Perhaps you would like to take over Pets' Corner, with your interest in animals."

Arthur explained that he would not. He knew that Carpenter

had no intention of giving up "Critic's Column". It was far and away the best thing in the magazine.

Arthur said he could not go to a party given by Mr Condiment, the proprietor of *Woman's Dream*, that evening, because he had a lecture. Carpenter knew that.

"What's the subject?"

"Education for Peace."

"Jolly topical, what with the Berlin crisis."

As Arthur was going out, Carpenter said:

"This Dorkins piece – aneurisms aren't anything to do with cancer, are they?"

"I don't think so. It says something about rupture of the arterial coats."

Although Doctor Dorkins was unable to enter into correspondence on individual cases, he received about fourteen letters a week, almost all from middle-aged women enquiring whether they had got cancer. Any mention of the disease was banned.

"Sounds all right. Have a good meeting."

Even Carpenter did not dare scoff at the idea of Peace, although at times he came perilously close to it.

"Before Mr Besant arrives, I should like to tell you of our future arrangements. Next week and the week after, we are going to hear Mr Thomas Gray, the well-known campaigner for racial relations, talk on his subject, racial relations in the modern world. Mr Gray is an American of African descent who now works for U N E S C O and is a leading spirit behind the movement for better race relations in America. The week after, we are having a man from the Egg Marketing Board who is going to talk about egg production and distribution in the – er – modern world. We are hoping to arrange a visit to Slough where we can see for ourselves how eggs are actually produced in present-day conditions. Then at the end of the month, on Friday, 21st, we are having a single talk from Mr I. G. Andreyer, the well-known Soviet agronomist, on Soviet advances in agriculture. This will include lantern slides on new methods of crop rotation and soil fertility programmes which have never before been seen outside Russia. I think we shall discover that there is a great deal that we in the Western world can learn from the other side of the Iron Curtain, and many of our preconceptions on these vital matters will be challenged."

Arthur faced the alert row of faces, and congratulated himself again on such a rich and varied programme. Out of fourteen people enrolled for the course, sixteen had turned up. One of the extras was obviously a tramp, who had come in from the cold and probably hoped for a cup of tea. The other was a lean, hatchet-faced young man who sat taking notes furiously. Arthur made a mental note to ask him for one and sixpence attendance fee. It would pay for his petrol both ways.

Ferdie Jacques made a signal from the door of the Assembly room. Mr Besant had arrived. Arthur was well used to these entrances. Tall, benevolent, and stooped Mr Besant roamed absent-mindedly into the room.

"Good evening, everybody. I hope I haven't kept you all waiting." Besant was the only man in the world whom Arthur respected. Like Arthur, he was an idealist, who kept his passionate beliefs hidden under a mask of urbanity and genial distinction.

"Mr Besant needs no introduction from me," said Arthur. "You already know more about him than I dare say he knows about himself." Only Mr Besant chuckled. Arthur made the same joke each time he introduced the Director of International Peace Studies. "Mr Besant is not only the Director of our movement. He is also the inspiration behind it and countless other schemes to educate us for peace. Although an extremely busy man, he always tries to put in an appearance in the course of each – um – course to see the students and answer any questions they might have." Arthur was never at his best in front of Mr Besant. Perhaps he was too anxious to create a good impression.

"Well, I don't really believe much in making speeches," said Mr Besant. "After six weeks of your nine-week course, you must have a pretty good idea of what it is all about. But before I pass the ball into your court, as it were, I should like to say a few words about the new concept of Peace. Up to now, people have been prepared to accept Peace as meaning little more than the absence of war. With post-war developments, like nuclear weapons and the great hungry masses of Asia and Africa on our doorstep, we are going to have to re-define our ideas about peace in terms of what we might call modern reality. Peace should be something tangible, like cheese, not something abstract, like hot air. Peace is something living, an organism deriving its nourishment from international goodwill. It is not peace if there is disagreement under the surface.

"The one vital pre-requisite for peace is World Government, and there can be no World Government while there are two opposed systems in the world. First, we must build the base. There are three alternatives – the full blooded Stalinist system; the somewhat *arcane* capitalist system which we know; or the effective compromise between the two, pioneered by Khruschev in Russia.

"I am sometimes asked where I stand. You may say it is impertinent, but I am not ashamed of anything. I am a Liberal. I have not always been, but as one gets older, one realizes what every intelligent person must realize, that we have a lot to learn from the other side, if only we can persuade them to trust us and teach us.

"We may even teach them about fish and chips, in time, and Association Football."

Mr Besant sat down, smiling benevolently at the titters which greeted this sally. With his lean face and silver hair, he might have been the Chairman of an Insurance Company or a Cabinet Minister. But he, like Arthur, had decided to devote his life to improving the world. Throughout the Victoria Assembly Room, the air was charged with the electric sensation of people taking part in important events.

Much the same atmosphere prevailed in the Princess Ida Room of the Savoy Hotel, where Mr Condiment, Chairman of Strand Publications, was entertaining his senior executives.

"We've gained three thousand from *Woman*, but *Woman's Own* are still putting on weight. Why's that?"

"I think it was the eight-page cosmetics pull-out. Ours is scheduled for the end of July, for people to take on holiday with them."

"Cosmetics are old hat. What we want is new men with new ideas." Everybody began to feel uncomfortable, as they always did in Mr Condiment's company after seven o'clock. "What is the modern woman really interested in?"

Mr Carpenter felt he was being put to the test.

"Romance. Animal stories. Children. Home hints. Cooking. Body beautiful. Personal problems. Fun with the stars. . . ." It was no good. He was not putting himself over. "Illnesses. Cancer," he finished hopelessly.

"Cancer," said Mr Condiment. "You may have something there. This is just an idea mind you. What about a shock issue: *The Cancer-Ridden Society*. Or, put it another way: *Have I got cancer?*"

"I hardly think . . ." said Mr Carpenter.

"Of course you don't," said Mr Condiment wittily. The idea was taking shape. Soon it would become an inspiration. "List all the symptoms. Make it fairly comprehensive – we don't want anybody to be excluded. Tiredness after work, occasional headaches, sore feet after excessive walking. Hangover after a night on the tiles. General feeling of being not so young as you used to be."

"Tingling in the fingertips," said Mr Carpenter.

"Brilliant," said Mr Condiment. "Then get hold of a few real cancer patients, and let them explain in their own words how it feels. Give diagrams of all the places cancer can get at you. Get all your medical experts on the job. Who's your chief man for medicine?"

"He's called Arthur Friendship. But I don't think. . . ."

"We know you don't think. Leave this one to me. I am going to take personal charge of a shock issue – *Cancer In Our Time. Woman's Dream* joins the crusade to keep cancer out. Send Mr Friendship to see me on Monday morning."

18

This request particularly annoyed Mr Carpenter. He thought it a very bad thing that his subordinates should be on speaking terms with the managing director. He comforted himself with the reflexion that Arthur would have to answer all the eight or nine thousand letters from cancer enthusiasts.

"The present Berlin crisis, again, is typical of the sort of world we live in," said Mr Besant, in answer to a question by Miss Margaret Holly, eighteen.

"But aren't the Russians being a bit aggressive, shutting off access to West Berlin like that?" said Miss Holly.

"Well, we must try and look at it from the East German's point of view," said Mr Besant, very maturely. "We wouldn't like it very much if half of London was suddenly occupied by the Russians, for instance. That is what the American occupation of West Berlin looks like to them. Of course, they may be being unreasonable. But they have done everything they can to prevent incidents. The Berlin Wall, which Western propagandists have exploited so unscrupulously, was built with the very good idea of preventing incidents which might escalate into warfare. We must try not to be taken in too much by our own propaganda."

"Mr Jacques," said Arthur, slightly embarrassed. Jacques was always embarrassing.

"Why can't the Americans get out of West Berlin?"

Mr Besant smiled indulgently. "We shouldn't be too impetuous. That is, of course, what must happen eventually. But the Americans don't want to lose face, any more than any of us do. We must give them time."

"Now, I think it is time we adjourned for refreshment," said Arthur. "Oh no. Miss – ha, ha – Elizabeth Pedal."

No wonder Arthur laughed nervously. It was not so much that Elizabeth Pedal was beautiful. She had that radiance, that perfection in every feature and exquisite assurance which marked her out as semi-divine. Every lecture was an agonizing struggle for Arthur between desire to feast his eyes on her and embarrassment lest she should discover him staring. How such a person came to be attending the nine weeks' course on International Affairs organised by UNESCO and Education for Peace was anybody's guess. No doubt she coveted the diploma which was thought to be a recommendation in certain kinds of employment. But such an angel had only to smile once and every diploma, degree or doctorate that had ever been invented would fall into her lap.

Mr Besant seemed less impressed by her loveliness. "Yes, Peace Education also functions behind the Iron Curtain," he said, almost abruptly, in answer to her question. "Indeed, much of the inspiration originally came from there, so it is scarcely surprising."

"Mr Milchiger," said a voice. It was the fair, hatchet-faced stranger.

"We have no time for any more questions. If Miss – ha, ha – Elizabeth Pedal is satisfied with her last answer, we shall now adjourn for tea and coffee next door.

When he was alone that night in Albany Chambers, Arthur put on a record of Tchaikovsky's Sixth Symphony, softly, so as not to disturb Ferdie Jacques next door. On second thoughts, he put it up slightly louder, reckoning that it would do the youth good to hear some first class music. There could be nobody so insensitive as to be unaffected by it. As the melody surged around him, he stood in front of the mirror where he cleaned his teeth in the morning and addressed himself to the under-developed nations of the world. His face softened in compassion.

"Come to me," he said, "come to me."

When the record came to an end, he climbed into bed and tried not to think of the hauntingly lovely Elizabeth Pedal.

Chapter Two

SATURDAY MORNING WAS NEVER THE LIVELIEST OF OCCASIONS in Albany Chambers. Mrs Quorn made no secret of the fact that she preferred her gentlemen to be asked away for the week-end. It just so happened that this week Arthur had decided to stay in London. His many friends who were giving houseparties in the country would be disappointed, of course, but, in an odd sort of way, Arthur found he liked the peace and quiet of London in the week-end after all the bustle and turmoil of the week.

Mrs Quorn was not impressed. Arthur had produced the same excuse for the last fourteen weeks. He had two grand friends. One, Lord Hargreaves, worked as a Management Consultant for Shell and lived in Purley. The other was the close friend of a cousin of the Queen Mother, which gave Arthur a personal insight into the affairs of the Royal Family.

"Such a sweet girl, Alexandra," he would say. "We were all so pleased she decided to marry Angus Ogilvie."

Mrs Quorn liked that, but it did not quite make up for everything else.

Captain Starter always spent his week-ends playing golf. This annoyed Mr Dent, who would have liked to talk about the news from Berlin. But Captain Starter believed quite firmly that world affairs came to a halt on Friday evenings. Mr Dent did not consider Arthur or Ferdie Jacques important enough to discuss anything, so after cheerfully assuring them that they would all be reduced to radio-active dust by the evening he climbed into his grey Ford Cortina and went to a film called *Naked as Nature Intended* in Tooting Bec.

"Serve him bloody well right if he is blown up," said Ferdie. Arthur said nothing, because he felt Mrs Quorn might be listening. He reflected that Ferdie would not mind much if the whole world was blown up, so long as his own survival was assured. All the young man required out of life was a Wimpy Bar, a record player, an endless supply of tipped cigarettes and a few teen-aged puppets of either sex with whom he could shout appropriate slogans in moments of excitement.

It was inconceivable that anyone so base could understand the great and wonderful vision of Mr Besant: Peace, as tangible as cheese, the inspiration which kept Arthur Friendship alive in the fullest sense of the word through all the indignities of having to earn his own living and write about women's monthly periods. There was nothing that Arthur did not know about women's monthly periods. But it was all for peace.

Arthur reflected that it was also impossible to imagine Ferdie alive in the ideal society which he and Mr Besant were striving to build. There would be no ugliness, no rancour. All the nations of the world would work together in loving harmony. He, Mr Besant and the lovely Elizabeth Pedal would sit watching the world go by, smiling serenely at each other, their labours accomplished.

"What did you think of last night's meeting?" he said.

"It didn't achieve much, did it?" said Ferdie. He had wanted to propose a motion condemning West German militarism. Arthur felt it was nothing to do with the course of studies.

"We are strictly non-political," he said. It was like explaining to a Dominican inquisitor of the Counter-Reformation that he was strictly non-sectarian. "I saw you making friends with that new arrival."

Ferdie bridled. He did not believe in being friends with people. It suggested weakness.

"He was a nut case. I think he may have been queer."

"What was he called?"

Ferdie produced a bit of paper from his pocket.

"Mr T. Milchiger," he said. "He told me to call him Johnny the Milkman."

"I wonder why," said Arthur.

"He seemed to have developed a passion for Mr Besant. Said he had never heard such a lucid and brilliant speaker. Wanted to know all about him, what he had done in his life, where he was going to speak again."

"Probably a foreigner," said Arthur, reflecting on what a wonderful thing it was to be able to inspire men. Nobody – Napoleon, Henry V, Shakespeare himself – could possibly inspire Ferdie Jacques. "I don't know why you should think he was a homosexual." Arthur was particularly sensitive to this form of innuendo. He was aware that in this unsatisfactory age it had become customary to marry younger than was considered usual before, and that as a bachelor of thirty-two, he was immediately suspect.

But he was not a homosexual, nor anything remotely resembling one. He generally found younger people of his own sex particularly revolting. And Ferdie Jacques was no exception. As he sat in his dirty flannel trousers, the mysterious line around his jawbone bristling indignantly, Ferdie seemed to personify all the horror and moral depravity conjured by the words "homosexual acts between consenting adults in private".

"We've got some very good talent in this course of lectures," said Arthur.

"What?" said Ferdie.

"The birds," said Arthur.

"What birds?"

"You know, the girls." It was very difficult to communicate with the younger generation. They did not seem to understand even their own ridiculous idiom.

"What are you talking about?" said Ferdie, as if he suspected an insult.

"I said that one or two of the girls in evening class are extremely attractive."

"Who would that be?" said Ferdie, becoming interested.

"You know. Miss What's-she-called. That small, neat, dark one with the lovely skin. Miss – ah – Miss – yes, that's it, Miss Pedal. Ha ha."

"You fancy Liz Pedal, do you?" said Jacques thoughtfully. "Yes, I thought I might have a shot at her myself."

Arthur hardly took in Ferdie's words at first. His heart always missed a beat when he uttered the divine creature's name, and he was recovering from the shock. He thought he had handled it well – lightly, carelessly, almost flippantly. Then the full import struck him, and he was aghast.

"Do you love her?" he asked.

"Steady on," said Ferdie. "I hardly know her. She looks quite easy-going, although I am not sure she is very mature yet. I sometimes get the impression she isn't being serious. But strictly speaking, she is the sort that appeals to me."

Arthur was appalled. The young man could surely not mean that he planned to have sexual intercourse. What else could he mean? "How far would you propose to go?"

"As far as she'd let me."

"You must be mad. You can't just go round having sexual intercourse with anyone you like."

"Why not?"

Arthur was out of his depths. Ferdie was only ten years his junior, but they had no common ground for argument at all. Arthur knew that Ferdie was not a Christian, but he had mistakenly supposed that he was at least a human being. Ferdie saved him the trouble of replying.

"Sorry. I forgot you were an R.C. But young people today who are not R.C.'s just aren't like you any more. If they have a meaningful relationship with a girl that's really meaningful, then they are not doing anything wrong because they are educating themselves."

Arthur had heard it all before. *Woman's Dream* remained orthodox on these matters, but some of the other women's magazines in the group, for the younger type of woman, had pioneered this line of reasoning as long ago as the 1950's.

"What makes you think she would look at you, anyway?" The man who finally conquered Elizabeth Pedal's heart – speculation was agonizing, but one had to be realistic – would have to be as

24

brave as a lion, as tender as a dove, as handsome as Apollo, as gay as Alcibiades, as wise as Solon . . . there could be no doubt, Ferdie Jacques did not fit the bill.

"I don't know, you know," said Ferdie. "Most girls are the same. Basically all they want is two legs and a thruster."

As if she had been waiting for a cue, Mrs Quorn burst into the room. "I don't know how long you young gentlemen propose to sit here," she said.

"As a matter of fact, we were just going," said Ferdie, as if delivering a tremendous snub. "Come on Arthur."

Arthur loathed and despised Jacques, but fascination held him. "Where to?"

"We might go and get a snack in the National Gallery, if you could give me a lift on your scooter." As they mounted he said: "You know, Arthur, you ought to have been a priest."

Mr Besant was being kept very busy at his suite of rooms in the Hilton. Nobody had informed him there was going to be another Berlin crisis, and he was offended.

"How can I conceivably have my preparations made if I am not informed of what is happening?" he said testily into the telephone. "A lot of my work is being undone. What do the East Germans think they're doing? Nobody told me anything until Thursday evening, when it was too late."

The voice at the other end spoke for several minutes.

"Of course the English don't want to be involved," said Mr Besant. When he rang off, he sighed. He had a meeting to address in the afternoon, an appointment at the Foreign Office immediately afterwards, and now his superiors wanted him to arrange a meeting with the Prime Minister. There was a discreet buzz from his desk, as if a grasshopper had stirred in its sleep.

"Yes," he snapped.

"There is a Mr Milchiger on the telephone who wishes to speak to you. He has rung several times."

"Tell him it is impossible. I am too busy."

"He says it is urgent."

"I have never heard of him. Tell him to write in the normal way and arrange an appointment."

"I am sorry, Mr Milchiger," said the Secretary, who was Sinhalese, down the telephone. "I am afraid Mr Besant is out. I suggest you try again this evening. Goodbye."

All the tenderness and yearning of young love were in that "Goodbye", but Mr. Milchiger, who was in a telephone box in Park Lane, threw down the receiver with a curse.

Arthur had played with the idea of becoming a priest when he was converted to Rome five years before. But, on reflection, he did not think he took his religion quite as seriously as that. The celibacy of the clergy was a point in its favour, but some of the other aspects of a vocational life dismayed him. He had a horror of babies and the thought of having to baptise them by the score every week for the rest of his life was a strong deterrent. Even the Editor of *Woman's Dream* had not yet submitted him to this particular indignity.

Also, his conversion had been conditional on the truth of the major proposition. Even when Mgr Potinue had sprinkled his head and intoned the sacred words, Arthur was aware that he was only ninety per cent convinced that there was such a thing as a God; if there was such a Thing, he was prepared to go the whole hog and accept Heaven, Hell, Purgatory, limbo – the lot. Even if there was not such a Thing, his ten per cent margin had reasoned, there was nothing to be lost by pretending there was. If, after death, all the fury and passion of Arthur Friendship's soul was extinguished like a candle – and commonsense recoiled from the idea – then there would be no-one to mock him for his credulity. But if Arthur Friendship's soul, transformed into an object of exquisite purity after death, browsed through fresh fields and pastures new, then it was he who was going to laugh, and the non-believers – Ferdie Jacques, Mr Besant, the unspeakable Ronald Carpenter – who were going to look silly.

However, with the passing of the years – and Arthur felt he had matured more than most – there was a shift in the margin. After the Vatican Council, piously deplored by all sane Catholics, and the brief but terrible reign of Good Pope John, the Catholic Church seemed to offer little which the other Churches hadn't got. With the threat to remove Latin from much of the Mass, and expose its ancient subtleties to the banality of tired English phrases, Arthur found that the proportion of his conscious mind which was prepared to accept that the whole structure was built on make-believe had grown to around forty per cent. He was still ready to defend his Church against Anglicans, whom he particularly detested as hypocrites and prevaricators, but against frank paganism he was more reticent.

In any case, most of his idealism was taken up nowadays in the campaign for World Peace.

When Ferdie and Arthur reached Admiralty Arch, they were stopped by a policeman who said that Trafalgar Square was closed to traffic for a public meeting.

"Oh boy," said Ferdie, rubbing his hands, "who are they?"

"Beatniks," said the policeman. Arthur took his number.

They parked their scooter outside the fluted elegance of Carlton House, and ran into the square.

Although there had been only three days in which to organise the demonstration, there was a good turn-out, and high spirited groups with banners filled the square.

"Labour, Labour, Labour," shouted Ferdie. "Who's organizing this demo?" When he was told, he said: "Christian bloody Action."

A pleasant young man had his arm round the waist of a girl with a banner which said "Verwoerd OUT."

"I know," he said, "but they had the square booked, and we had to go somewhere for this Berlin business. Nobody's prepared."

"Peace is indivisible," boomed a voice down the microphone. "We cannot blame the Communists, we cannot blame the Americans. . . ."

Loud boos, and shouts of "Peace, now. Peace, now."

27

". . . We must blame ourselves. Now let this mighty throng stand in silence for two minutes, while we all pray, in whatever manner we know, for peace in Berlin."

"Peace, now. Peace now. Peace now," shouted the Young Anarchist League from Bromley. Obviously, they did not favour the contemplative method of prayer.

Next to them, the group of Young Communists from Eltham was trying a more sophisticated slogan requiring organization and initiative. "We don't want to be YANKED into war. We don't want to be YANKED into war."

But the effort was too much, and only one voice continued the message, when all around had faltered. It came from a girl of about twenty, who looked most appealing in a black plastic mackintosh. Arthur loved her at first sight, but then he fell in love with most pretty girls he saw at a distance. Somehow, her presence reassured him that beauty, wisdom and goodness resided in the cause of Peace. When he was with Ferdie, he was not quite so sure.

"We don't want to be YANKED into war," shouted Arthur loyally, above the babble of noise.

At one moment, it looked as if there was going to be a scuffle between the Anarchists from Bromley and the Communists from Eltham over their rival slogans, but it was broken up by the Catholics Against Nuclear Warfare who said "Sh. . . ."

They carried a banner showing an enormous portrait of Pope John, with the caption, somewhat unhappily chosen, PEACE IN OUR TIME.

Arthur supposed that his place was to be marching alongside the Catholics Against Nuclear Warfare. But they did not look a particularly enticing crowd, and, besides, he liked to preserve his independence.

After two minutes' silence, described in the *Daily Telegraph* next morning as the most moving and eloquent moment, another voice floated out from the loudspeaker over the crowd:

"As we meet in this time of troublous strife, we must not lose sight of what we are working for. Peace is not just our ideal. It is our goal. It is not something abstract, either, like the hot air we breathe. It is as tangible and real as a piece of cheese. And like cheese, too, it can be a source of nourishment, both physical and spiritual, to the nations of the world."

"Christ, Besant has gone religious," said Ferdie.

"Shut up," said Arthur. "I want to listen."

Mr Besant appeared carried away by the enormous throng and his own popularity. "We must march for peace, we must fight for peace. We must die for peace."

"Peace now," shouted the multitude. "Peace now. Peace, now."

A tall man with fair hair and a hatchet face pushed past them.

"It's Johnny the Milkman," shouted Ferdie.

The man turned round, looking preoccupied. "Milchiger," he said.

"Old Besant is doing his stuff. Just listen to him."

"It is amazing," said Mr Milchiger. "Such magnetism. People would follow him to the ends of the earth." He had a camera round his neck, and was pushing his way through the crowd, presumably to photograph his idol.

"I call that rather disgusting," said Ferdie. "Besant is at least twice his age. Do you think he sticks the photographs up in his bedroom?"

"Not at all," said Arthur. "And it is absolutely true. Mr Besant has magnetism."

"Well, it takes all sorts to make a movement," said Ferdie, giving him an odd look.

After Mr Besant had finished his piece, a rather dim Labour politician from the Midlands stood up and started talking about Britain's moral leadership of the world; when he moved to the starving millions of Asia, Ferdie and Arthur began to think of their lunch.

The National Gallery canteen was nearly deserted. They ate fried fish fingers with tomato ketchup, followed by a pork pie, and drank tea.

29

"Nobody here," said Ferdie. "It's funny how the slightest threat of war sends everybody visiting their old aunties in the country."

"Do you think the Russians are really serious this time?" said Arthur, beginning to feel a little frightened.

"Of course they are," said Ferdie. "None of us is going to war for a lot of Huns who are mostly ex-Nazis anyway."

They both sensed that they were veterans of the Hitler war. One of the reasons they felt so bitterly against Spain and Portugal was because they had fought through six long years to preserve Britain from that kind of thing. A few even extended this vicarious involvement to the Spanish war, but that was not the consensus. Arthur, who was ten when the war ended, and Ferdie, who was not yet born, tacitly agreed that they had been present at the liberation of Belsen, and had seen for themselves the logical consequence of policies which are right off centre.

"Some people say the Germans have changed," said Arthur timidly.

"Why should they have changed?" said Ferdie scornfully. "Nazis have still got all the top jobs. They have suppressed the peace movements in West Germany. Many of the war criminals are still alive, just waiting for an amnesty. If people think we're all going to be incinerated for that crowd, they've got another think coming."

After lunch, they wandered round the gallery, engaging in a desultory conversation about modern art.

"I just don't think it's beautiful, that's all," said Arthur, becoming bored.

"People didn't think Leonardo da Vinci was beautiful at first. All artists are ahead of their times," said Ferdie.

"Some people thought Leonardo's work was beautiful," said Arthur, wondering if he was going to spend the whole day with Ferdie.

"Some people think John Sturgeon's work is beautiful. And Dave Williams's," said Ferdie, naming two fashionable abstract painters of the time. "Me," he added.

"No, you don't," said Arthur. "You can't."

They were standing in front of the Madonna of the Rocks. Arthur had not meant to speak loudly, but he was so bored by the conversation that he had tried to put some feeling into his voice, and the result had sounded like a challenge to a fight.

Nothing loth, Ferdie turned to face him. "Who says I can't?"

For a moment, they each read the hatred in each other's eyes. When the moment was passed, they forgot it again. Looking over Arthur's shoulder, Ferdie said: "Why, look who's here," in a slightly American voice.

It was Miss Margaret Holly, eighteen, and another girl of the same age.

"Fancy meeting you here," said Ferdie suggestively.

"Hello, Ferdie, I don't know what you're doing here, either," said Miss Holly coyly. Most of human communication is made through such inane remarks, reflected Arthur sombrely. "This is Susan," said Miss Holly, as if reluctant to impart the information.

"Hello," said Susan.

"Arthur and me were wondering just what two such lovely girls were doing all alone on a Saturday afternoon," said Ferdie.

"We're not alone. We're with each other," said Miss Holly.

"Come and join us for a cup of tea," said Ferdie.

Arthur's stomach turned over at the thought, but he was willing to pay any price to avoid another dialogue between himself and Ferdie. "Yes, do," he said.

Both the girls looked at him, and Arthur blushed. They looked back at Ferdie. "We haven't had our lunch yet."

"Have it on us," said Ferdie magnanimously.

They went back to the canteen and ordered more fish fingers.

"Fish fingers," said Miss Holly. "I think they're jolly good."

"Yes, aren't they?" said Susan.

"It's funny you know," said Arthur, to get a conversation going. "I don't care for them all that much."

"Not care for them?" said Miss Holly. "You must be mad."

"I like them," said Susan.

"You don't want to pay any attention to Arthur," said Ferdie.

Under the table, he had just put his hand on Miss Holly's thigh. "He's a bit peculiar in what he says. He loves the things, really."

"No I don't," said Arthur, the controversial voice. "I have never much liked them."

"Yes he does," said Ferdie, who was stroking Miss Holly's thigh, and had exchanged glances with her. "He had some for lunch."

"He didn't," said Miss Holly, half-heartedly shaking Ferdie off. "Did you really?"

"I like them," said Susan. "I like the sauce, too."

"Did you really have them for lunch?" Ferdie's hand was back, unresisted.

The controversial voice was silent.

"You see he did," said Ferdie.

"He must be bonkers," said Miss Holly. "Fancy saying you don't like something, then ordering it for lunch."

Arthur could not be bothered to point out that the events had not occurred in that order. It was too undignified and trivial. In any case, something – whether the fish fingers or not – had brought on an acute discomfort.

"Excuse me a moment," he said.

When he came out of the lavatory, Ferdie was standing by the washbasins. He moved up to the next washbasin.

"I didn't like to ask you in front of the girls," said Ferdie, "but you don't happen to carry a spare protective around with you, do you?"

"A spare what?" said Arthur, while his mind tried to sort out the implications of this request.

"French letter. Sorry, I forgot you were R.C. I always carry them around myself, but left them back at Ma Quorn's. I can't take Margaret there. You'll have to run me over and fetch them." While Arthur was deliberating, Ferdie said: "Hurry up, or the girls will think something peculiar is going on. You go out first."

When Arthur returned to the table, Miss Holly said: "Where on earth have you been?"

Arthur said: "I'm sorry, it was the fish fingers," and he sat down.

Susan was wiping her plate with some bread to catch the last sauce. "They were delicious," she said. "Thanks very much."

The remark addressed his attention to a bill on the table, for seven shillings and tenpence. Arthur picked it up and paid, swearing inwardly.

When Ferdie came out, he said: "Where shall we all go to?" He and Miss Holly looked at each other and smiled.

Susan looked at Arthur, who blushed. She looked him up and down. He blushed deeper, and counted the toes inside his shoes.

"Actually I think I've got some letters to write," she said.

"Oh, don't go," said Ferdie, insincerely.

Susan looked at Arthur again. "I am afraid I must, really," she said.

Damn, thought Arthur, just my luck. "I've got to get back, too," he said. "Lots of work to do."

"Oh dear, must you leave us, too?" said Miss Holly, with a hint of mockery.

"It's an extraordinary thing about Arthur," said Ferdie. "He's always working. Writes these reviews, you know. Never knows what hour they're going to be needed. But don't go yet, Susan. Arthur's got to take me back to fetch something."

For the first time, Miss Holly looked uncomfortable. "Be quick," she said.

"It's an extraordinary thing about Ferdie," said Arthur maliciously. "He never seems to know when he's going to need things."

But the joke fell flat, as nobody seemed to know what he was talking about.

On the way across Trafalgar Square, nothing was said. When they reached Carlton House, Arthur spoke:

"Do you know Margaret well?"

"Only spoken to her twice before this afternoon."

One part of Arthur was appalled by this callous immorality. The other was intrigued. As he drove down the Mall, he debated to himself whether "immorality" or "amorality" was the more appropriate term. At Buckingham Palace, the sixty-per-cent pure

33

Christian had asserted itself, and he began to wonder whether he was sharing in the guilt of Ferdie's sin. He remembered the ways in which it was possible to share the guilt of another's sin – by counsel, command, consent, provocation, praise and flattery, concealment, being a partner, silence and by defending the ill done.

If he did share the guilt, it was most unfair, as he had none of the fun. On the other hand, if Ferdie were treated, casuistically, as an amoral animal, then there should be no guilt to share. Conversely, it would be possible to share in the non-existent guilt of two amoral animals if one derived pleasure from assisting them in the act. Arthur decided that he derived no pleasure, and that his conscience was clear.

At Albany Chambers, Ferdie bolted upstairs on his bestial errand, and Arthur reflected that he would be alone again that evening.

"Goodbye, Margaret, have a good time," he said suggestively when they were outside the National Gallery again. But Margaret thought the remark in bad taste, and Ferdie did not seem to hear it. "Goodbye, Susan," he said.

"Goodbye Arthur. Thanks again for the lovely lunch." Susan genuinely seemed sorry to see him go.

If she wants me to make love to her, thought Arthur savagely as he drove away, she should say so. In any case, he had far more important things to attend to than womanising.

He drove to the King's Road, where he watched *Kind Hearts and Coronets* in the Classic Cinema, for the fourth time. The newsreel had not yet caught up with the Berlin crisis, and its main feature was a beauty contest in Blackpool. As he went into the Chinese restaurant next door for a lonely supper, he saw the evening newspaper placards: "German guns open fire".

He bought a copy, but there was no mention of war on the front page. On an inside page there was reference to the fact that some German artillery units sent to Wales for exercises had started practice on the ranges. Arthur realized that he had been tricked out of threepence, and swore never to buy another evening newspaper.

After supper he felt slightly ill, as he always did after Chinese food. In his own bedroom, he stared dismally at himself in the mirror above the washbasin. Ferdie was not back. Presumably he was pursuing his meaningful relationship in Miss Holly's flat. He looked at himself again, but found he had nothing to say.

Wordlessly, he climbed into bed.

In another part of London, east of Whitechapel Road, a second lonely figure was preparing himself for bed. As Ferdie had predicted, the walls were covered with photographs of Mr Besant, at different moments in his career.

In one corner of the room, a hatchet-faced man covered his head with his hands and prayed.

Chapter Three

ARTHUR SELDOM RECEIVED A TELEPHONE CALL AT ALBANY Chambers, and Mrs Quorn's interruption during breakfast caused a minor sensation.

"You mark my words, he's courting," said Captain Starter, who always took the charitable view.

Mr Dent was not interested. Ferdie Jacques, who had returned to the Chambers at four o'clock in the morning, was totally self-absorbed.

"Go on with what you were saying," said Mr Dent.

Captain Starter, to illustrate his point, had built a little house out of Mr Dent's visiting cards.

"The whole Far East is like a house of cards," he said, after a little thought. "Each of these cards represents a country. This one is Laos, this one Cambodia, this one Thailand, these are the two Vietnams, and at the very bottom here is Indonesia, Malaysia and the Phillipines."

"These ones here," said Mr Dent intelligently, poking at them with the stem of his pipe.

"Now, I want you to see what is going to happen if I take one of them away."

"They're all going to fall down," guessed Mr Dent.

"Exactly," said Captain Starter. He removed Indonesia, and they all fell down.

"Then what happens?" asked Mr Dent.

"Exactly," said Captain Starter, "then what happens."

"We all get blown up," said Mr Dent, highly tickled by the idea.

"Not necessarily," said Captain Starter.

"What's the point of the Far East, then?" said Mr Dent.

"Anyway, we're all going to be blown up because of these Huns. Now then, Jacques, you're an intelligent young man. Which would you rather be, blown up for a lot of Huns, or be raped by a battalion of Chinese soldiers? Heh heh."

Ferdie scowled. He knew he was intelligent. "The Chinese do not permit homosexuality," he said.

"Hard luck on old Davy Crockett, that," said the irrepressible Mr Dent. "No wonder he's so keen on peace at any price."

"Still, we hope it won't come to that," said Captain Starter." You had to be quite mature in his job. "And we don't know for certain that Friendship is queer."

It was the odious Mr Carpenter on the telephone.

"I'm afraid I can't tell you what Mr Condiment wants to see you for. No doubt he will tell you himself."

"That's all very well, Ronald, but he must know that it is extremely inconvenient for me. My whole day is thrown out. Can you tell me if it is urgent?"

"Now put yourself in my shoes, Arthur. I can't betray my Chairman's confidence. If I did that, I wouldn't be here." Enjoying all that prestige and importance, thought Arthur bitterly. "Can't you wait for Mr Condiment to tell you himself?"

"Please, Ronald," said Arthur, with a sob of mortified pride. There was he, the Captain of School Fencing, on his knees, metaphorically speaking, before Farter Carpenter, the most unpopular boy of his year. "Please, Ronald. Can you tell me if it is anything to do with my review of that Elsie Peartree book."

"It may be and it may not be," said the vile Carpenter. "You must wait and see Mr Condiment."

It would be the first time Arthur had ever met Mr Condiment. He could not help feeling a little important, as he walked back to the dining room. He would certainly give the Chairman a piece of his mind. On second thoughts, perhaps it would be more prudent to try the cool approach.

Only the amoral animal Jacques was left in the dining room. "Who was it," said Ferdie. "Elizabeth Pedal?"

"It might have been, and it might not have been," said Arthur.

The atrocious Mr Carpenter always kept Arthur waiting ten minutes. At Strand House, he was kept waiting thirty-five.

"I hope you weren't kept waiting, Mr Friendship. There was a Board Meeting. Now, what have you come to see me about?"

"I was told you wanted to see me, Sir."

"Well, so I do. I am always glad to meet my employees."

However humble, thought Arthur bitterly.

"What do you think it was all about?"

Arthur explained the Elsie Peartree episode. Mr Condiment heard him out. He always heard his subordinates out.

"So what?" he said at the end. He always liked to keep his subordinates on their toes.

Fortunately, Arthur had his answer ready. "If there is any question of a libel action, I suggest we should fight it on the alternative plea."

"Alternative plea," said Mr Condiment.

"We should argue (a) that I did not accuse Miss Peartree of unnatural vice and (b) even if I did, it would have been absolutely true, and fair comment on a matter of public interest."

"You may have something there," said Mr Condiment automatically. He was wondering why he had asked this garrulous young man to see him. He sucked a cigarette while Arthur remained silent. "You mentioned a kangaroo," he said thoughtfully.

"The kangaroo was in the book," said Arthur.

"I don't care where the kangaroo was," said Mr Condiment, becoming dynamic. "It might have been in the bottom of Loch Ness for all I care. The exact location of that kangaroo is a matter of no interest to me whatever." He grinned. "But when a young man comes talking to me of kangaroos, I say to myself, here is a young man who's obviously interested in animals. And you can write. That much we've established. Now I'm going to offer you

38

a job on one of our magazines, *Woman's Dream*. You can take over the 'Pets' Corner', starting immediately. What do you say to that?"

Mr Condiment leant back in his chair and sucked.

"I am already on the staff of *Woman's Dream*," said Arthur. "I do the 'Padre's Hour', 'Doctor's Diary' and an occasional book review."

"I see," said Mr Condiment. "Are you Doctor Dorkins?"

"Yes," said Arthur.

"Now I remember what I wanted to see you about. We'll forget about 'Pets' Corner' for the moment, but keep it in mind. Cancer."

"Ah, cancer," said Arthur. He wondered whether the managing director was going to ask him to diagnose tingles in the ends of his fingers.

As Mr Condiment's inspiration unfolded, Arthur became excited. It was impossible not to be inspired by such a dynamic man as Mr Condiment.

"Every modern woman has a sort of feeling she might have cancer," said Mr Condiment finally. "It is your job to go into it in detail, and allay the anxieties of those who are perfectly all right, while hastening the diagnosis of those who are afflicted, as the case might be."

But far the most attractive part of the assignment in Arthur's eyes was that the obscene, anti-Christian hermaphrodite, Ronald Carpenter, would have no control over it.

"I think you can rely on me to produce quite a challenging report," he said modestly, as he shook Mr Condiment's hand.

"That's right, Doc," said the visionary.

"Now before Mr Gray arrives, I want to give a little talk about the purpose of his visit. Although he comes from America, he is of African descent and is a great champion of what he likes to call the 'Negro' world movement. We all know that the greatest immediate threat to world peace comes from the middle of Europe, in Berlin, but we've come here tonight because, even in this anxious time, if we have any faith in destiny, we must look to the future. And it is the opinion of many people who have studied world affairs that future wars will be fought as a result of the racial tensions being built up today. So we must all do everything in our power to understand racial problems, particularly the problems of the – er – Negro.

"I know that you are all too intelligent here tonight to be influenced by feelings of racial prejudice. I also think you are all too nice." Arthur beamed round the hall. "But I would like you all to make a special effort tonight. We must remember that the American negro is the product, all too often, of generations of neglect, and he is often very sensitive indeed. We must all make a big effort to show Mr Gray not only that we are unlike other whites he may have met, but that we are genuinely concerned to see all the wrongs committed against the coloured people over the centuries put to right. We must be specially friendly, and give him a special welcome. That's all."

It was a simple and moving address. When Arthur sat down, he took pleasure in seeing their eager, attentive faces. The adorable Elizabeth Pedal had her sublime face set in a friendly welcome. It was so nice, thought Arthur, to be on the right side. Even Jacques was looking serious.

"Yes, Miss Holly." He allowed an austere chill to edge into his voice when addressing the fallen woman.

"Please, Mr Friendship, will we get an opportunity to meet Mr Gray after the lecture?"

"Yes, Miss Holly. There will be the usual discussion over coffee afterwards."

"Mr Milchiger," said a voice.

"I know," said Arthur. "Well, what is it?"

"Will Mr Besant, the Director, be coming this evening?"

"No," said Arthur. "He only comes once in a course of lectures. I'm sorry to disappoint you."

"I have made a mistake. I was told he was definitely coming."

"I'm sorry."

Mr Milchiger left the room. There was an awkward titter.

Arthur reflected that it takes all sorts to make a movement. He saw a beautiful little hand. It came from a slender wrist, an arm like a doll's. Arthur did not need to follow it further.

"Miss ha ha. Who's that there? Ah yes, Miss ha ha ha ha Elizabeth Pedal."

As she spoke, Arthur stared enraptured at her lovely face. Beauty, wit and virtue were stamped indelibly on it. Not virtue of the priggish, narrow sort, but more the type of virtue associated with loving and giving.

"I am terribly sorry, I did not hear your question," he said.

"I said, will we be able to ask Mr Gray to sign copies of his book?" Her voice was clear and musical. Even blindfold, or over the telephone, Arthur would have been able to tell that it was the voice of a transcendently lovely woman.

"Of course you may, Elizabeth." Arthur spoke too violently, and his voice sounded unnatural. He wondered where the strength of his feelings lay: irritation with anyone who supposed that Elizabeth Pedal should not produce books to be signed; defence of Elizabeth Pedal's right to have books signed; general defiance of anyone who opposed Elizabeth Pedal in any way.

Ferdie Jacques, from his position by the door, was watching her in a manner which seemed to say: "Strictly speaking, Liz, you're my type of girl."

Elizabeth Pedal was speaking again. Arthur wondered whether she had cancer, but dismissed the thought. For the first time, he was really interested in his work for *Woman's Dream*. Margaret Holly was a much more likely candidate for cancer. She might well have caught it from Ferdie Jacques, whose enigmatic beard seemed to proclaim disease in every bristle.

"I am terribly sorry, Miss Pedal. I did not hear your question."

"She said will you get him to sign it for her," shouted Ferdie rudely from the other end of the room.

"Certainly not. You must not be shy. He is just like everyone else, and we must all go out of our way to be friendly. I will introduce you to him, Elizabeth, after the talk."

A signal was given, and Mr Gray walked in accompanied by

41

Mr Besant. Ferdie started to clap, and everybody else clapped to overcome the shock. There could be no doubt that Mr Gray was very black indeed.

As he clapped, Arthur reflected that it was just like the entrance of the Christmas pudding in the hospital where he had once spent Christmas. Mr Gray did not actually have a holly leaf stuck in his head, not did blue flames lick around his skin, but his face was very shiny, and he made a puffing noise.

"Before I introduce Mr Thomas Gray, who really needs no introduction, I must say how delighted we are to see Mr Besant again this evening. It is a sign of the importance which the leaders of our movement attach to this very important question of race relations that Mr Besant, our very busy director, should find time to come and see us."

Mr Besant looked up and smiled. He seemed a bit tired under his distinguished white mane of hair, and Arthur swelled again with pride and loyalty.

In fact, the Director of Peace Education had had a bad day. The Prime Minister's Office said that the Prime Minister would no doubt be delighted to see him when he was less busy. Mr Besant had no wish to push himself forward. Then, immediately afterwards, he had been visited by a man from Security. Mr Besant was extremely angry and had immediately contacted friends extremely high in the security services. They had made enquiries, and assured him that the check was purely routine, but Mr Besant felt the indignity keenly.

People were behaving in such a high-handed way over Berlin, that he felt inclined almost to wash his hands of the whole crisis. There were plenty of fish in the sea. Mr Besant leaned back and let the waves of African oratory flow over him.

Arthur, too, leaned back, and stared at Elizabeth Pedal.

"It was very kind of your secretary to introduce me at all. He could not help making mistakes, because he is English. However enlightened and well-wishing, it is impossible for members of an ex-colonial race to understand what is going on in the minds and hearts of Africans the world over. He said my name was Thomas Gray and that I was an American. Very well, you may think, now we've got this strange, wild man neatly docketed in the right file. My name is not Thomas Gray and I am not an American. My name is Toe-mass Gray and I am a Negro. Not even half American. Not even quarter an American. I am a one hundred per cent pure buck Negro. You may call me a Nigger."

Arthur made a deprecating face and a wave of embarrassment swept over the hall. Only Miss Holly, eighteen, giggled.

"You can call me that if you like. Everyone else does. I don't mind, because I know you are frightened of me. All the white races of the world are sitting on their fat refrigerators, rubbing their hands, but they are frightened of us Negroes. So they give us money. That is all they understand. They think they can *buy* our friendship. We don't mind. We take your money. We are not too proud. We are only one of the lesser breeds without the Law."

Again, Arthur made a deprecating face, and from somewhere in the hall there was a murmur of disagreement.

"I didn't write that. *You* wrote that," shouted Mr Gray pointing at Ferdie.

Very wide of the mark there, thought Arthur. The adorable Miss Pedal was concentrating so hard that she might almost be going to burst into tears. He wondered if she ever wrote poetry. The thought was too sensuous to be entertained. Elizabeth was a notoriously difficult name to write poetry about.

> "A sweeter woman ne'er drew breath
> Than my son's wife, Elizabeth."

Inappropriate to the circumstances, decided Arthur, although someone would presumably be able to comfort himself with the thought when beloved Elizabeth laid down her virginity on the altar of matrimony to some whey-faced poltroon of a dentist in the suburbs. Such speculation was too poignant. Far better she should die of an incurable disease in the first flower of her youth.

Consumption was romantic, but cancer more fashionable. He wondered if she would consent to be photographed in colour for the shock-issue of *Woman's Dream*. The caption could be: "Must I die, asks 22-year-old secretary Elizabeth Pedal. Her predicament is typical among millions of cancer-sufferers."

Suddenly Arthur felt ashamed of himself.

"You counsel moderation," shouted Mr Gray at Ferdie, whom he had chosen as the spokesman for all the subterfuges of the Ku Klux Klan. "We are not going to be moderate. We are not going to wait while our brothers are exploited. We want action, not today or tomorrow, but NOW. And if we don't get it, if we are put off again with paltry sums of money and promises, I can promise you there is going to be such an explosion as the world has never seen. In the confusion, a lot of things may be done which we would regret afterwards. But if the white man is swept off the face of the earth, it will be his own fault for not paying attention in time. That is the choice facing you all. Act now, or. . . ." He clicked his fingers to indicate total extinction of the white races.

Arthur was very pleased he had asked Mr Gray to speak. They had seldom heard such an eloquent or challenging speech. Now they all knew just to what extent they were sitting on a volcano. With the European races outnumbered five-to-one by Negroes – he was not sure of the exact figures – it was obviously time they devoted serious thought to the matter. Clearly, if wealth were not immediately distributed more evenly among the nations of the world, there would be little chance of the world peace they were all looking forward to. Such temporary crises as Berlin paled into insignificance beside the enormous threat of the Negro explosion. Were there any questions?

"What sort of action does Mr Gray think it possible or desirable for us to take?" Miss Holly put an insolent boldness into the question which Arthur found irritating.

"What sort of action should we, or ought we to take," he interpreted. Arthur thought of his own share of capitalist excesses. Sixteen pounds a week from *Woman's Dream* – no doubt he would be paid more for the shock issue – eight pounds a week from

44

Education for Peace, plus an extra guinea or two whenever *Woman's Dream* printed one of his book reviews. After tax and stamps, he reckoned on a steady income of seventy-five pounds a month, of which sixteen was paid to Mrs Quorn. Still, that was enough to support fifteen Negro families in Africa, if the figures published by UNESCO were true. What could he deny himself? He seldom had anything more nourishing than sandwiches for lunch. The cinema was a great economy, because it prevented one from spending money on other things during the two hours one watched it. Cigarettes were essential for his work. He thought of the fish fingers which had been followed by a quite unnecessary pork pie. Voluptuary! No wonder the coloured races were seething.

"I don't want you to do anything at all," said Mr Gray mysteriously. "Just you sit right there where you are in that chair and wait for something to hit you."

Miss Holly squirmed and giggled.

"I think one thing we might do is to make a really big contribution to the various Peace organizations in Africa," said Mr Besant, taking charge. He had a deep, sexy voice and behaved like a retired General giving a talk on television about the last war. "There is the Rhodesians for Peace movement, at present exiled in Tanzania, the Congolese Peace Headquarters, whose mission is to bring peace to the former Belgian Congo. They are at present stationed across the border in Brazzaville. The East African Peace Offensive is working actually inside Kenya, Uganda and Tanganyika respectively, and is in desperate need of medical supplies and other weapons to carry on the fight for peace. Then there is the Angolan Freedom Movement to consider. I assure you there is no shortage of areas where we can be active. Mr Friendship will take round a collection now."

Here I sit, thought Mr Besant, fiddling while Rome burns. There were a million other causes – the North Vietnamese Peace Forces, Hands Off Cuba Campaign, United Africa Against Apartheid – all demanding his attention, yet he wasted his time talking to fifteen mentally deficient post-adolescents in a draughty hall. And while great events were happening in the world, his dreams were perilously close to being shattered, tantalisingly close to being realised, he had to occupy himself with the affairs of over-excited Negroes, half-witted in their conceit and self-importance.

Miss Holly gave ninepence. Elizabeth Pedal gave ten shillings. Arthur's hand shook as he took it. Ferdie gave half a crown. Most surprisingly, the tramp gave sixpence. He seemed to have joined the course of lectures. Perhaps he was an eccentric millionaire, thought Arthur, who always inclined to the romantic interpretation of events. The total was twenty-four shillings. Arthur gave it to Mr Besant, who added a pound of his own and gave it to Mr Gray. The poet smiled and pocketed it.

Martin Starter was working late at his office. As a general rule, he made a point of knocking off at half-past-five, but with his Captain to Major exam approaching and nothing much to do in the evening, he judged it prudent to stay.

Work was slack in the South-East Asia Office. Some photographs on his desk showed a lot of buildings which had gone up near Weti, in the Northern half of Zanzibar. They might be barracks, but they could scarcely be missile sites. And even if they were, what the hell? They could only be used to blow up a lot of turbulent Africans. One day someone would learn that Zanzibar was not in South East Asia. He marked the photographs "Commonwealth Office – Africa" and put them in his Out tray.

He started using calendar cards to build a house representing the political structure of South East Asia. A telephone rang and the house collapsed.

"Starter." Terse, eager, intelligent Starter.

"Martin, it's Dick. I was thinking about taking some girls out tonight to the Crazy Elephant. You care to chip in?"

"Who are they?" Eduction, evaluation, decision.

"One of them's my sister, actually."

"Sorry, old boy. I'm afraid I'm rather tied up tonight."

"'Fraid you might be. Shouldn't have left it so late. By the way, you know that Home Office bod we've got attached to us here.

Well, I gave him your tip about Mr Besant, and they've done some enquiries but there doesn't seem to be anything in it. He may be a Commie now, but there's no evidence he ever belonged to the Party, or any other organization except U.N. – bloody – ESCO. Apparently he was attached to the old League of Nations Committee on Slavery when they were recruiting for the new outfit in Geneva. Couldn't find out much about his early years, and he wasn't exactly helpful."

"Did you try the Foreign Office?" Captain Starter did not like the sound of Mr Besant. This was something he and Mr Dent had cooked up together over breakfast.

"No change out of them. So long as you haven't actually belonged to the Communist Party, you're all right there. You know the place is riddled with Left-Wingers."

"Steady on." Captain Starter liked to think that he was Left of Centre himself. "What about Berlin?"

"They're just not going to let the convoys through. Simple as that. We're all splitting our pants in here."

"What?"

"Laughing. They're letting the English and French convoys through, and telling the Yanks to sit on the roadside."

"You don't think the Americans will do anything silly, do you?"

"Might do. You can never tell with the Yanks. But we must try and convince ourselves they're not all nuts. World opinion wouldn't stand for anything at the moment. The Prime Minister is going to make a statement tonight praising them for their restraint and all that twaddle, calling for a peaceful settlement."

"About time, too. Sorry about tonight. The truth is, I'm a bit skint at the moment."

"Aren't we all?"

"Mr Gray, I'd like you to meet Miss Elizabeth Pedal." Arthur was holding her by the hand in a paternal way. Her hand was so tiny and so soft he could scarcely bear to let go of it. She smiled into his eyes gratefully and affectionately. He was masterful and

47

unconfused. "Miss Pedal has a book she'd like you to sign."

"I always like signing books for pretty ladies," said Mr Gray with old-world courtesy. No doubt learned on the slave-plantations of the deep South, thought Arthur. "And what would you like me to write?"

"Whatever you like," said Elizabeth demurely, giving him a smile of such dazzling brilliance that Arthur felt his confusion returning.

"I am afraid I forgot to bring my copy," said Miss Holly.

"Then I must sign it for you another time," said Mr Gray gallantly. Really, thought Arthur, it just shows that Negroes have the best manners in the world. They are so poised, so charming. He simply could not understand colour prejudice.

"Oh will you really," said Miss Holly. "I love having books signed by the author."

"Now we must attend to the book of the beautiful Miss Pestle."

"Elizabeth," she said.

"Elizabeth," said Mr Gray. "Tell me, did you like my talk?"

"Very much," said Elizabeth. "I particularly liked the bit about how our civilization was on the way out, like the Greeks and the Romans and the Egyptians before them. And how the new race with the will and energy to succeed came from Africa."

Arthur felt so proud and happy. Here, he felt, he was showing his African the very best sort of intelligent and good white person. It must soften the Negro's harsh judgment of the English.

"Ah yes," said Mr Gray. "The original African civilization was a beautiful thing, before you white men turned up and taught us to lust after money and be ashamed of the colour of our skins. But it will come back, it will come back."

"Of course it will," said Miss Holly, "and I hope to be there to see it."

"It's interesting what you say about colour prejudice," said Ferdie. "Have you found much of it in England?"

"Everywhere," said Mr Gray.

"There are some boarding houses which refuse to take in coloured people," said Ferdie. "We could work on them for you."

48

"Ah, now, I would not suggest anything violent," said Mr Gray. "That would have to come from you."

"We could inform the police first about landladies operating a colour-bar, then if nothing happened we could make things unpleasant."

"In America," said Mr Gray, "we use petrol. But I would be the last to suggest such a course of action."

"Police, then petrol," said Ferdie happily.

"I do not know what makes you think the police are on your side," said Mr Gray.

"Petrol," said Ferdie getting excited.

"Now don't be foolish. You are very young. You must give warnings first."

"I wouldn't give any warnings. They don't deserve it," said Miss Holly, who was being left out of the conversation.

"You must give warnings," said Ferdie, "or people don't know what they're being attacked for."

"They don't deserve it," said Miss Holly, and the argument continued.

"I am not sure what to write in this book," said Mr Gray. "Perhaps you can help me."

"I don't know," said Elizabeth, looking over his shoulder at the bare fly-leaf. Arthur thought of moving closer to look too, but something in the enormous expanse of black neck put him off.

"Perhaps I should take it away and think of something," said Mr Gray. "Then I could send it round to you, or have it delivered."

"You could take mine, too, if only I had remembered to bring it," said Miss Holly.

"Or I could deliver it myself," said Mr Gray, who looked at Elizabeth steadily. Once again she smiled that bewitching, happy smile. Arthur was prouder and happier than he cared to say. He had asked everyone to be friendly, but friendliness from Ferdie Jacques might have done little to soften the black man's heart. As it was, he felt sure that even Gray would soon find himself quite liking the English.

Elizabeth gave Gray the address of the flat she shared and her

49

Fremantle telephone number. Arthur could have given them himself. They were engraved on his heart from the students' register.

"Tomorrow evening, then," said Mr Gray.

"Fair warning, then petrol," Ferdie chanted, with a gleam in his eye.

Arthur returned to Albany Chambers in a highly emotional state. It was one of those rare moments in the life of an idealist when he could feel he had genuinely done some good in the world. He scarcely noticed Ferdie clinging like an octopus to his back as they drove down Victoria Street on the scooter.

They climbed the stairs in silence. Arthur shut the door of his room and went straight to his record player. The Nutcracker Suite was too flippant; the prelude to La Traviata would be falsely sentimental. There was no need for music.

He stood in front of the mirror where he cleaned his teeth in the morning and regarded himself with fond, foolish old eyes. In every human being, he felt, there was a little furry, woolly thing struggling to get out. He knew in his heart that this tremendous potential for tenderness existed even among the under-developed races. If only Arthur Friendship were the controller of the world's destiny, how soon would the various races of the world live together in harmony and brotherly love. Love would reign supreme.

The moment was too poignant for words. After a few minutes contemplation he put on his pyjamas and went to bed.

Chapter Four

ENGLAND WAS BEGINNING TO BE BORED BY THE BERLIN crisis. As Christmas approached, the newspapers prepared to be indignant about office parties, road accidents and the commercial exploitation of Christmas.

"It's quite simple," said Captain Starter. "They just aren't prepared to let the Yanks through until they've been searched. It's perfectly legal, and nobody's got anything to complain about." All the newspapers showed pictures of American G.I.'s standing by the roadside in their underpants while Comrades searched their lorries, and there were many good-humoured jokes about how the Frauleins' mouths were watering. Everybody felt the Americans were being very mature.

Captain Starter began to worry about the Inter-Services Squash Racquet Tournament, and Mr Dent, after a regretful sigh, looked hopefully to the Far East.

Mrs Quorn's dining room was not a place where the men were supposed to hold general discussion groups after breakfast. "It's ten to nine," she said.

"Christ, what a bore," said Ferdie Jacques.

"If you're going to be rude, you can find a bed somewhere else. There are people queueing up for the rooms here. I would have no difficulty in getting someone to pay double the price."

"Mrs Quorn," said Ferdie, choosing his words carefully, "I wonder if you have ever considered the possibility of having coloured guests."

"I don't know what you're talking about."

"I notice," said Ferdie, "that not one of your guests here is coloured."

"Very observant young man," said Mr Dent. "You mark my

51

words, he'll go a long way. I'm not coloured. Are you Starter? Don't think so. As for old Friendship, it's harder to tell. Never seen him in the raw. But his little bald patch looks quite white to me."

"I suppose," said Ferdie insinuatingly, "it's just coincidence."

Mrs Quorn was on the defensive. It was bad enough, she thought, lodging beatniks. "I'm not having any more friends of yours here, Mr Jacques, coloured or otherwise. You're enough trouble as it is, and we haven't got any room."

"That's all I wanted to know," said Ferdie.

"What is all you wanted to know?"

"That you refuse to take coloured people in."

"I never said any such thing."

"Yes, you did."

"I never heard her," said Mr Dent. "Did you Starter?"

"I don't think so," said Captain Starter. "There used to be a coloured chap at Sandhurst. Brilliant at rugby, but he could never tell his left foot from his right. Funny thing, you know, but apparently a lot of coloured chaps can't."

Ferdie was quelled. He ground his teeth and made his beard bristle. "Evidence," he thought. "I must have evidence."

Mrs Quorn watched her guests depart, feeling sad and unprotected. Her husband, who died of a seizure in dramatic circumstances, had become very merry one evening and thrown a young medical student out of the window of the room now used by Arthur Friendship. The student was behind with his rent, and there had to be an inquest. After that episode Mrs Quorn resolved to board no more students. They were untidy, as well as being notoriously prone to suicide.

Christmas is a time above all others when Christians realize that their religion is not one of "Don'ts" and "Ifs" and "Buts", wrote Arthur. When we think of that oft-repeated miracle of the act of giving birth, so familiar to all of us through our television screens, it is indeed moving to reflect that the same sort of thing was going on so many thousands of years ago when Christ was born in a stable at Bethlehem.

Modern advances have removed the terrors of childbirth from motherhood. It is now a joyful, happy occasion. Something to be looked forward to, prepared for, and remembered as one of the happiest moments of one's life — for many people the happiest moment.

So it has come about that Christmas is a happy occasion, a time when one can forget the worries and irritations of the week and rejoice with the whole family in the certain knowledge that our Saviour has been born.

Last year, I reminded you of the country's 600,000 lonely old people to whom Christmas is just another day of solitude. The year before, I mentioned the thousands of millions of underdeveloped peoples, from whom a plateful of turkey and Christmas pudding is a far cry. This year, while always mindful of those poor unfortunates who are less happily placed than ourselves, I would like you to eat your Christmas dinner in a spirit of optimism and hope.

Optimism, that we shall soon be able to feed the world's hungry millions as well as we like to feed ourselves; hope that in time, with better nourishment and medical attention, the spirit of amity will prevail, and Love will reign supreme among the nations of the world.

The Rev. Cliff Roebuck seldom received any letters as the result of his weekly column in *Woman's Dream*. Occasionally, there was one from a vicar's wife complaining about her husband; or one from a vicar, taking him up on some obstruse theological point. More often, Arthur himself wrote a letter to the Editor in disguised handwriting, to say how the column inspired him; he signed these letters Phyllis Chulmleigh or Sylvia Grantley. Once, in a flight of fancy, he wrote to say that he had read the column while working as a prostitute in London's Soho, and, on the strength of it, had decided to abandon the vile profession and dedicate his life to care of the elderly. He signed the letter Margaret Holly, eighteen.

The Editor was too mean a man ever to show him these letters. But Arthur derived secret satisfaction from the knowledge that he was appreciated.

Ferdie Jacques was feeling particularly temperamental when he reached his office in Berkeley Street. His creative director, Mr Isinglass, was prepared to tolerate a certain amount of temperament. Artists were well known to be moody and unpredictable. But they had to produce the goods, just like anyone else. There was a long queue of moody, unpredictable people waiting to join the firm.

"It's no good, Ferdie," said Mr Isinglass. "You've been working on this 'power – punch' theme for two weeks now and nothing has come out. I think you may be going stale on the idea. Why not give it to Nina, and we'll find something else for you?"

Ferdie handed him a sheet of paper. On it was typed: "Anglo-American has power behind that punch."

"Not bad, Ferdie. Quite arresting. Quite original. Petrol is not an easy commodity for a young man to handle. You need to get the feel for it. I remember the first slogan we handled for Anglo-American – 'You get more MPG's and no pinking'. We had two asterisks, explaining what MPG stood for, and what we meant by pinking. And that was only ten years ago. It reads like Chaucer, now. All right, so Anglo-American has got power behind that punch. Where's the suggestion of sexual virility?"

"Power," said Ferdie.

"Fair enough. And where's the suggestion that you'll be scoring off the Jones's if you buy Anglo-American petrol?"

"Punch," said Ferdie.

"Good. You're coming on. You didn't think that Anglo-American might *pack* power behind that punch."

"Too many P's," said Ferdie. "Peter Piper picked a peck of pickled pepper."

"You may be right," said Mr Isinglass. He brooded. "It lacks something," he said, becoming artistic himself.

Ferdie knew that it lacked nothing. What was there for it to lack? Whenever one of his ideas was turned down, he sneered openly. It meant that Mr Isinglass was losing touch with youth and young ideas. Both of them knew that as soon as this happened, Mr Isinglass would have to retire. Probably he would become a book reviewer or a theatre critic, or end his days as a lavatory attendant. The advertising industry had no place for faded *cocottes* who were stuck in the mud.

Ferdie despised his profession, but knew that with his temperament, he had to work in a creative field. If he had been born in the sixteenth century, he would have been a poet; in the seventeenth century, a Protestant theologian; in the eighteenth century, a patron of the arts; in the nineteenth century, a revolutionary. Now, in the second half of the twentieth century, he was a junior advertising executive, and there was no question of his resigning.

"We all know that Anglo-American has power. That statement, as it stands, is tautological. We established it in last year's campaign. The new insight is 'punch'. Anglo-American has *punch* behind that power."

"Exactly," said Ferdie. "That is what I said."

"No you didn't. You said that Anglo-American has power behind that punch."

"It is the same thing."

"You may think so."

"Your version doesn't make sense."

"There are a lot of things which only make sense when you understand them."

On that Delphic note Mr Isinglass indicated that the conversation was at an end. He had often thought of writing a monograph on the distinction between inspiration – genius, call it what you will – and technical competence. No doubt he would get round to it during the lean years ahead, as a book reviewer or lavatory attendant.

Ferdie stamped off to pour more scorn on Nina Cattermole's idea of non-violent revolution.

"Mr Carpenter won't keep you a minute, Mr Friendship."

"I am afraid I am in a bit of a hurry and can't wait."

"I am afraid Mr Carpenter really is engaged."

Fiddlesticks, my pretty little kitten, thought Arthur. Since being given sole responsibility for the shock issue of *Woman's Dream* devoted to the vexed question of cancer, Arthur felt a greater confidence in himself. Unless he was mistaken, the attractive secretary was already looking at him with a new respect. Admiration had taken the place of sweet, sad longing in her voice.

He walked breezily into the Editor's office. What he saw deflated him somewhat. Mr Condiment was in there, with Mr Besant.

"Can you come back in twenty five minutes, please?" said the uniquely horrible Mr Carpenter. Arthur was disappearing when Mr Condiment saw him.

"Ah, come in, Doc. Dr Dorkins, I want you to meet my very good friend Walter Besant."

"Mr Friendship," said Carpenter.

"William," said Mr Besant.

"William Besant," said Mr Condiment.

"I know," said Arthur.

"Mr Besant has got this idea that we should have something to uplift the housewife morally. I don't know if there's anything in the idea. What do you think, Doc?"

"Well, we have 'Padre's Hour' by the Rev. Cliff Roebuck," said Arthur.

"This would replace it. Walter's idea is that we should have a weekly column by a coloured person giving his views on moral problems."

"Well, it's an idea." Arthur was quite game to have his face treated with burnt cork. He had been finding the *persona* of the Rev. Cliff Roebuck rather burdensome of late.

"He's got this man called Thomas Gray."

"Toe-mass. I know him well. He's a poet."

"I'm not too keen on the idea," said Mr Carpenter in a kind of whimper. "Many of our readers haven't too much respect for coloured people anyway."

For the first time, Arthur felt himself in agreement with the ineffable Editor. Not for the same reasons, of course. They were beneath contempt. But he genuinely did feel that the magazine

56

needed a Christian voice. And there was also the small matter of eight pounds a week which he was paid for the Reverend Roebuck's column.

"Think of the appeal it would have to the million coloured immigrants in this country. They would all take *Woman's Dream*. It might even stir them into some action." Mr Besant's last sentence was an aside to Arthur. He knew he ought to be rallying behind his chief in the cause of peace. But it was not as simple as that, and his mind was then taken up with cancer.

"Less than a third of them are women, and very few of the women can read English." Mr Carpenter was looking even pastier than usual. "It's all a question of image. Many of our readers might feel we had hired a black man to write for us because we couldn't afford an Englishman."

"Our readership is surprisingly unsophisticated." Arthur agreed that Mr Besant was barking up the wrong tree. "We might publish a poem by him."

"That's an idea," said Mr Condiment. "Just to show that black people can do it too, if you see what I mean. You've got to educate people slowly for peace, you know. It's no good rushing things."

"Well, Mr Gray will be most disappointed. But, I'm sure you'll pay him properly for his poem."

"We'll put it on the front cover of our Christmas number, won't we, Ronald?" Mr Condiment obviously felt that a poem was sufficient moral uplift. "We'll pay a hundred pounds for the exclusive world rights."

After Mr Condiment and the Director of Peace Education had gone, Ronald Carpenter said: "We can't have these blacks coming over and stealing our jobs, can we, Arthur?"

Arthur was appalled by this coarseness but found himself smiling. Perhaps it was the first time he had heard Carpenter express a recognizably human sentiment, however base. Normally, he talked about images, consensuses, TAM Ratings and other sub-human, anti-Christian drivel.

57

"Who is this Mr Besant anyway?"

"He's only about the greatest Englishman living," said Arthur quietly. "If, and this is a very big if, we are saved from being blown up over Berlin, it will largely be due to his efforts." Arthur did not normally talk to his Editor in this way, but he was elated by the way things were happening. After the shock issue of *Woman's Dream* in the New Year, he would be famous, or at any rate Dr Dorkins would. His acquaintance with Besant, Condiment and Toe-Mass Gray seemed to put him at an advantage. And Ronald Carpenter was looking even unhealthier than usual.

"Here's my Christmas message from Roebuck. Doctor Dorkins for the Christmas issue will be with you later. And I've got the review of a book of carols, if you have room for it."

"I think we might," said Mr Carpenter. Some of the spirit seemed to have gone out of him. His blue hair lacked lustre. "That Negro will have to be very quick with his poem if he wants to catch the Christmas number. It is only nine weeks to Christmas. We can't possibly take any copy after November 1st."

"I'll tell him," said Arthur. "As a matter of fact, I'll be seeing him tomorrow evening."

"You're as bad as my friend Arthur," said Ferdie. "He seriously believes that nothing violent need ever happen if we all get together and love each other."

"Love," said Nina Cattermole. "Yes, I think there is definitely a place in any non-violent revolution for personal relationships."

"I agree," said Ferdie. "There's this girl called Elizabeth Pedal in the class who I am beginning to think seriously about. But I never let that sort of thing interfere with one's political beliefs."

"Don't you?" said Nina, looking him in the eyes. Ferdie smiled. She might have something. One did get rather bored sitting in the office for hours on end, doing nothing.

"But seriously," he said, "I am not sure that I want a revolution anyway. And if I did, my experience of revolutions is that they have to be pretty violent. You will never goad the inert grey masses

58

of the English proletariat into doing anything violent, so you might as well give up any ideas of a revolution."

"This is what I have been trying to say all along. *Because* the English working class is so inert, grey and inarticulate, it will put up no opposition to a revolution provided it is non-violent. As soon as you start shooting people, or hanging them, the English fill up with Dunkirk spirit and make trouble. But if you just quitely take over the Government and start passing laws, nobody would notice. They would complain about it in the pubs, of course, and a few people would write letters to the *Daily Telegraph*, but everybody would realize in their hearts that we were being progressive."

"And how are you going to quietly take over the Government?" Scorn poured off Miss Cattermole's back like fat from a basted duck, leaving her slightly browner and tastier than before.

"By a gradual process which need not even be conscious. It is happening all the time, although, of course, it will be speeded up a bit when the younger people like ourselves begin to make themselves felt in politics."

"That is the most complacent and hypocritical thing I have ever heard. Young people today simply aren't prepared to wait while their elders bumble around. We are already making ourselves felt in the arts and entertainment, and we are not going to be put off by politicians. We don't want to take the lead today or tomorrow but *now*. And if our demands are not met in full, there is going to be an explosion such as the country has never seen."

"I think this is true about sex," said Nina. Really, there could be no doubt about it, women were much more mature than men. "Younger people have certainly broken right away from their elders over sex."

"Exactly," said Ferdie. "We're not prepared to be told not to do things just because they say it's wrong. The elder generation have got no right to preach at us, seeing what sort of a mess they've made of the world. The sooner they make way for younger people like you and me, the better it will be for everybody."

"I think they're prepared to admit it about sex," said Nina. "Some of the older generation try to imitate us. It's rather pathetic, really." She thought about Mr Isinglass, and his fumbling advances. "But it will take a long time before they admit that we are right about everything else."

"Half the younger generation are nearly as feeble as they are," said Ferdie. "Every time I read about Young Conservatives, I want to be sick. They're the sort of people who should be put in mental homes."

"Me too," said Nina. "But they probably come from unhappy backgrounds and feel insecure."

"I would give them something to be insecure about." Ferdie had no time for the nineteenth-century sentimental approach. "Look at Arthur Friendship. Admittedly, he's thirty-two and belongs to an older generation, but he's taken up religion. It's difficult to believe he lives in the same age as ourselves. He isn't able to think any thought for himself until he has cleared it with the religious authorities."

"Poor Mr Friendship," said Nina. "He's probably unhappy about something. I dare say he needs a steady relationship."

"He needs about ninety." Ferdie was beginning to be bored by all this talk about steady relationships. "It's nearly lunch hour. Shall we go out and have some lunch?"

"On the Dutch?"

"No, I'll pay."

Nina hesitated. She was not one to shirk obligations, but there were practical difficulties. "All right," she said recklessly. She, too, found it boring to sit in the office and do nothing all day.

Arthur was in a fury of creative activity:

Cancer, then, is not confined to any one part of the body, nor is it confined to any one social class. It can strike with cruel suddenness, or it can creep with insidious slowness. Most people know if they have caught it within two months, but with others it takes longer, and in two cases out of four it is already, at the time of discovery, too late for surgical treatment to be one hundred per cent effective. Many of us may carry around with us an incipient, dormant carcinoma which is only waiting for the right conditions to breed and flourish. Nobody knows, at present, what these conditions are. On the other hand, our tumour may be non-malignant, and we are worrying unduly.

There are six ways in which we can discover the presence of a growth, whether malignant or otherwise:

1. *Straight X-Ray.*
2. *Barium meal in combination with X-Ray. This will reveal gastric tumours, as well as ulcers, etc.*
3. *Bronchoscopy. For cancer of the lung, throat, pleura, etc.*
4. *Surgical investigation of the rectal passages.*
5. *Blood count, followed by cell culture in laboratory conditions. For leukaemia, etc.*
6. *Personal observation of the skin.*

It will be noted that only one of these methods may be employed without the assistance of a doctor. Obviously, it is not possible for doctors to test every single woman every single day, as we would like. That, of course, would be ideal, but our Government would have to delegate a much larger part of its resources to medicine before we even began to approach such an ambitious target.

But there is this one method—superficial inspection of the skin—which is within everybody's reach, and there can be little excuse nowadays for women not to examine every part of their body whenever, for instance, they take a bath.

I think, thought Arthur, that we can discount the old-fashioned theory that hot water baths cause cancer of the skin, while still bearing it in mind. He derived a certain amount of pleasure from the thought of so many millions of women inspecting their bodies in the bath on his advice. He could not say why. The idea appealed to him.

The shock issue of *Woman's Dream* was not only going to be good journalism, making money for Mr Condiment and his shareholders. It was also going to serve a good moral purpose.

Arthur had decided that it was all too easy, in modern conditions, to lose sight of the inevitability of death. Flippancy about death was the only thing which really shocked people any more –

61

not that Arthur had any intention of being flippant – and even serious discussion of death was considered in bad taste. Yet they were all going to die, every one of his happy little readers. If they died in a hospital ward, they would be hustled out on a trolley before any of the other patients could see them and reflect on the human condition. If they died in a road accident, they would be removed in an ambulance within twenty minutes, the broken glass would be swept up, the wrecked motor cars would be towed away, any blood on the road would be covered with sawdust, and nobody would benefit. If they died at home, an undertaker would remove the corpse to his own private mortuary within hours. Death was left in the hands of a few professionals. No longer were the old crones of the village called in to lay out the corpse, no longer did it lie in state in the front room, visited by all its relations. For many a modern housewife, death might as well not exist.

If his article caused one of them to pause for a moment and reflect on the precariousness of human survival, Arthur felt it would have served a good purpose. Without awareness of mortality, there would be no religion, no morals, no true humility.

Examining his conscience, Arthur found it clear. He was working for peace; he had paid his newsagent's bill; he had resisted the sin to fornicate with a girl called Susan despite flagrant temptation.

Morality-wise, there could be no doubt, he was flying high, fast and fearless.

Ferdie chose an Italian restaurant in Curzon Street, where the spaghetti only cost two shillings and ninepence, because he knew the proprietor.

"Hello, Marco. I've got a new customer for you," he said jauntily. "And there's somebody else."

"Who is it?" said Nina.

Ferdie walked over to where a hatchet-faced man was eating soup in the corner, with a beautiful girl of oriental appearance.

"Hello, Johnny," said Ferdie.

The hatchet-faced man stood up. "Teyve Milchiger," he said.

"I just call him, Johnny the Milkman," said Ferdie.

"Have you met my fiancée, Miss April Kalugalla, from Ceylon?"

Miss Kalugalla smiled deliciously. "We're not actually engaged yet," she said, in a soft, American voice. "I'm working as secretary to Mr Besant at the Hilton."

"We were talking about Mr Besant, actually," said Mr Milchiger.

I'm not surprised, thought Ferdie, you dirty old pervert. What on earth was he doing with such a delectable girl? "I know Mr Besant, too," he said. "Perhaps I'll be seeing more of you, April."

"Perhaps," said Miss Kalugalla. Her tone, though sweet as a crystallised plum, did not seem to hold out much hope. Her eyes, beautiful onyx saucers, were all for the pervert.

"I suppose she's his mistress," said Ferdie, when they returned to their table. "Ninety-eight per cent of Sinhalese females have V.D."

"They should be given contraceptives," said Nina automatically. "Actually, the Government is getting round at long last to making it part of their foreign aid programme."

"Too little and too late," said Ferdie. They both looked at the lovely Miss April Kalugalla, and wondered if she had been the recipient of any largesse.

The spaghetti arrived.

"It's a funny thing," said Ferdie. "At any moment, as we sit here, we might all of us be blown to smithereens."

"I prefer not to think about it," said Nina.

"Escapism," said Ferdie affectionately. Then they tucked into their spaghetti. Ferdie finished before Nina was half-way through, and she said she did not want to finish the rest. No, Ferdie did not want to finish it for her. He had eaten too fast, and was feeling slightly ill. "It just seems a pity, that's all."

"Never mind," said Nina. "I think I could manage an ice-cream."

This infuriated Ferdie. He would not have minded so much if

she had finished her spaghetti and then demanded ice-cream because she was still hungry. But to leave her spaghetti and order ice-cream was wanton extravagance at his expense. And she seemed to think she was doing him a favour by asking him to spend one and threepence on an unnecessary luxury.

"One vanilla ice, please, Marco," he said coldly, beard a-bristle. He looked away in distaste from the spectacle of gourmandism.

April Kalugalla was sitting with her head very close to the Milkman's. She was telling him something which he seemed to find absorbing. He took notes, pausing occasionally to squeeze her thigh under the table. Ferdie reflected that there was no need to squeeze Nina's thigh. She probably would not notice it, anyway, as she wolfed her ice-cream. Or it might produce more unfortunate results. He really detested women for their stupidity, their pretentiousness and their greed.

When they came out into the street, Ferdie said:

"Wait a minute: There's something I must get from the barber's." Nina waited outside the Ministry of Education buildings, brooding about the possibility of a non-violent revolution.

"Here's Doctor Dorkins for Christmas," said Arthur breezily, as he walked into the office. He scarcely bothered to nod at the pretty receptionist these days.

Carpenter was sucking a blue tablet that smelled of gentian violets.

"What's it about this week?"

"Children's upset tummies. Haven't time for anything punchier this time, I'm afraid. Too busy with the cancer scare." Arthur wondered if the disgusting sweets which Carpenter sucked were responsible for the colour of his hair. If so, someone should tell him.

"You know, Arthur, I'm not too keen on this cancer idea."

"Mr Condiment is."

"I know. But it's all very well, there may be a few of our readers who genuinely are worried about the dangers of cancer."

"Of course. It will be of particular interest to them."

"Yes, but you can't make a joke of it. Cancer is a pretty serious thing. There will be a good number of people who have lost husbands and mothers and aunts from the disease. Very few people haven't."

Arthur exulted. Ronald Carpenter, he decided, was the quintessential woman. No doubt he was worried about cancer himself. His reactions were the typical modern woman's reactions. That was how he got his present job, with all its prestige and importance.

"Nobody's going to joke about cancer, Ronald. This is dead serious. Of course, people are going to be frightened and indignant. But they are also going to be interested. This is what gives it readership appeal."

Readership appeal was one of the phrases Carpenter used when he was being at his most nauseating. It is also going to make them think about death, thought Arthur savagely. Even you, Ronald Carpenter, surrounded by all your pomp and circumstance, by all your prestige and importance, are going to realize for a moment that you are mortal, that you must die. And what then? You can't take your pile carpets across to the other side. Not all the buzzing telephones and pretty receptionists in the world are going to be of any use to you there.

"Readership appeal isn't everything," said Carpenter. No doubt he means there were also images, TAM ratings and consensuses to be considered, but to Arthur it sounded as if he had just heard the Devil sing a Te Deum.

When Nina and Ferdie returned to the office, everyone else was still out to lunch.

"I can't thank you enough. I can't remember such a delicious lunch for a long time," she said, sitting down at the desk.

Ferdie watched her suspiciously. Had she forgotten who had paid for the lunch?

"Where shall we go?" he said.

65

Nina looked up, met his eye and smiled. She was not one to shirk her obligations, although the spaghetti and ice-cream lay rather heavy on her stomach.

"We could go in the Ladies."

"Are you mad? What on earth would people say if they saw me coming out of there? That's the trouble with this office, there's nowhere to go when you want some fun."

"We could use Mr Isinglass's room. He won't be back 'til after three. There's a carpet."

"And get me the sack? Thank you very much."

In the end, they decided on the Gentlemen's lavatory. Ferdie locked the door and whispered:

"It's too cramped to do anything in here."

"Not at all," said Nina, adjusting herself and resourcefully climbing on the pedestal.

Once again, youth showed the way.

Chapter Five

"I THINK THE BEST TIME TO TALK TO THE PATIENTS WOULD be when the cocoa goes round at eleven-fifteen. The only two which will be of interest to you are Mrs Van Craven in the far corner and Wendy Moose by the door. There's nothing much wrong with any of the others. Mrs Van Craven has got cancer of the spine, poor dear, and she's paralysed from the waist down. Mrs Moose had it in her colon, or big intestine, and she's been operated on, so we're all waiting." Sister Blossom was a strikingly handsome woman in her late thirties. Arthur was terrified of her. "Now don't mention to them what they've got, there's a dear. And whatever you do, don't get in conversation with Mrs Janks, half-way down on the left. She's a bit disturbed, I'm afraid."

"Excuse me, please." A much less pretty nurse wriggled past, carrying something disgusting wrapped up in a towel.

"Ah, Pearson," said Sister Blossom. "Will you look after Mr Friendship and take him round? He's writing an article on surgical malignancies for *Woman's Dream*, and Matron has agreed to co-operate. Introduce him to Mrs Van Craven and Wendy Moose. But you mustn't let him frighten them."

"Very well, Sister," said Nurse Pearson demurely. "Mrs Moose has just been sedated, and I thought of leaving her alone for a bit."

Sister Blossom looked at her watch. "That is the second sedation today. She will be come an addict."

"Mr Petrucci altered the dosage on his rounds this morning."

"Let me see. Pethidine, 150 mls, four hourly × 5, then morphia 1/3rd grain four hourly × 5 then heroine 2/3rd grain *si opus est*. Oh dear."

"Yes, I'm afraid so."

"Well, perhaps it would be better not to trouble Mrs Moose too much, if she isn't feeling up to it. Just see how she feels."

When Arthur was left alone with Nurse Pearson, he realized that the object she carried was a hypodermic syringe in a kidney bowl. He felt sick. Anything to do with injections always affected him. Once, when all the staff of *Woman's Dream* were forced to be inoculated against poliomyelitis as a publicity stunt, he had fainted. He often thought that one of the reasons for his compassionate attitude to other people was his peculiar hatred of pain in any form. A visit to the dentist usually entailed something approaching a nervous breakdown. On the last two occasions, he was unable to go, as the nervousness affected his stomach and he had to stay in bed.

"Poor Mrs Moose is on what's called a terminal dosage," said Nurse Pearson.

"Oh, really?" Arthur tried to sound interested. Actually, he was too disgusted by the hospital atmosphere. He dreaded having to walk round the Annie Zunz Ward and pretend to take an interest in the patients' affairs. Disease was ugly and sinful. Sick people should not be allowed to clutter the world up, making ordinary, healthy people embarrassed in this way.

"Come and have a cup of tea," said Nurse Pearson. "They're just finishing the dressings in the ward, then the cocoa goes round."

"Thank you," said Arthur, not because he wanted tea. They went into the sterilization room, where nurses' tea was served.

"Yes, I'm afraid Mrs Moose won't be with us very long."

"You mean she's getting better?"

"No, that's just it. Mr Petrucci said he had to cut so much out of her, there's nothing left. Of course, she's too old to take that sort of thing in her stride, anyway."

"You mean she's going to die?"

"Sh!" Nurse Pearson put her finger on her lips. "Mr Petrucci says it won't be more than thirty-six hours."

How perfectly disgusting, thought Arthur, she expects me to go and interview her when she's just about to die. He had discovered again and again that there was no limit to the appetite for publicity among ordinary men and women.

"I don't know how successful your interviews are going to be," said Nurse Pearson. "One of the patients, Mrs Van Craven, is under morphia, and the other one is under pethidine. You may get some rather odd answers."

That is how the truth has been hidden, thought Arthur, of what it feels like to be suffering from cancer. Never mind, it was his job as a journalist to arrive at the truth, although, of course, in the most compassionate way possible.

Another nurse came in.

"Mrs Janks is calling for a bed-pan again," she said. "It's the fourth time since I've been on duty. Honestly, I'd like to throttle her. She never does anything. And if you don't bring it her immediately, she manages to wet herself. I don't know how she does it. Pearson, will you attend to her."

"Sister told me to look after Mr Friendship, from *Woman's Dream*," said Nurse Pearson.

"Well, will you do what you're told to do, just once, for a change," said Staff Nurse Anderson.

When Nurse Pearson had gone, Staff Nurse Anderson said: "Honestly, I don't know. Some of these young student nurses haven't got a clue."

They both laughed heartily over that, then Arthur found himself left alone in the Sterilization Room, also called the Sluice. Nurses came and went on mysterious errands. Occasionally, strange noises filtered through from the corridors. But for ten minutes, Arthur Friendship was alone with his soul.

"How does it feel?" Arthur asked compassionately.

"Not so bad, now I've had my injection," said Mrs Van Craven. "It's the pain in the kidneys I don't like."

"How do you think you got like this?"

"It was the work. My husband told me I shouldn't go out to work, but of course, I wouldn't listen. Now I wish I had, of course."

"Of course," said Arthur warmly. "Do you remember the first symptoms at all?"

"It was the pain," said Mrs Van Craven. "Nothing sharp. Just a nagging pain at the top of my bum. I didn't tell anybody, not at first, then it got worse. Now I can't move my legs or anything."

"What does your husband think?"

"He wouldn't be so interested, now, of course, being dead, like." She cackled to herself for a bit. "But there's my daughter. One thing I'll say for her, she is interested. She comes to see me, always asking after what's happening now. She told one of the nurses I was getting the wrong treatment, which made me laugh. She's a secretary, you see."

"Oh really?" said Arthur.

"One thing I can't understand about her is why there's no children," said Mrs Van Craven. "Her husband, Carl, doesn't want any, of course, but then no man never does. I only had one, and that was by letting my man get drunk on a Saturday night so he forgot himself. She says she's sitting on the fence, but you'd have thought she wanted a couple. It's not as if they can't afford it."

Arthur felt that he was wasting his time. It was really no concern of his enquiry how Mrs Van Craven's daughter proposed to limit her family.

"Send me a copy of *Woman's Dream* if you mention me," she said, when she saw he was going to leave. "Will there be a picture?"

"I don't know," said Arthur. All that would have to be decided at a Pictures Conference later on.

"This is Mrs Moose. Cheer up, Wendy, we've got a visitor for you," said Nurse Pearson.

"Who is he?" said Mrs Moose.

"It's a man," said Nurse Pearson, as if there could be any doubt.

"Arthur Friendship," said Arthur, taking charge. "From *Woman's Dream*."

"That's not my man," said Mrs Moose in a small voice. "There's been a mistake."

70

"I'm a man from *Woman's Dream*," said Arthur sympathetically. "And I've come to help you."

"I don't need any help," said Mrs Moose. "The only thing I'm worried about is who's supposed to get the tea for my man in the mornings back home."

"The almoner's looking after all that," said Nurse Pearson.

"He always likes to have his tea before he goes out to work."

"Does he?" said Arthur. "Well I suppose we all like our nice, homely cup of char. Nothing better in the world."

"And his sandwiches," said Mrs Moose. "You can't expect a working man to get his own sandwiches."

"No," said Arthur. "We all like our sandwiches." He prided himself above all else on having the common touch, but he could not see that this conversation was getting them anywhere. "Tell me, Mrs Moose, how do you feel now?"

"Not so lovely," said Mrs Moose. "Still, I expect I'll pull through, won't I nurse?"

"Of course you will," said Nurse Pearson indignantly. "We'll have you better in no time. Then you can see all your grand-children again. They're all preparing surprises for their granny when she gets home."

"That's right," said Mrs Moose.

"Now, I think it's time you had some rest," said Nurse Pearson. "You don't want to be over-excited when your grandchildren come this evening. See if you can get some sleep, Mrs Moose, dear, and I'll pull the curtains round for you."

Mrs Moose shut her eyes obediently with a happy look on her simple, red face.

"Aren't you coming to look at me," shouted the dreadful woman called Mrs Janks from the other side of the ward.

"No. He isn't interested in you," said Nurse Pearson.

"My operation scar hasn't healed. Nurse, show him the dirty dressings they took off me this morning. I'd like him to see my operation scar."

"It's no good, Mrs Janks. He isn't interested in you."

"Well he's bloody well got to be interested in me. That's what he's here for. I'm not going to be pushed around. That's not what I'm here for, either. Tell him I'm not interested in him."

A woman in the bed next to Mrs Janks started sobbing quietly to herself.

"What's she got to cry about?" shouted Mrs Janks. "She's going out next week. It's us as stays in here have got something to worry about."

Another woman, further down, took up the sobs, and soon the whole ward was weeping. "It's the poor children I'm sorry for," wailed Mrs Janks. Only Mrs Moose slept serenely through.

Arthur was dismayed by the havoc he had caused in the ward, but Nurse Pearson reassured him.

"They often get like that," she said. "After cocoa."

On the way out, she said: "Such a pity about poor Mrs Moose. She's the sweetest old dear."

"Never mind," said Arthur. "With the news from Berlin, it looks as if we'll all be blown up before Mrs Moose can get much worse."

Such talk was obviously above Nurse Pearson's head. "That's right," she said.

Mrs Quorn may have been dimly aware that social advance and the irresistible processes of Thought had altered the status of the Negro in the modern world. On the other hand, she did not approve of callers, and any caller for Mr Friendship was doubly suspect. So it may not have been white racialist passion which accounted for the scowl on her face as she climbed the stairs, although Ferdie, who always inclined to the more dramatic interpretation of events, decided it was.

Arthur was standing in front of the mirror with a silly look on his face when Mrs Quorn burst in. He had been addressing a message of compassionate love to the cancer sufferers of the world, and it took him a little time to realize what was happening.

"There's a visitor to see you, Mr Friendship. A most *unusual* visitor. I told him to stay outside until you had come down to see him. There's no room to talk to him downstairs, as you know I don't like the dining room used as a public lavatory."

Arthur blushed, stung by the injustice of the charge. On reflection afterwards, he decided that his landlady had run out of words, and, like many garrulous people, decided that the volume of sound compensated for lack of meaning. Perhaps she had been at a loss for a word to follow "public". She might just as well have said "public prosecutor" or "public nuisance", but Arthur, who was particularly sensitive about the motions of his bowels, felt offended.

"I was not expecting any visitors, and I am extremely busy," said Arthur.

"I'll tell him to go away then," said Mrs Quorn triumphantly.

After she had gone, Arthur found that curiosity got the better of him. Undoubtedly, he was extremely busy, but he very seldom received any visitors, and he had not meant to be taken too literally.

He leaned out of the window from which, ten years before, Mr Quorn had thrown a medical student who was behind with his rent. An enormous open Cadillac was drawn up outside Albany Chambers. In the front was a chauffeur, in the back, wrapped in furs like a film star of the 1930s, was the unendurably beautiful Liz Pedal. Mr Gray stood on the pavement, shouting and gesticulating at Mrs Quorn.

"Hullo," said Arthur.

"Hi, there," shouted Miss Pedal, waving a glove rather affectedly. "Toe-mass, do look. There's Mr Friendship."

Everybody looked at Arthur, whose little bald patch gleamed in the cruel winter sunlight.

"This bitch says you're out," said Mr Gray.

"Oh no," said Arthur cheerily. "I'm not out."

"He told *me* he was," said Mrs Quorn. "You'll have to stay outside if you want to talk to him."

When Arthur joined them, Mr Gray was talking to his chauffeur. Obviously, he was in a sulk.

"Hello, Elizabeth, ha ha," said Arthur.

73

"Hello, Mr Friendship," said the divine beauty, with a sweet, gay, friendly smile.

"Ha, ha, ha," said Arthur.

"I'm showing Mr Gray round London," said Elizabeth. He's only here for a fortnight." She sighed. Arthur could not bear to look at her, she was so ravishingly beautiful. Yet he was hopeful. There seemed an especial bewitchment in the way she smiled at him. Perhaps she had taken rather a fancy. Arthur would not be at all surprised. He was terrified of betraying the violence of his emotions; his approach should be light, devil-may-care. An experienced seducer toys with the idea of sniffing this pleasant little flower which presents itself to his nostrils. But a serious thought struck him.

"If you incur any expenses while taking Mr Gray round, please hand them in to me. The Movement should pay for that sort of thing. I must say, I think it is extremely kind of you to put yourself out like this."

"That's all right. Toe-mass is paying for everything," laughed Elizabeth. "He's even giving me dinner this evening at the Hilton."

Well really, thought Arthur, I don't see how he can possibly complain, even if he is coloured. It was typical of such a kind, sweet good person as Miss Pedal to take trouble. He only hoped Mr Gray appreciated it.

"Here, you," said Mr Gray.

"Me?" said Arthur.

"Aren't you Arthur Friendship?" The poet sounded sarcastic.

"Yes."

"Well then."

Conversation seemed to die. "We're all looking forward to your talk, this evening, Mr Gray. I hope Miss Pedal's looking after you properly."

"I know all about that," said Mr Gray. There was no mistaking the nasty, satirical edge on his voice. "Aren't you the Editor of *Woman's Dream?*"

Arthur beamed. It was true that he occasionally contributed

book reviews to that journal, but he would hardly aspire to the prestige and importance . . .

"Anyway, I've got something for you. It's a poem. Mr Besant said you would pay me two hundred guineas."

"One hundred pounds," said Arthur. It was curious how artists were often vague about money. The sum was as much as Arthur earned from *Woman's Dream* in six weeks.

"Then I shall keep my poem. One hundred pounds is an insult," said Mr Gray.

"Well, of course I would pay more," said Arthur. "But I am not in charge of contributions accounts."

"Never mind," said Mr Gray. "You can't buy a poem for a hundred pounds." He spoke as if there was some Charter of International Rights forbidding it, as if Arthur were a nineteenth-century slave-owner. It made Arthur feel like one, and he cringed. "Well, shall we say a hundred and fifty guineas," said Mr Gray.

"I can't," said Arthur desperately. "You'll have to see the Editor."

"Honestly," said the adorable Liz Pedal. "Mr Friendship can't do anything. Toe-mass is very sensitive about his poetry. It's a wonderful poem."

"The beautiful Miss Pedal has intervened on your behalf," said Mr Gray. "Then you shall have my poem for a hundred guineas. For no other reason." With a flourish, he handed Arthur a sheet of the Hilton Hotel writing paper. Elizabeth smiled dazzlingly, and the limousine edged away, making Ebury Street look like a Calcutta slum.

> For Elizabeth
> When I am with you, I am glad
> When I am away, I feel different
> You are my catechumen.

"Very nice, no doubt," said Mrs Quorn. "I like the way it's typed." The poem was written on an electric typewriter. "Who's Elizabeth?"

Arthur said nothing. His breast, that stout and manly object, was a turbulence of unwholesome emotions.

"I expect it's the Queen," said Mrs Quorn. "All coloured people are supposed to be very keen on the Queen. I don't know what she thinks about it all, though. All those black men writing poems about her. Oughtn't he to call her 'Majesty'."

"Ma'am is the normal form of address," said Arthur. "Although, if you were dedicating a poem to her, you would probably write it something like this: 'To the Queen's most excellent Majesty: Ma'am, when I am with you, etc.' "

"That certainly seems better. Does she like poems?"

"The Queen Mother is extremely interested in all the arts. She is keenly alive to the latest movements in painting, music, sculpture and poetry. Her daughter, the Queen, has less time, of course, for such things, being weighed down by onerous burdens of State, but she still takes a lively interest. That is one of the nicest things about the Royal Family, I always think. They are wonderful in that way."

"And Prince Philip?"

"Prince Philip is particularly interested in the more modern-minded aspects." Arthur was improvising, but he had no doubt that he was right. "He feels particularly that the younger artists should be given more opportunity."

"And Princess Margaret?"

"Ah, well, since Margaret has married Tony, she has had to take a certain amount of interest. Not all of us were too pleased when we heard about the engagement, but, as things turned out, it seems the best solution for both of them, really."

"That's what I said. I suppose the younger ones are too young to take much of an interest in poetry and that sort of thing."

"You'd be surprised. Charles is a much brighter young man than you might suppose."

"Well, you're the literary expert. What *does* it mean?" Ronald Carpenter was being a bit cocky today, thought Arthur. His blue hair was still dull and his face was pastier than ever, but he sat over his enormous executive desk with a pathetic attempt at jauntiness, like a diseased bull-frog.

"In the first line, I think, he's trying to say how much he enjoys this person's company."

"All right, that's thirty-three pounds six and eightpence worth."

"In the next line, I think he is trying to give some impression of the enormous gulf of separation he feels when they are apart. It's a very difficult thing to put this sort of thing into words when you're dealing with emotions."

"All right, that's another thirty-three pounds six and eightpence worth. Who's this girl he's writing about?"

"It's been suggested that it is either the Queen or the Queen Mother."

Suddenly, the placid heap was animated.

"It's the Queen," said atrocious Mr Carpenter decisively. "We've got a special colour pullout of the Queen Mother in four weeks' time. This one can go with the new full-length portrait of the Queen commissioned by the Royal Air Force Dental Corps."

"The Queen Mother is particularly keen on poetry and the works of the younger poets," said Arthur.

"Rubbish. This is a moving tribute to the Queen from one of her humble Commonwealth subjects."

"Toe-mass Gray is not a Commonwealth subject."

"I thought you said he was coloured."

"He is a coloured American."

"I suppose you are trying to tell me that America is not a member of the Commonwealth." Mr Carpenter's tone was so contemptuous that Arthur did not dare agree that this was his intention. So America became a member of the Commonwealth.

"I don't think it right that he should refer to the Queen by her Christian name. I mean, I know we all do in private conversation, but I think this is a bit different."

"You're out of touch," said Carpenter, using another of his

77

revolting phrases. "You haven't moved with the times. The great thing about the Commonwealth nowadays, and particularly these junior Commonwealth people, is that they're so informal. Prince Philip always wears a leopard-skin, or dances in his underpants when he goes to one of their receptions."

"Yes, but this is the Queen. And I don't think he dances actually in his underpants."

"I was speaking figuratively," said the genius. "Of course, he has other things on, too."

"The proper mode of address is 'Ma'am'," said Arthur.

"No, I think it is charmingly informal of these coloured people to refer to her as Elizabeth. We couldn't get away with it, of course. We're supposed to know better. Now let me see. When I am with you, I am glad." Grotesque Mr Carpenter was reading in a sensitive, poetic voice. "That's very good. When I am away, I feel different. Yes, I like that. You are my catechumen. What do you think he's trying to get at there?"

"The catechumens, in early times, were Christians under instruction who had not yet been received into the Church by baptism."

"I see. What are they nowadays?"

"Much the same sort of thing."

"That sounds all right. I thought he might be suggesting that the Queen was his – ah – girl friend, you know mistress. Only poetically speaking, of course."

"You are confusing catechumen with concubine," said Arthur.

"No I wasn't. We all know what concubine means. But you can't tell with poets. They are liable to say things which just wouldn't go down well with our readers. Sometimes when they speak figuratively, they are taken literally. But there it is. A magnificent tribute to the Queen as head of the Commonwealth by one of her far-flung subjects."

"You know, America really isn't a member of the Commonwealth."

Carpenter looked incredulous: "You mean to say you believe that?"

"I promise you. The United States is not a member of the British Commonwealth."

"I never said the British Commonwealth," said Mr Carpenter craftily.

"What sort of Commonwealth, then?"

"The Commonwealth. Don't you know that America is now practically the leading member of it? You can't have opened your eyes for twenty years."

"America is not a member of the Commonwealth," said Arthur. Obviously it was settling down to one of those boring arguments about fact. They tried looking it up in the *Guinness Book of Records*, but that was inconclusive.

"I'll ask Xandra," said the fatuous Mr Carpenter. He picked up one of his executive telephones, and soon a winsome little receptionist came in. "Will you assure Mr Friendship that America has joined the Commonwealth, and we are no longer living in the nineteenth century."

Xandra looked from one to the other. She obviously did not have the slightest idea. Arthur tried to look dominant, virile, sexually aware.

"I always thought it had," she said. "Certainly, they were on our side in the war, In think. In fact I know they were."

"Thank you very much, Xandra." There was no need to paint the lily, or to throw a perfume on the violet. "Now Arthur, I think we have wasted enough time. Mr Condiment wants you to re-write your 'Christmas Padre's Hour' to deal with the dangers of office parties. That is what I really wanted to see you about. Thank you for the poem. I will see that it goes into our Christmas Number as a Commonwealth Tribute to the Queen. You may not credit us with much but I do think we know how to edit a woman's magazine better than some other people. I'll see you tomorrow with the revised Christmas Message, if I might."

Arthur was dismissed. He scowled at Xandra on the way out. Now he knew why Farter Carpenter had been so cocky. What on earth were the dangers of Christmas office parties? He had never been to an office party.

The real reason for his misery was different. Somewhere he had gone wrong with Elizabeth Pedal. Was it his aloofness that had driven her into the arms of a second-rate Negro poet? Had he been too stern, too unyielding?

"Elizabeth," he moaned, as he walked into Temple Underground Station. "You are *my* catechumen."

"Before Mr Gray gives us his second talk on this important matter of race relations in the modern world, I would like to say that I have been able to arrange with the South East Authority for us to visit the Egg Packing Station and Egg Repository at Slough. That will be in November, and should give us an important insight into the packing and storing of eggs under modern conditions. Most unfortunately, Mr I. G. Andreyev, the well-known Soviet agronomist, is unable to be with us the week after next as he has caught a chill, but Mr Besant is trying to get someone from the Soviet Embassy in London to give us a talk on Soviet Foreign Policy and the International Peace Offensive. Now Mr Gray will give us what promises to be a punchy and thought-provoking talk on the Negro question. He has been in England a week now, and we must hope that his experiences among the English have softened his judgments a little."

It was no good. Nobody understood the reference, and Arthur did not dare look at Elizabeth Pedal to see if his shaft had struck home. Few people seemed to have been paying any attention to Arthur at all. They were watching the chief speaker.

Arthur had absolutely nothing against coloured people; in fact rather the reverse. But he thought it showed exceptional maturity to be able to discriminate between them, preferring one to another. A natural corollary of this position was that one should be allowed, always within the bounds of Christian charity to dislike a particular Negro. Such an attitude, thought Arthur, should always be qualified most carefully. Thus, one's dislike of a particular Negro was to be no reflection on one's attitude to Negroes as a whole, of whom one warmly approved. That said, he could admit to his innermost self, although nowhere else, for fear of damaging the cause, that Gray was a conceited, second-rate fornicator.

No doubt Elizabeth was motivated by the purest desire to improve race relations when she took up with him. If that was so, it was most unfortunate that Peace Education had chosen such an arrogant, unrepresentative member of his race. Elizabeth's politeness merely swelled his conceit. When they walked into the Hall, Elizabeth on Gray's arm, Arthur could swear that the poet had caught his eye and given Elizabeth a conceited pinch on the bottom. And Elizabeth, the sweet angel, had done nothing but smile back at her tormentor.

After the talk, which was punchy and thought-provoking, Ferdie approached Gray where he was standing with Elizabeth.

"I think I've found a lodging-house which refuses to take in coloured people." He produced Mrs Quorn's name and address.

Gray held the piece of paper between his thumb and little finger, wrinkling his face eloquently. "Naturally," he said.

"I find it hard to believe such places exist," said Margaret Holly, eighteen. "What sort of people can possibly want to live in them?"

"Well, Mr Friendship for one," said Gray. Everybody looked at Arthur, who blushed.

"Honestly, I never knew Mrs Quorn didn't take in coloured people," he said. "I've never had any difficulty."

"Nobody ever does know," said Gray sarcastically. "They just find it convenient not to know. And nobody ever troubles them. Of course, you wouldn't have any trouble. *You* are white. *You* have got the upper hand. You don't want to share your bedroom with a nigger, do you?"

As usual, this word produced a ripple of horror through the room. Only Margaret giggled. Arthur warmed to her. Elizabeth gazed adoringly at Gray.

"No, I don't. That is to say, I don't want to share my bedroom with anybody." It was very difficult to explain how sensitive he was about personal privacy. Margaret Holly looked at him oddly. "Of my own sex, that is to say."

81

"He doesn't mind sharing a room with a coloured lady. Then he can do what he will with her and pay her afterwards. But not with a nigger. Oh no."

"I didn't say that. If I had to share my bedroom with someone, I wouldn't mind whether he was coloured or not. But I would prefer not to share with anyone."

"You're the sort of person who brings about race riots," said Miss Holly.

"No, I'm not," said Arthur.

"I think we ought to warn Mrs Quorn," said Ferdie.

"And who could be a better person to do it than Mr Friendship, since he lives there?" Arthur could not understand why Gray was so unpleasant to him. His attitude to the coloured question was unimpeachable, with the one reservation about Thomas Gray. And that was a secret reservation.

"So does Ferdie Jacques," said Arthur.

"I think we all ought to warn her," said Ferdie. "As a deputation."

"Yes, let's," said Margaret.

"Then the fire next time," said Ferdie.

"Fire next time," said everyone.

"I can do nothing," said Mr Gray. "In my position it would do too much harm. Nor can I urge you to do anything. I can just say what is done in the United States. Perhaps, you will want to follow suit. Perhaps you won't. I leave it entirely to you. For myself, I know nothing about it."

He was as subtle, thought Arthur, as a lame hippopotamus.

"Let's go tonight," said Margaret Holly. "All of us."

"I can't come," said Gray.

"Nor can I," said Elizabeth, looking at him questioningly. "I have to go with Toe-mass."

"Why?" said Ferdie.

"She's staying with me at the Hilton," said Gray. There was an awkward silence. After that exchange, some of the life went out of the meeting.

"I hardly think we can rush into this sort of thing," said Arthur.

"We ought at least to form a committee and collect all the available evidence. Then we ought to make a list of lodging-houses all over London which turn down foreign immigrants. Then, when we've got all the evidence and they haven't a leg to stand on, we can have concerted action."

"Petrol," said Miss Holly stubbornly.

"Yes. Fire next time," said Ferdie.

"I propose Mr Ferdinand Jacques as Chairman of the anti-intolerance committee," said Margaret. Since nobody objected, it was obvious that he was chairman.

Thrust into great office, Ferdie suddenly became disconcertingly mature. "We mustn't rush our fences," he said. "We must plan a co-ordinated campaign."

"If you are getting down to the details, I must take my leave," said Gray. "My next talk, I think, is on Friday. I look forward to seeing you all then. But remember, my name must not be linked with anything you may decide to do."

He took Elizabeth Pedal's arm. It was a tender, fragile thing. He put his arm around her waist, and they left together.

As soon as the door had shut, intolerant landladies were forgotten. "Do you think they are sleeping together?" said a small, suet-faced girl called Bernadette.

"Of course not," said a tousle-haired one who smelled of rats. "The Hilton wouldn't allow it."

"Of course they are," said Ferdie. "They wouldn't tell the Hilton, or they could just sign the register as man and wife."

"Gosh. I can't believe it," said Bernadette.

"Neither can I," said Arthur. "Elizabeth isn't like that at all. Besides, what on earth can she see in him?"

"They say they're very good in bed," said Margaret Holly.

"Yes, they are," said the tousle-headed girl who smelled. Her name was Gladys, but nobody had ever asked her.

"You don't know," said Margaret angrily.

"I never said I did," said Gladys.

"Who are good in bed?" said Ferdie.

"Negroes."

"Well, they're not. They're no different from anyone else. That's how silly little girls get taken in."

"I'm not taken in," said Bernadette. "I think it's disgusting."

"You're all wrong," said Arthur. "Elizabeth is simply not like that at all. She's just going to have dinner with him."

"Funny time to have dinner," said Margaret. "Personally, I don't blame her. I think he's quite attractive."

"Aren't we all being a bit hypocritical?" said Ferdie. "Why on earth shouldn't Liz go to bed with him if she wants?"

"They might have coffee-coloured children," said Bernadette.

Ferdie looked at her and sighed. No matter what strides had been made in the emancipation of youth, no matter what serious thought had gone into a Young Persons' Charter of Rights, there would always be such girls as Bernadette Reilly to make sure that nothing ever changed. Ugly, stupid, reactionary, ignorant Bernadette Reilly. The gas chamber was too kind a fate.

Personally, he disagreed with Elizabeth's choice. But he would have died, or fancied he would, for her right to make it. That Gray was a Negro made no difference. If anything, it made the choice more poignant. Ferdie himself, he was prepared to admit reluctantly, was not a Negro. But he was confident that he knew all there was to be known, and had the better performance. It seemed a pity that Elizabeth had allowed herself temporarily to be dazzled by the glamour of having an affair with a Negro. But his time would come.

Meanwhile, it was impossible to converse with people who seriously believed that children were born as a result of going to bed. Such ignorance was invincible.

When Ferdie and Arthur returned to Ebury Street, they sat in the dining room for a time while Ferdie smoked a tipped cigarette.

"What I don't understand is how that black man can afford to stay in the Hilton, let alone keep Liz there, too."

"Education for Peace pays."

"Where do they get all the money from?"

"I don't know, really. It's a world-wide movement, of course, and all those sixpences add up. I think UNESCO coughs up quite a bit of money, or some other branch of the United Nations."

"I thought the U.N. was bust."

"It is, but they still have enough money for really important projects."

"Like the bedding of Liz Pedal. I quite agree. I only wish I had the resources of the United Nations behind me."

"You don't really think they are going to bed together, do you, Ferdie?"

"I have no doubt whatever. Wish it was me, that's all."

"But what on earth does she see in him?"

"Like I always say, all you need is two legs and a thruster."

"But everyone's got them."

"And the confidence. All girls are the same. They just need to be shown there's no nonsense."

"You mean to say that if I went up to Elizabeth Pedal, she'd go to bed with me?"

"Of course she would. All girls are the same. A few have got religious objections, of course, like Bernadette Reilly, but that's only because no-one has ever tried her. Then a few expect to be taken out to dinner half a dozen times before they'll do anything, but you don't want to waste your time on them."

"You may be right," said Arthur. "I don't want to waste my time on them."

Later, they talked about intolerant landladies. "I don't think we want to make things too difficult here," said Arthur. "After all, it is vital to have a base for operations."

"I hadn't thought of that," said Ferdie. "We would look a bit silly if we burned it down while we were still living here. But I think we ought to show that old bitch where she gets off. We can wait until we leave, then burn it down without saying why."

"Yes, I think that would be the better plan," said Arthur. He began to think of going to bed, and of his work tomorrow. "Have you ever been to an office party?"

"Yes, often."

85

"What's wrong with them?"

"Horrible people. Not enough to drink."

"Anything else? I mean, from the moral angle."

"Oh, sex," said Ferdie. "There's a hell of a lot of sex. Feelings which have been corked up throughout the year come out. You see people snogging all over the place. Sometimes it gets quite out of hand. I don't care for it much. Prefer to do my dirty deeds in private."

"Neither do I," said Arthur. "I had no idea they were as bad as that." He resolved to go to the next *Woman's Dream* office party and wondered about Xandra. "It seems a shame about Elizabeth."

"Not at all," said Ferdie. "Try it yourself. I am hitting the hay. Goodnight."

When he was in his bedroom, Arthur prayed for Elizabeth Pedal's soul, and that she would die in a state of grace. Then he climbed into bed, and wondered drowzily how one should set about seducing her. He dreamed of green fields in early summer, where cattle browsed around him and pigeons called to each other in the woods.

It was three-thirty in the morning when the Night Sister was called to Annie Zunz Ward. Nurse Harding, on Night Duty, had already summoned the porters and prepared the papers for her to sign.

"Who is it?" she whispered.

"Mrs Moose, the gastrectomy."

"Careful not to wake up the ward. There'll be hell to pay if Mrs Janks hears anything."

The trolley clattered in.

"Careful there. Easy. You take the bedclothes down, Harding. Leave everything tidy. And remember to get the cupboard emptied."

"Are there any relations?"

"There's a husband. Not on the telephone. I thought we'd leave it until tomorrow morning."

86

"All right. I'll get everything tidied up downstairs. That's the second we've had tonight. Remember to enter it in the book."

The trolley was wheeled into the theatre lift, and taken to the second basement floor. Nurse Harding resumed her letter to a friend who had emigrated to South Africa. Without so much as a whimper, Wendy Moose had departed this life.

Chapter Six

MR BESANT ALWAYS WORE LIGHT BLUE SHIRTS. THEY complemented his impressive light blue eyes, and reflected the genial sparkle which lurked in the recesses behind. His smell, a curious mixture of bay rum, cloves and other oriental spices, was most impressive. He always greeted his secretary in the morning with a conspiratorial chuckle.

"Do you think you could get Colonel Wukovski on the telephone for me? I don't think he'll be at the Legation. Try the other number in Kensington."

He watched Miss Kalugalla bend to her task. She was an extremely attractive little piece, but Mr Besant fancied that he was mature enough to have mastered his baser urges. In the old days, of course, he would have chucked her under the chin, put his hand up her skirt, told her to take her clothes off. But everything was changed. Sometimes, like all men in later middle age, he sighed for the old days. But he was a passionate, almost fanatical believer in progress and man's destiny, as well as being dedicated to a cause which allowed no time for the playful diversions of his youth.

"Hello, Stahsh? Willie Besant here. Yes. I just wanted to say that there is going to be a reporter at the Hounslow meeting tonight. The *Sunday Times* are doing a piece about the movement, and I've told them that one of your men is giving a talk there on Soviet Foreign Policy tonight. Better send one of the better talkers, as we don't want them to get the wrong impression. After Hounslow, he goes to the Victoria group, who are an extremely bright lot, and will take practically anything."

Mr Besant listened for a while, a slight frown of concentration framed in the silvery plumage. Even when he was alone, he assumed that half a dozen eyes were upon him.

"Big news from Germany this morning. What about all these heavy troop movements behind the East German lines, eh? Ha, ha." Mr Besant frowned. He had forgotten how pompous and humourless some Eastern Europeans could be. "No, of course I don't believe a word of the reports. Naturally, I assumed it was nothing but camouflage for Western aggression. My dear fellow, I wouldn't dream of disputing the People's Republic's right to take necessary counter-measures. The only thing which interests me is the Peace angle, and of course we're all scared stiff that those maniac Americans will start taking counter-counter-measures. Of course America would be wiped off the face of the earth, but so would we all, and that isn't quite what we're after, is it? I mean, is it?"

He enjoyed baiting Eastern Europeans, and despised them for their cretinous ideology and their optimism. But listening to the loud explosions at the other end of the line, he reflected that they did at least possess that robust quality of self-assurance which was so essential in the scheme of things.

When the conversation was over, Miss Kalugalla replaced the receiver in her office next door and stared inscrutably at a mural depicting Holborn in the eighteenth century. A bumblebee buzzed.

"Can you spare me a moment, please, Miss Kalugalla."

Submissively, she collected paper and pencil and clicked through the dividing door.

"I want you to round up all the usual people. Letters to *The Times*, telegrams to President Johnson, the Soviet Premier. Open letter to the Prime Minister from forty M.P's."

"What about the Secretary-General of the United Nations?"

"I don't think we'll bother about him this time. It is extremely expensive sending telegrams all the way to New York every time things warm up a bit. You might ask the Ministry of Works what chance there is of a mass meeting of all peace-loving peoples to march on Westminster and demand the resignation of the Government. I'm afraid we've left it too late, as usual. If only they would give us some notice."

"I have already enquired about that," said Miss Kalugalla. Any other employer would be astounded at her efficiency, but Mr Besant always suspected her of impertinence. "Saturday has been booked by the Keep Britain out of the Common Market Committee, and Sunday is reserved for clearing up."

"We might try and join the anti-Common Market people," said Mr Besant. After all, they were both intellectual movements.

"I spoke to Mr Droitwich, the general secretary, and he said he was not interested in the idea."

The Director of Peace Studies began to be irritated. He secretly despised women. Either garrulously pretentious or dumb, they were incapable of original, conceptual thought. But then, there were few classes of people whom Mr Besant did not despise, and it would never do to treat them all harshly.

"Very well, then, my dear. Go off and organize the letters and telegrams," he said kindly.

When she reached the door, April Kalugalla turned round. There could be no doubt she was a most striking young woman in her tight skirt and jersey. A less mature man than Mr Besant would have been profoundly affected.

"Is there any particular message for these telegrams and letters?"

A less self-assured person might have suspected that he was being mocked. It was perfectly true, Mr Besant had forgotten to say what the letters and telegrams were about. He frowned again. It was most becoming. He lifted one eyebrow, drew in his breath and paused. Miss Kalugalla, a lily in the doorway, swayed slightly, exuding a delicate perfume.

"I want them to make four points," said Mr Besant decisively. "I want all hostile activities to cease. I want America and Russia to come to an agreement immediately which is amicable to both sides. Obviously there will have to be a certain amount of give and take; I suggest an independent chairman, such as Bertrand Russell or one of those Indian chappies should settle the terms. Then he could move on to settle all outstanding problems, such as Israeli aggression in the Middle East, the struggle for self-determination among the freedom-seeking people of the Far East and all that sort of thing."

Mr Besant obviously felt he had settled world problems for the day. He leaned back and beamed.

"Point three?"

"You've had point three."

"Point four, then."

"Oh, that we should withdraw from NATO immediately and all other aggressive alliances and live in peace and harmony with each other, channelling all the resources wasted on the arms race into aid for the underdeveloped nations of the world in their battle against neo-colonialism, starvation and that sort of thing."

The details of his schemes always bored him. Mr Besant was the architect of grand designs. The pity was that grand designs only took about half an hour to formulate, and the rest of his time had to be occupied in troublesome details. He shuddered occasionally to think of the indignities to which his idealism led him: embarrassing dinners with absurd, conceited Negroes; speeches delivered to a handful of shivering adolescents in a draughty hall; interminable conversation with cagey, left wing civil servants; clandestine meetings with dull and pompous embassy officials from behind the Iron Curtain; his monthly assignation in Finsbury Park Underground Station with a near-moron from the Central Intelligence Agency; the gruesome and inarticulate Air Force general who was his only contact in the Pentagon; the neurotically over-intelligent official in the Foreign Office who kept accidentally revealing major secrets in his lunch-time conversation under the impression that he, the Director of Peace Studies, was a Russian spy.

"By the way," he said to the departing sylph. "Have you been troubled by any more telephone calls recently from the invalid who wants to see me?"

"No, Mr Besant. Not since last Monday. He seems to have called off."

"Quite right. Dreadful nuisance. I suppose everybody in public life suffers from that sort of thing. What was he called? Milchiger? Mikilker?"

"Something like that," said the sloe-eyed enchantress. Lily-like she drifted from the room, to western eyes as inscrutable as ever. Perha s fellow-Sinhalese could have known that her pulse was beating slightly faster, that her legs felt weak and her whole tiny body, sheathed in tasteful wrappings, was yearning for the lunch hour when she would meet her hatchet-faced lover. But Mr Besant was no Sinhalese; in fact he rather despised the Asiatics for their total inability to do anything except sit on international committees. They could never breed a truly great man, one who would sway the world. But then, it was scarcely to be expected that they should.

At this time of the year (wrote Arthur) *it is natural that our spirits turn to joyousness. People, even old grannies who seldom look at liquor throughout the year, may get a tiny bit tiddly over the Christmas bottle of port, and I should be the last to blame them. The Christian religion, as I never tire of saying in these columns, is not a religion of "Don'ts" and "Mustn'ts". It is a joyful religion, urging all its followers to have a good time in a Christmas spirit.*

To this extent, whatever our old-fashioned notions, we should try to move with the times. Indeed, we must, if we are to survive in this modern world of "mods" and "rockers" and nuclear bombs, and the population explosion of the underdeveloped masses, and rockets to the moon, and all the other exciting and wonderful things which would not have been dreamed of in our parents' generation.

Few people, nowadays, would say that it was sinful to get a little bit tiddly unless you were going to drive afterwards. On the other hand, there are other temptations which can be more serious. I am thinking of office parties. Few of my readers, I hope, will have any ideas about office parties at all, beyond what they have read in the newspapers. Others may have instinctively decided that office parties are "not for them".

But as this is a time of year at which office parties are frequently given and attended, it seems a suitable time to write about them. When I was

a curate in the East End of London, I think I saw the seamier side of life.
There were prostitutes and teenagers brought down by lorry drivers from
the North. There were Negroes living with other Negroes in flats. There
were unmarried teenage girls who habitually carried contraceptives in their
handbags. Yes, I am not trying to shock you; this is true. And there were
the meths drinkers. All these people used to come to me for help and
encouragement.

So I think I can claim to be speaking with some experience when I say that
OFFICE PARTIES ARE DANGEROUS. *Things may get out of hand at*
them, and things may be done which would be regretted afterwards. So my
advice to you . . .

What is my advice? thought Arthur. To take a contraceptive in
your handbag? To stay at home and drink meths? It was an intolerable imposition to expect him to write Christmas messages to
order. One had to *feel* a Christmas message, to *live* it. Under his
superficial veneer of cynicism, Arthur knew in his heart of hearts
that he was an artist. He had once read a book about Michelangelo
by an American writer, and it had touched a deep chord. He knew
all about the agony and ecstasy of creative travail at first-hand. He
reviewed the book for *Woman's Dream*, but the review never
appeared, being superseded at the last minute by an advertisement
for dog food. Perhaps that was why he did not like animals. He
was a warm-hearted person by nature, but for some reason animals
did not touch a chord. Or perhaps dislike of animals was just
another fascinating clue to his many-sided genius. The review had
hinted that he, Arthur Friendship, was just such a one as
Michelangelo. And so he was, but for the life of him he could not
think of any advice to give his followers on the subject of office
parties.

The *Woman's Dream* Christmas party was being held this year
on October 12th, so that photographs and a description of it could
be included in the New Year's number. Arthur had managed to
secure five tickets from Xandra, but he could not think of four
people he wanted to ask.

His great friend, Lord Hargreaves eventually received one, and
so did his other friend, whose friendship with a cousin of the Queen

Mother made him particularly suitable. The third went to Mr Besant, at the Hilton Hotel.

Arthur nursed the remaining card, and thought longingly of Elizabeth Pedal.

"Before Mr Gray gives us the third of his talks, I would like you to have details of the arrangements for Slough at the end of the month. A char-a-banc has been hired which will leave the Victoria Assembly Rooms at 11 o'clock on Saturday morning. At 11.45 we shall be met at the Egg Inspection Centre and taken round before lunch, which will be an egg meal demonstrating the various ways of preparing eggs under contemporary conditions. After that we shall visit the egg chilling plant and the warehouse vaults where eggs can be kept for almost indefinite periods, under modern methods, without any deterioration in the nutritional value.

"I think this visit will be of exceptional interest, and ties in with the related problems of the world food problem and the population explosion in Africa and Asia. One small aspect of this problem is being dealt with tonight by Mr Gray, who will continue his talk on race relations, in which we hope some positive suggestions will be made to ease the very genuine dislike, amounting in some cases to total abhorrence, which unhappily exists between races in the modern world."

Arthur was becoming extremely tired of Thomas Gray. He had seen through the poet, and it irritated him that everyone else could not. When he watched Elizabeth Pedal's adoring face and happy smile, he reflected on the many ways in which possession of a superior intelligence could be a disadvantage. How often he had wished he could be like other men, taking pleasure in the simple things which seemed to keep them happy. Whenever he heard two labourers conversing in their stumbling, unaffected way about the weather, or football, or television, or some other subject of general working-class interest he yearned to be able to participate. But his occasional attempts had been uniformly disastrous. He wished he could enjoy the television serials which so diverted the entire working class of Great Britain, and were enjoyed by those blessed with an inferior intelligence in every class. There could be no doubt about it, stupidity and a low level of sensitivity were the greatest levellers of all, and the most precious assets in the modern world. If only Arthur Friendship could take Elizabeth Pedal in his arms and thrust her, or whatever Ferdie's expression had been, how much happier everything would be. Arthur would reap the unimaginable joys of sexual intercourse with the world's most beautiful woman, and Elizabeth would not have to waste her charms on a charlatan. But he was too sensitive, too intelligent, too civilized. If Elizabeth were as intelligent as he, she could not conceivably be as beautiful as she was. There was nothing so sexually repulsive as intelligence. That explained why Negroes were found attractive. Not for the first time, Arthur passionately wished that he were a Negro.

When Mr Gray stood up, he remained silent for a full minute. It was most effective. Nobody dared to move except Margaret Holly, who giggled, and Ferdie, who cleared his throat. It was the worst thing he could possibly have done. Something about the noise seemed to infuriate the poet. Perhaps it reminded Gray of his great-grandfather's life on the slave plantations in South Carolina.

"Mr Friendship," he said, pronouncing the words sarcastically, as if any normal person would find them funny. Only Margaret Holly giggled. "Mr Friendship talks about easing race relations. What does not seem to occur to him is that race relations cannot be eased. They are here to stay. And furthermore," he shouted, banging the table, terrifying Arthur out of his wits, "they've only just started." He went on more quietly, in a sinister, soft whisper. "We can all of us talk about easing race relations if we want. And we can still be talking when we're lying in bed and a man arrives at the front door to slit our throats. Because you'll all have talked too much. I can talk, too. But I don't. I'm not going to say a word. To anybody. Not even to you. BECAUSE I BELIEVE IN ACTION."

The shouted words fell like pancakes round the draughty hall. Not even Margaret Holly giggled. A spotty-faced young man who

95

sat next to her removed his arm from her shoulder and straightened his tie.

"But what can I do, you will ask yourselves. What can I do to prevent the full brunt of this from falling on me?" When he was describing how his listeners would address themselves, he impersonated a stage homosexual, fluttering his eyelids and wriggling his behind. Perhaps we do talk to each other like that, thought Arthur. He hoped not.

A sigh of merriment went through the hall. Elizabeth Pedal, God bless her, laughed outright. Margaret Holly nearly fell off her chair. Greatly encouraged, Gray left his place by the table and minced up and down the platform, carrying a handkerchief daintily before him.

"Please, Mr Gray, what can I do? I'm so dreadfully frightened. I really think some of these people intend to harm me. What can I do?"

Everybody was in stitches. "Ha, ha, ha," said Arthur. One good thing about the English was that they did know how to laugh at themselves. But they were not allowed to laugh for long.

Gray bounded back to the table and struck it a blow which would have broken any white man's hand.

"You can do NOTHING," he shouted. "Everything the white man can do has been done. You have enslaved a continent and exploited an entire race. Now is the time for other people to be doing things."

Arthur removed the smile from his face and began to feel resentful. This was really worse than a white racialist's nightmare. He was prepared to concede that the coloured races had had pretty tough stretches in the past, but it was time they began to get over that.

"All you can do is attempt to delay the explosion. You can appoint Negroes to all the top positions in government and civil service. You can buy us off – for a time – until you have given over every penny. You can offer us your women – daughters, wives and mothers. You can plead with us to take everything and only spare you. But it is too late. The explosion will come, no matter how long you manage to put it off. You can't alter history, and we are the people of the future."

Arthur was no cynic, but he very much doubted if the situation was quite as desperate as that. Of course, it was always interesting to hear other opinions, and he welcomed controversy.

"The only thing which has prevented our coming into our own sooner has been lack of organization. Now, with modern methods, we are organized, internationally. You try it. Spit in a Negro's face in Tennessee, or in Montreal, or anywhere you choose and you will be a marked man not only in Africa, but all over the world. In London, Paris, Rome, New York, Washington, Moscow, Peking, Belgrade. We will be watching you and we will get you. There is no escape. All over the world, we are waiting. Some of the West is so effete it buries its head in the sand and pretends to see nothing. Others are frightened, and offer us money to try and buy us off. That is all right. We can wait."

On that almost unbearably sinister note, Gray sat down. Arthur was at a loss for words. Anything he said would be an anti-climax. He decided to play it for laughs.

"Well, that was a very disturbing talk. Since it seems there is nothing to do about the race relations explosion, perhaps the best thing would be to lie back and enjoy it." Roars of laughter. Never had one of Arthur's little jokes gone down so well. He attributed it to dramatic relief, like the Porter's scene in *Macbeth*. Elizabeth Pedal blushed and laughed, the cynosure of admiring glances. Emboldened, Arthur went on: "We thought when we came here, we were going to get some food for thought, but it turns out we're going to end as food for the hungry millions, ha, ha."

A few laughs this time; not so many and perhaps attributable in the main to people who had not finished laughing over the first joke. Never mind.

"And I hope when Mr Gray's friends come to take away all our women – sisters, daughters and mothers – they won't forget to take away my Great Aunt Eliza."

No laughs at all, this time. Rows of puzzled, stupid faces. Of course, Arthur had no Great Aunt Eliza, nor any other relations at all. He had invented her in a spirit of fun, to demonstrate the lighter side of the loss. Great Aunts, he had been brought up to believe, were notoriously dull.

"She is a perfect nuisance," he explained. Again, no laughs. They seemed to be expecting further explanation. "I absolutely detest her. She is a pain in the neck. When she comes into the room, I walk out. I hate her."

Wonderment had given way to embarrassed surprise. Arthur realized that perhaps he was talking too passionately.

"Not that she's as bad as all that, really. She's just a bit talkative, I suppose. But I think if Mr Gray's friends really want to take away our womenfolk, the person they should not leave behind would be my Great Aunt Eliza."

It was no good. He had lost the audience. Gray was looking restless.

"If there are any questions before we go through for coffee, perhaps we could hear them now."

There was the usual pause. Then Ferdie cleared his throat.

"What makes you so sure that the – um – Africans are going to win this great racial explosion. I mean, if there was a war between us and the Africans, we will probably win. After all, I know that there are fifty Negroes in the world to every white man, or something like that, but we have got nuclear weapons. Not that we'd use them, except as a last resort. But even in conventional weapons, I think I'm right in saying, we have got the lead."

"Good question. That's what I like to hear. You won't win because you don't want to win. Of course you've got the weapons, but you won't use them, because you have too much respect for world opinion. World opinion wouldn't stand for it. And world opinion," said Gray with a sarcastic grin, "is us."

"And I don't think any of us are advocating immediate genocide," said Arthur hastily, to put the record straight.

"Exactly," said Gray, triumphantly.

"Granted all that," said Ferdie doggedly, "I still think we will put up a fight before we allow you to take away all our kiddies." Ferdie had no kiddies and obviously did not know what he was talking about. His questions were always embarrassing.

"We don't want your kiddies," said Gray. "If you brought them to me on a plate, I would ask you to take them away," he said, holding his nose. Everybody tittered. One good thing about the English was that they did know how to laugh at themselves. "It's you that's going to ask us to take away your wives and womenfolk. You're going to give us all your weapons, because you've got no self-confidence, and we have. It's happening even now."

"If there aren't any more questions, I think we might adjourn to coffee," said Arthur. He did not want to snub Ferdie, but one had to be mature.

"I have not finished yet," said Ferdie. His beard bristled aggressively, and Arthur knew that something unpleasant was coming. But Ferdie adopted his reasonable manner.

"Now, you know I'm no white racialist, and I don't agree at all with the sort of dirty crack about Mr Gray's personal life which we have just heard Mr Friendship make." There was a heightening of tension. Elizabeth Pedal looked proud and demure. Suddenly, it occurred to Arthur that his first most successful joke was open to a dirty interpretation, and he blushed to the crown of his shiny, bald head.

"I believe a man's personal life and his public affairs should be kept separate," said Ferdie. Arthur gazed at Elizabeth, imploring forgiveness, and was met by the proud stare of a woman who has been wronged. "Nevertheless, I do sincerely feel" – as if anything he sincerely felt must be pretty important – "that if the situation is as grave as all that, we should go into the attack. I mean, we could wipe out the entire continent of Africa if we really felt like it. And Asia, too. And as for the coloured minorities in Europe and North America, well, they could be disposed of overnight."

There was a general movement of repugnance. Even Ferdie had overstepped himself. Paradoxically enough, Arthur felt himself warm to the strange young rebel. But he had to show the right spirit.

"How would you dispose of them?" Arthur's voice was crisp, modulated, reasonable. Only more intelligent members of the audience could appreciate the depth of sarcasm behind it. Margaret Holly certainly didn't. She leaned forward, anxious to learn.

Ferdie realized he was out of step, and began to withdraw. "Well, there would have to be a Ministry of Disposal," he said. "And that would take a little time to get up. I'm not saying it should be done, but just that it could be done. I mean, I think there's still hope."

"Well, thank you very much," said Arthur. "And now, I think, the coffee."

Gray looked unaccountably perturbed and hurt. Perhaps he has not had time to think it all out, decided Arthur. He was prepared to admit that it must be hurtful to make a speech in favour of race relations and then hear a member of the audience propose that you should be annihilated. Arthur felt a pang as he saw Elizabeth slide her arm sympathetically through the Negro's. She was too beautiful and fragile to be sacrificed on the altar of race relations.

"Well, you made a fool of yourself," said Arthur.

"I think I was quite right. We should drop our bombs on Africa and Asia, before it is too late," said Ferdie.

"There was no need to tell Mr Gray that."

"You don't think he took it personally, do you?" Ferdie was appalled. "I didn't mean it that way. Not like you making cracks about Elizabeth Pedal. I am very keen on the Negro movement. I was just talking about Western policy, that's all. Perhaps I had better go across and make it all right with him. Besides, I have got a scheme."

Arthur watched him stride across the room. However base the young man's morals, he certainly had confidence. It was just as well that the nation's affairs were not entrusted to Ferdie, or he would try and blow up the under-developed nations. It all stemmed from lack of maturity.

"I say, old chap, I hope you don't think there was anything personal in my remarks just now," said Ferdie. You would never guess that he was an extremely young man addressing someone who was probably the world's greatest living Negro poet. "You know I'm on your side. I was just talking about possible Western strategy."

"That's all right, old man, I quite understand," said Gray, in the tone of a person who has been deeply offended.

"Actually, I've got a scheme I would like to put to you," said Ferdie. "You know the crypto-racialist landlady I was telling you about in Ebury Street? I think we ought to tackle her together. . . ."

Arthur found himself standing alone with Elizabeth Pedal.

"Hello, Elizabeth. You're looking very pretty tonight." Afterwards, he could not understand how he had the courage to say it.

Elizabeth beamed. She was not very pretty. She was divinely, intoxicatingly beautiful. Although Arthur realized that she was somebody else's property, or at any rate that her present attachment to somebody else made her less immediately available, the socialist in him felt most strongly that an object of such beauty should be public property.

"I hope you don't think there was anything personal in the remarks I made just now – about you and Mr Gray."

"That was all right. I thought it rather funny myself."

"Why was that?" Arthur could not conceive how Elizabeth thought it funny. The morals of the younger generation never ceased to amaze him. But his curiosity was aroused, and he enjoyed frankness, being a life-long opponent of humbug in any form.

"Well, it's not as if I am trying to keep anything secret." She really must be quite extraordinarily immoral.

"No, of course not. After all, times have changed."

Elizabeth looked puzzled, before turning her sparkling eyes on him. "Have they?" she said. Perhaps he imagined it, but there seemed to be something almost provocative in her manner. He laughed knowingly, but he felt weak at the knees.

"What I wondered is whether you would care to come to a little do we're having tomorrow night."

"What?"

"Well, it's a sort of office party. We're having it early this year before Christmas."

"Oh dear, it's very kind, but I really don't see that I can. You see, I don't know what Toe-mass is doing."

"I don't expect he would mind if you disappeared for just one evening. After all, he sees you all the rest of the time." Arthur leered.

"Well, I'll have to ask him. I'm afraid there isn't much chance."

"I'll telephone you tomorrow and ask. I've got your number."

"Yes, do. I'm out of the flat, just at the moment, and staying at the Hilton. You have to ask for Mrs Gray; I don't know why. But I'll let you know tomorrow."

"We could have some dinner afterwards," said Arthur, astounded at his own savoir-faire.

"I'll have to ask Toe-mass."

Arthur leaned over the washbasin and raised his eyebrows. It was true, of course, that he was a trifle bald, but baldness was a sign of intelligence. That was why Negroes were seldom bald. And his face, although unremarkable at first glance, rewarded closer study. It revealed a wealth of humour, kindness and honest fun. Arthur rolled his eyes merrily and chuckled at his daring. He could be the best company in the world, when he was feeling in the right mood. It was a shame his fellow-creatures took such little advantage of it. No doubt they were put off by his austere public face. You had to get to know Arthur extremely well before his full potential was revealed, and nobody had ever got to know him extremely well. It was the world's loss.

For his part, Arthur delighted in his own company, and scarcely knew the meaning of loneliness. He never ceased to surprise himself. On one occasion, he stood in the centre of the room and dropped low curtseys to his pillow. Perhaps there were other men in their early thirties, living alone in rented accommodation throughout London, who possessed the same ability to divert themselves, but Arthur doubted it very much. He was unique, and knowledge of his own uniqueness bolstered his belief in the existence of a deity to whom he was directly and personally responsible. There was no question of applying to blue-haired Carpenter who passed his application to the maniac Condiment who might remember to mention it at his next meeting with God. The hot line ran straight from his bedsitter in Ebury Street to Supreme Headquarters.

Arthur found himself pleased with this conceit, and made a note to include it in the Rev. Cliff Roebuck's Message for New Year.

Tonight, he felt curiously restless. He surveyed his gramophone records, wondering which would catch the mood of the moment. Mozart was too mathematical. He wanted something powerful and impulsive, perhaps concealing its latent violence under a theme of almost deceptive simplicity. The Kreutzer Sonata.

There could be nothing remarkable in the fact that he had just asked the most beautiful woman in England out to dinner. Such incidents were commonplace in the life of a man whose daily work and social round took him among the greatest in the land. While the first movement played its solo violin adagio, Arthur wondered whether Elizabeth Pedal would be a suitable person for him to take to the Palace, as one day, he supposed, he might have to. He decided she would. As soon as she had accustomed herself to the strangeness of it all, and overcome her natural awe at the magnificent surroundings, she could not fail to get on with that other Elizabeth whom Arthur always thought of as Lillibet.

Ferdie returned to Albany Chambers bristling with excitement.

He burst into Arthur's room waving a bit of paper. The confidant of Royalty was lying asleep on his bed, fully clothed with his mouth open. The gramophone, after a long tarantella in sonata form, hummed to itself with the pointless clicking noise of a satisfied woman. Ferdie removed the record, making a terrible sound like tearing paper.

"What on earth are you doing? Don't you know this is my bedroom? You've ruined my record." Arthur nursed himself back to life. "What time is it?"

"Two o'clock and a fine blustery morning," said Ferdie, wiping his hands on his bottom, as if the gramophone record had contaminated them.

"What on earth do you mean by crashing in on me at this time of night?" Arthur could tell that Ferdie was drunk, and began to fear for his safety.

"I went back to the Hilton with Toe-mass and Liz. Lovely suite they've got there. We were talking about leadership of the white resistance movement, and the need for someone to give a lead to white liberal thought in the battle for negroes' rights."

"You've been drinking," said Arthur.

"We decided that leadership was needed. Toe-mass thinks it's between you and me for who shall take the whites back to sanity."

"Oh, does he?"

"Quite honestly, Toe-mass wasn't sure you had got the fire in your belly. We've got a plan for tomorrow, to tame Mrs Quorn. Would you like to take part?"

"You know I'm going to be extremely busy tomorrow. What are you going to do?"

"Just give her a piece of our mind, and let her know that it is the fire next time. We're coming round in the evening."

"Well, I'm afraid I can't join. I've got a reception tomorrow evening, and then I said I would give someone some dinner."

"Who?"

"Liz Pedal, actually."

Ferdie whistled. He really was a most boorish young man.
"Does Toe-mass know?"

"Why should he?"

"Well, I noticed he wasn't too keen on my speaking to Liz this evening. He kept trying to interrupt."

"I don't know whether Liz has told him or not. She may have done."

"You should be careful, you know. These negroes are tremendously jealous. Wasn't there a famous case of one who strangled a girl because he found one of her handkerchiefs somewhere?"

"There may have been. But there is no reason why he should ever know anything about this little *affaire*."

"It isn't as if there is only Toe-mass. He runs a sort of secret service, to revenge any wrong done to a black man anywhere. They hunt you down."

Arthur looked very mature. "I think we're being just a tiny bit dramatic about it all, don't you?"

"I don't know. They're organized, you know. It's just a question of time before they strike. Of course, I'm on their side, but I think the Western Powers ought to do something about it while we still have the upper hand."

"What sort of thing?"

"First of all, get all the Africans there are back in Africa. Then, if they're still making trouble, blow them up with a hydrogen bomb." Ferdie started looking mature, too. "Of course, one doesn't like to think about it, but there's no good in not looking facts in the face."

"Don't you think it would be better just to learn to love them?"

"Of course it would." Ferdie paced up and down the room. "But they don't want to be loved. Toe-mass was telling me. The more people that hate them, the more they like it. We've got to respect them."

"Well, let's respect them, then." Arthur resented having to listen to political harangues at two o'clock in the morning.

"If you don't mind, Ferdie, I've got a lot of work to do."

After Ferdie had gone, Arthur went to his desk and wrote:

My advice to you is to leave office parties well alone. Or, if you must play with fire, give your own office party at home – just for the family. It will be easily as much fun, and you are less likely to regret it afterwards.

Chapter Seven

"THERE WAS A LOT OF EXCITEMENT LAST NIGHT," SAID MR Dent. "Were you having a party, Starter?"

"Who, me? No, I didn't hear anything," said Captain Starter.

"Slamming of doors, raised voices, music; all at two o'clock in the morning."

Arthur pretended not to hear them. He had a most important telephone call to make.

"I thought war must have been declared. What do you think it was, Starter?"

"Beatniks, I expect. It's a pity they abolished National Service. It's not as if they are any happier with their coshes and leather suits," said Captain Starter. "One of the reasons they're so unhappy is that they have nothing to do. Most young people need a challenge. We used to organise basket-ball games at Aldershot, to keep the men occupied. Of course, many of them were of pretty low intelligence."

"But at least it prevents them from annoying everybody else."

"Exactly," said Captain Starter. "An idle man is a discontented man, and a discontented man means trouble."

"I wonder if young Jacques there has ever thought of basket-ball. You have to put the ball through a kind of basket," he explained to Ferdie, who looked preoccupied. "Of course, you'll all be in uniform soon. It looks as if we'll have to have general mobilisation if things go on the way they are. What do you think, Starter?"

"Hard to say," said Captain Starter, as if he knew the answer and wasn't prepared to give away a military secret. "Of course, the danger is the Russians would interpret it as a provocative action. They're very touchy about that sort of thing."

"Still, if we're going to fight them, it doesn't matter what they feel." Mr Dent was not to be put off.

"Hard to say. If there is a war, of course we'll fight. But you don't want world opinion to say we started it. The days of gunboat diplomacy are over, you know. You've got to think of the risks of escalation."

"Heh, heh," said Mr Dent. "By the time we're all a pile of radioactive dust, you won't know who's escalated into whom."

Arthur walked out of the room. He simply could not sit and listen to people talking like that. Besides, he had an important telephone call to make.

"Davy Crockett was rather on his high horse, I thought, this morning," said the irrepressible Mr Dent. "Probably scared he is going to be mobilized. Do they still make the recruits do press-ups?"

"Oh yes, and basket-ball. The idea is to combine physical fitness with mental agility. Of course, a lot of the recruits are pretty poor material."

"Still, I'd like to see old Davy Crockett doing press-ups."

"He might be quite good, actually," said Captain Starter thoughtfully. "A lot of those bald people are."

Ferdie left the room.

"Must have been quite a night," said Mr Dent. "He doesn't normally leave for work at quarter to nine."

"What were they up to? Do you think it's all right leaving those two together on the top floor? It's not as if they are the same age."

"I don't mind what they do, as long as they don't make a noise about it. We should talk to Mrs Quorn. She told me she wouldn't mind losing one of them if she could find someone to take the room."

Arthur came back into the room.

"Have either of you got six pennies for a sixpenny bit?" he asked defiantly.

"Mr Friendship wants to spend a penny," announced Mr Dent. "Sorry, old boy, I've only got three."

"I want four."

"I've got two."

"Thank you very much. I will repay you tomorrow."

"Not at all. Have it on me."

"If you wish, you can have the sixpence and owe me the the balance."

"Steady on, old chap."

"Or I shall owe you respectively one penny and three pennies."

"No need to lose any sleep about it. We all get taken short sometimes. Have it on me."

"It is for the telephone," said Arthur with dignity. "I shall repay you tomorrow morning."

"Queer cove, that," said Captain Starter, when he had gone.

"I'm going to talk to Mrs Quorn about him," said Mr Dent.

"This is Mr Gray's suite. Mr Gray is out. May I take a message?"

"Um. Ha, ha. Is that Miss, ha, ha, Pedal?"

"Who is speaking, please?" There could be no mistaking the silvery tone, although she was trying to sound impersonal. Arthur wanted to weep into the telephone.

"This is Mr Friendship. I was hoping to talk to Miss, um, ha, ha, Elizabeth Pedal."

"Oh, Mr Friendship, Liz Pedal here."

"Ha, ha, ha," laughed Arthur. "I wonder if you have reached a decision yet."

"A decision?"

"Whether you can come out with me this evening."

Elizabeth had obviously forgotten about the whole arrangement. "Oh dear, I'm afraid I really can't. You see, I haven't asked Toe-mass."

"Toe-mass is busy this evening. He won't be able to be with you."

"Oh, all right then. I'd love to come."

"I'll collect you in a taxi at six."

Arthur put down the telephone, his heart singing effervescently.

"Mr Carpenter won't keep you a moment," said the pretty little pussy cat curled up around Reception.

"Can't wait, I'm afraid. I'll just pop in and see how he's getting on."

Humming merrily to himself, Arthur popped in.

The Editor of *Woman's Dream* was drinking sweet tea with Miss Roger Barracks, in charge of Family Fairground and Home Hints. She was his confidante and the only member of the staff with whom he occasionally shared his blue tablets, which smelled of violets. They decided to ignore Arthur, although Miss Barracks watched him apprehensively.

"It was the last scene I particularly enjoyed, when it turned out that the ghost of Trenkettering Castle was in fact the mother-in-law. I couldn't have borne it if the story had an unhappy ending."

"No stories in *Woman's Dream* have unhappy endings," said Carpenter smugly.

"It was so clever the way we were kept guessing until the very end – was Richard a murderer, and had Sally taken on more than she bargained for, when she married into this old Cornish family with its terrible legends? I honestly cried when she fell into his arms at the end over the corpse of the terrible mother-in-law. I suspected the housekeeper myself."

Miss Barracks was a terribly sentimental old thing, but Ronald was fond of her. Something about her deep voice and warm woollen jerseys touched a chord. "I think it was a good serial, too. It illustrated in a very striking way the problem which arises among many young couples today, of the possessive mother-in-law."

"That scene in the ruined vaults under the great hall of the Castle, when Richard said: 'I am the last of the Trenketterings,' and Sally said: 'Need you be? Trust me, Richard.' Then of course the old butler had to arrive, carrying a lighted candelabrum."

"Many young couples find it difficult to be alone. It comes from living on such a crowded island. No wonder you have these appalling scenes in the London parks. The long-term answer, of course, is contraception. But not among the unmarrieds – yet, at any rate. We may get round to that, of course. But I feel our young girls should be protected." Carpenter spoke as if he was being controversial, but in point of fact the entire staff of *Woman's Dream* knew that this was editorial policy. Other women's magazines had taken the plunge, and said that teenage daughters, after frank and free discussion with their parents, should make up their own minds as to whether to be fitted with contraceptives before marriage. *Woman's Dream*, by ignoring the debate, had decided that teenagers should be protected, at any rate until the population problem grew worse.

"Morning, Ronald," said Arthur cheerily.

"The great problem, you see, Rodge, which any woman's magazine editor must face sooner or later, is how far can we go?" Carpenter continued with dignity. "On the one hand you have people who say that any mention of contraceptives encourages promiscuity among teenagers, on the other you have the people who say that more knowledge would result in less casualties. That is the sort of question we try to deal with in our stories and feature articles. Of course, we can only nibble at this stage."

"I never really believed in the Monster of Trenkettering," said Miss Barracks. "You never find ghosts in the magazine. You may get them in real life, but never in *Woman's Dream*. They always turn out to be someone pretending."

"If we just wanted to go in for reality, we could show them photographs of Belsen, or Hiroshima victims," said Carpenter. 'But women don't like that sort of thing. They like love stories,, and things with a human interest."

"I've brought the Christmas message," said Arthur. "And the cancer number is finished, but I think I'd better take that straight to Mr Condiment."

"No, leave it here," said Carpenter sharply. "I would like to look at it first."

"I'm afraid Mr Condiment particularly asked me to take it straight to him," said Arthur happily.

"He would not wish you to by-pass me."

"Well, I think that was rather the whole idea. It is going to be something entirely different from the usual run of *Woman's Dream*. We are having five thirty-second spots on television to advertise it."

"I don't know anything about that," said Carpenter.

"I know," said Arthur, with a little giggle.

"Well, I'm afraid you're too late with your Christmas Message," said Carpenter. "It's already at the printers'. We had to use your earlier piece about Christian permissiveness, or something. The Chairman won't be too pleased. He didn't like Doctor Dorkins's contribution about Chilblains, either."

"Upset tummies," said Arthur. "Gastro-enteritis."

"Exactly," said Carpenter. "The Chairman thought it sounded old-fashioned. Not the sort of thing modern women are interested in."

"I've got the cancer number for them," said Arthur.

"I don't like this cancer idea at all," said Miss Barracks.

"Neither do I," said Carpenter warmly.

"Of course, it will only appeal to the younger, more modern-minded type of woman," said Arthur scathingly.

"I think it's appealing to their lower instincts," said Miss Barracks. "You don't want to pander to the masses."

"Exactly," said Carpenter. "On a responsible woman's magazine, it's our duty to educate them as far as possible. They don't want to be told only about the nasty things in life. Many of them have quite enough to put up with at home, poor things. You wouldn't understand about the ordinary, working-class sort of people, Arthur."

"Yes I would." He avoided the temptation to say that many of his best friends were from the working class. It was too obviously untrue. He was known to enjoy the friendship and respect of those close to the Royal Family, people who happened to be members of the peerage, and many others. But it was absurd to say that because he occupied an exalted social position, he was unable to mix with even the humblest members of the society on terms of friendship and equality. "As a matter of fact, I see quite a lot of ordinary sort of chaps."

"Have you tried talking to them about cancer? They don't like it," said Miss Barracks.

"As a matter of fact, they were quite interested." Both the Editor and Miss Barracks looked sceptical, but as neither had the slightest contact with members of the working class, they were in no position to contradict.

"Of course, we're really aiming for the middle incomes nowadays," said Carpenter. "Your background was all right for the old days, Arthur. But times have changed and you haven't. Nowadays they want to be shown what's bright and smart and new. You think of nothing but the world you knew with Dad wearing a cloth cap and taking sandwiches to work. Of course, it was the most splendid way of life," he added enthusiastically. "But it has passed."

Nobody knew about Arthur's background, and he was not going to tell them. The suggestion that it was anything but extremely respectable was preposterous. Carpenter's father inherited a chain of pork pie factories in the West Country, but they had not prospered much under his administration. He married a lady some years older than himself, and Ronald was their only contribution to the over-population problem. Arthur could not imagine how such a background was thought suitable to occupy a position of such prestige and importance.

"I'll see you all at the party this evening," he said.

Carpenter wondered how he had come by an invitation. Generally speaking, editorial contributors were asked by the editor, or not at all. Arthur was never asked.

When he had gone, Carpenter said: "Poor old Friendship. We should not hold his humble background against him, I suppose."

"After all, it might have been any of us. But still, I think the general tone of the magazine does need raising a little, and it isn't easy with people like him around. Perhaps there aren't many who would do the job. For the money."

"We can only use what material we have. I often wonder if the age of our sort of people isn't over," said Carpenter, helping himself to another violet-scented tablet.

Ferdie ignored the scowls of his friend the proprietor. "The spaghetti is particularly good."

"I do not eat spaghetti," said Gray.

"Then you must try the osso buco. It is excellent."

Little man, little man, is *must* a word to be addressed to Princes?

"I will have a steak," said Gray.

Ferdie cursed. The steaks cost fifteen shillings each, and were not particularly good.

"I still think we should bring a can of petrol, just to show her we mean business," said Ferdie.

"Not at all. I think there may yet be time for a peaceful settlement. I am a great believer in peace. I have lived for peace, and I am prepared to die for peace."

"Exactly," said Ferdie. "There can never be peace in this world so long as there are people like Mrs Quorn around. She and her sort are among the biggest obstacles to world peace that exist."

"I agree with you," said Gray. "But unfortunately my hands are tied. Nobody knows this yet, but my agent in New York received a letter yesterday from Sweden telling me that if I keep my hands clean there is a chance I might be in the running for a certain Peace Prize which I shall not name. So any violence must be done by other people, if you see what I mean."

"The Nobel." Ferdie's eyes shone. He had always rather fancied his own chances for this particular prize, although only half-consciously. Whenever he left Albany Chambers for a few days, he looked forward to opening his letters on return, just in case there was one from Stockholm telling him that his labours for world peace had at last been recognized. His hope for self-advancement was either that or the football pools, and as he

114

never filled in a coupon, his chances were slender. But Ferdie had never been entirely serious in his aspiration; he read the New Year's Honours Lists each year with the same sort of hope in mind. "Many congratulations."

He reflected that it was only because Gray was a Negro that he was being awarded it. Such poor white trash as he would never even be considered. Ferdie had been born in the wrong place and at the wrong time. In the thirteenth century, he would have been a Genghis Khan, conqueror of the world. In the fifth century, he would have been one of Attila the Hun's generals. As it was, he was no more than a junior advertising executive on the fringe of the World Peace Movement.

Gray looked modest. "Nothing is certain yet, they may even give it to someone else."

Both thought this most unlikely.

"That's all right. I'll look after the ugly side of things," said Ferdie. He had suspected Gray of cowardice for a moment. "Your name will never be connected with the fire."

"I do not even think you should burn down the house. Not after I have been there. Other houses, perhaps. You must hunt for other landladies who refuse coloured rights."

"Well," said Ferdie. "We'll see." He recognized a friend. "Why, there's Johnny the bloody Milkman. Come and meet my friend Mr Gray. He's probably the greatest American poet in the world, but nowadays he spends most of his time working for peace."

"Thank you, I know all about him," said Mr Milchiger. He was with a party. The Sinhalese secretary gazed at him adoringly. "This is Mr Abba Sapir. Mr Dov Allon. Mr Pinhas Barzilai. Mrs Golda Ben Almogi. Miss April Kalugalla."

"We know each other," said Ferdie, looking at Miss Kalugalla suggestively.

"Who are these men?" said the woman introduced as Mrs Ben Almogi.

"They are friends of Mr Besant," said Johnny the Milkman.

"Oh," said Mrs Ben Almogi. She was an incredibly tough

blonde in her early forties. Ferdie decided that she was probably French.

"I am a Negro," said Gray. It was a habit of his.

"I know," said Mr Milchiger. He had seldom looked so hatchet-faced. Miss Kalugalla was in raptures.

There seemed nothing left to say. "Well, we must be getting on with our meal. Nice to see you again."

"They didn't like me," said Gray. "I don't mind. I don't want to be liked. We coloured people can get on just as well without them."

"Oh, shut up," said Ferdie.

The Nobel Prizewinner looked hurt, then ate his steak in silence.

Liz was waiting in the foyer of the Hilton, ravishingly lovely in an elegant charcoal grey coat. Arthur shivered as she sat beside him in the taxi.

"Are you cold?"

It was his nerves. They always affected his stomach. "I think I may have a bilious attack coming on."

"Oh dear. Are you sure you want to go to this party?"

"I'll be all right." Gruffly, manfully. "How are you?"

"I'm all right."

Conversation faltered.

"You're sure it's all right with Toe-mass?"

"I spoke to him myself." Arthur was feeling reckless. Goodness, but the girl was immoral. He thrilled to her.

"You're shivering again." Her breasts, though small, were firm and high. Arthur could scarcely bring himself to look at her, in case she sensed the violence coiled up inside him.

"Bit of tummy trouble," he said lightly. "We're nearly there."

Elizabeth caused quite a sensation in the Princess Ida room of the Savoy. Everybody was there. Mr Condiment, the Chairman, Roland Cleghorn, the distinguished *Woman's Dream* columnist,

116

Mr Besant, beaming at the photographers, Ronald Carpenter, shaking his blue locks as he enjoyed a joke with Miss Roger Barracks, Tristram Catchesyde, the pushing young features editor, Lord Hargreaves, who happened to be a member of the peerage, Kenneth Dribblepick, the accountant, Lady Lewisham and Barbara Cartland. A bevy of beautiful girls was supplied by the agency which *Woman's Dream* sometimes employed for its cover photographs, but none came near to the lustrous, serene beauty of Elizabeth Pedal.

"What will you have to drink, Elizabeth?"

"Nothing, really."

"Go on."

"No, really. Well, some Coca-Cola then."

A waiter was sent scuttling to the cellars which stretched for miles in every direction, across the Strand to Covent Garden, under the Embankment to the Thames. Coca-cola was brought and everyone smiled. It was one of the most glittering occasions of the year. Elsie Peartree, the romantic novelist was there, in a tiara made of old-fashioned paste.

Arthur drank vodka and martini and ate stoned olives. "Do you know Roland Cleghorn, the distinguished author?" Even Arthur could not find it in his heart to disparage Roland Cleghorn. He was so utterly distinguished. Mr Besant himself seemed to recognize a competitor. They both had grey hair and crinkles around the eyes. Whereas Besant smelled of bay rum and cloves, Cleghorn smelled of roses but they both smelled distinguished. Arthur was torn between the two in his desire to emulate. His own smell, chosen with care, was called Silvikrin. Both represented what Arthur might one day become, but he was not sure which. One, the distinguished man of letters, summed up all his literary aspirations. The other, the public figure and elder statesman, was Arthur's *altera persona*. He sometimes felt the tremendous conflict which raged between the demands of his public life and his artistic compulsions. But there it was.

"Arthur writes all the Medical hints in *Woman's Dream*," said said the insufferable Mr Carpenter.

"And the book reviews," said Arthur.

"Isn't there something else you write?" said Carpenter.

"I don't know. What are you talking about?"

"I'm not sure. I just thought there might be something else." Even the atrocious Carpenter was not going to expose him as the Reverend Cliff Roebuck. Arthur took another drink, which turned out to be whisky and soda.

"Have some more Coca-cola."

"No, thank you. Really." Although immoral, Liz had the most beautiful manners.

"Ah, drinking Coca-Cola I see." Roland Cleghorn seemed to think it formed a bond. "So sensible. Not like many young girls today, if we are to believe what we read. Yet you are going to break a lot of young men's hearts before long, my dear. Never have I seen such a beautiful peach-coloured complexion. Tell me, where did you find her?"

"Liz and I have known each other for some time."

Elizabeth smiled, the sweet, gentle smile of one who has suffered.

"People like you, Elizabeth, make me wish I were twenty years younger." It was well known that Cleghorn had no time for girls, but he charmed them as a peacock might in its pride.

"Who is that extraordinary girl?" said Miss Barracks.

"Something Friendship brought along."

"She looks much too young to be allowed out alone with people like him. If I were her parent, I would ask her to bring the young man home first."

"So would I," said Carpenter. "She probably doesn't think her parents would approve."

"I'm not surprised."

"But seriously, Rodge, what do you think she sees in him?"

"There's a certain sort of girl who falls for that sort of man. It's a bit peculiar – they will go for anyone, lorry-drivers, postmen, bar-tenders. Psychologists say that they can only release their tensions by degrading themselves."

"But do you really think we are going to have a war over Berlin, Mr Besant? How fascinating."

"I'm afraid there's the possibility." Besant's eyes were shining. "We're not going to be able to hold the Americans in check much longer. If only we could assure the Russians that no matter what they do, we shall do absolutely nothing at all in retaliation, then we might shame them into doing nothing. But all this tough talk is just spurring them on."

"How terrible. You don't think we'll have rationing again? The Government wouldn't dare, would they?"

"I decided not to bring Jacquetta, my pet kangaroo," said Elsie Peartree. "She doesn't like crowds."

"Of course not," said Tristram Catchesyde sympathetically.

"And I was told there might be a black man coming. I don't think she'd like black men. She has probably suffered too much from them back home. Some of them are terribly cruel to animals."

"Are they?"

"The savage ones."

"Well, Mr Gray couldn't come at the last moment. He's a poet."

"I don't think she'd like poets. She's jealous enough of me writing as it is. I tell her it's all for her good. Otherwise I wouldn't be able to feed her."

"Of course not. What does she eat?"

"Anything at all. That's what is so wonderful. Corned beef, baked beans, Irish stew. She particularly likes marshmallows."

Arthur finished his drink. It tasted like brandy and ginger ale. Or it might have been champagne. "Won't be a moment," he said.

The corridor outside was long, wide and empty. Arthur trotted down it, humming to himself. His feet made no noise at all on the carpeting.

"Do you happen to know where the gentlemen's toilet is?"

"Indeed I do."

There was no end to the insolence of the working classes these days. Coming from a labourer, it was traditional Cockney wit, but a waiter should know better.

"Where is it then?"

"End of the corridor. Round the corner. Bottom of the stairs, on your left."

"Thank you so much."

"It's a pleasure."

Arthur trotted on. He knew that "Toilet" was the incorrect expression, but "lavatory" was too biological, "Gents" too familiar. "End of the corner, down the stairs, on your left and hoop-la," he hummed to himself. He opened the door and entered. A gathering of middle-aged men seated in chairs round the room started to clap. He went out again.

"Do you happen to know where the gentlemen's toilet is?" The man walked on.

"I say, do you happen to know where the gentlemen's toilet is? I say." Overcome with fury, Arthur ran after the man and seized him by the shoulder. He was tall, and hatchet-faced. "Oh, hullo. Don't I know you?"

"I am looking for the Princess Ida room," said Mr Milchiger.

"Top of the stairs, round the corner, end of the corridor, on your right and hoop-la," said Arthur helpfully.

Mr Milchiger looked thoughtful. "Does Mr Besant come to receptions here often?"

"Quite often, I expect. We all do. It's the normal place for receptions."

"The corridors are wide. There is access from both the Strand and the Embankment. From the Embankment it is easy to cross Blackfriars Bridge. Then you have the whole of South London open to you."

"Quite right. It's a capital place. I don't actually go to South London much. All my friends seem to live in the West End."

They separated. Arthur met a doorman.

"Are you waiting for anyone?"

"I am looking for the gentlemen's toilet, actually."

"The nearest public conveniences are situated in Temple Underground Station. Along the embankment, and on your left."

"Thank you very much." Arthur tipped him sixpence.

"Thank you, Sir. You should have no difficulty in finding them."

In Princess Ida room, the party was warming up.

"You're just the sort of girl we're looking for. We could make quite a big thing of you. I don't suppose you're ever free in the evenings?" Tristram Catchesyde was not one to miss an opportunity.

"Not often, nowadays, I'm afraid," said Elizabeth, with an enchanting smile.

"Honestly, we've got hundreds of vacancies for girls in the features department, on the secretarial staff, or, if you can't type, in the packing department. Even in the canteen."

"I'm not actually looking for a job at the moment."

"I suppose you want to become an air hostess," said Tristram bitterly.

"Wouldn't mind."

"Well, you stand a better chance than in modelling. But very few girls get through. Have a fag?"

"No thank you."

"Go on. I've got plenty."

"I'm afraid I don't smoke."

"Wise girl. You know, I think we've got a lot in common."

"Of course the Americans are mad. Absolutely barking mad, every one of them. But that is something we have got to live with. Peace, you see, is indivisible."

"Of course it is. They have got almost as much right to it as we have. But do you think we'll have the call-up?"

"I don't see how they can avoid it. Personally, I'm in favour."

"Oh, Mr Besant."

"If only to make people aware of the seriousness of the situation and the need to do something urgently."

"Still, it seems rather drastic. And petrol rationing?"

"No, I can't see any need for that at present," said Mr Besant generously.

"Some people say I talk too much about my mother," said Mr Cleghorn. "But I don't see how you can talk too much about someone you have loved."

"Jacquetta adores smoked salmon," said Elsie Peartree, filling her handbag with sandwiches. "She has never much cared for olives."

"I think that girl must look rather like Sarah."

"Sarah?"

"Trenkettering. She married Richard, the last of the Trenketterings and went to live in Trenkettering Castle, the gloomy old family seat in Cornwall."

"She's called Elizabeth Pedal."

"They always are." Roger Barracks made a poor-little-me face and called for more cider. Her powder compact fell to the floor. It had been a free gift, distributed with each copy of *Woman's Dream*.

When Arthur returned, he found himself standing with Mr Condiment.

"Have you received my cancer enquiry, Sir?"

"What's that?"

"My shock issue of *Woman's Dream*: 'Have I got cancer?'"

"Wait a minute. Have a drink. Now let's start at the beginning, shall we?"

"I am Arthur Friendship," said Arthur, taking a glass of what was probably gin and Dubonnet and Curaçao topped up with lemonade and vanilla essence. "I came to see you recently."

"That's right. You were interested in animals. I made a proposition to you that you should take over the 'Pet's Corner'. Am I right?"

When Arthur explained, Mr Condiment said:

"Ah yes. But the 'Pet's Corner' offer is still open, you know. I am particularly anxious to get someone young, with dynamic new ideas about pets. Would you be interested?"

"No," said Arthur.

Only then did Mr Condiment acknowledge Arthur's labour. "Let us drink to Cancer 1964," he said. "A new breakthrough in journalism." Even Mr Carpenter had to drink. Arthur finished his glass and took another, which was full of sweet sherry.

"I'm afraid I ought to go now," said Elizabeth Pedal.

"Aren't I giving you dinner?" Arthur was secretly relieved. He had put aside ten pounds for this purpose. "Then come back and have a drink at my flat." The bed-sitter only became a flat on very special occasions. This was one.

"No, really."

"Well, I'll get a taxi. We'll stop at Albany Chambers first as that is on the way." Arthur was planning to make a pass at her in the taxi.

"Who said I refused to take coloured people, anyway?" Mrs Quorn spoke nervously. The last one had been thrown out of a top window by her husband nearly ten years ago.

"Look, I am a reasonable man. Just show me the coloured people you have staying here and I will go away." The Nobel Prizewinner looked very reasonable, except that his foot was jamming the front door.

"Perhaps I don't choose to show you my coloured guests."

"Then I shall wait here until I see them."

"I will call the police."

"That would be most unwise. I am asking you to be reasonable. Look, I am being reasonable." Gray would not mind being imprisoned in America, where it would increase his chances of recognition, but he was less certain about England.

"I haven't any empty rooms. How can I take coloured guests if I haven't any rooms?"

"That's what they all say. You can either turn out one of your white guests, or put a coloured one in to share. We don't mind who we share with."

"If I had an empty room, I would give it you."

"You could give him Arthur Friendship's room," said Ferdie. "Arthur could find somewhere else."

"We don't want a scene," said Mrs Quorn. "Mr Gray shall have the next available spare room."

"Or come again tomorrow," said Ferdie. "But it is no good. Coloured people are not going to be put off. They want their rights now."

"Who asked for your opinion, anyway?" All Mrs Quorn's friends had deserted her. Mr Dent, deciding it was nothing to do with him, climbed into his grey Ford Cortina and drove to a cinema in Tooting Bec. Captain Starter emerged for a moment, told Gray of a Nigerian he used to know at Sandhurst who was unable to distinguish his left foot from his right, then went off to play squash racquets with a friend. Mrs Quorn was alone with her enemies.

A taxi drew up.

Arthur sat trembling with exhilaration next to the girl he loved. She could not fail to admire him, now. Arthur had been the life and soul of the party – its social and intellectual focus. As he left, shaking the pasty and listless hand of the abominable Carpenter in a friendly manner, there had come to him in a blinding flash of inspiration the knowledge that Ronald Carpenter was dying from cancer. It explained everything – pastiness, blue-hair, listlessness, the fact that he seemed to derive no pleasure from the importance and prestige which attached to his position. Perhaps the blue tablets he sucked were some quack remedy.

Nobody was as compassionate as Arthur where the sufferer deserved pity. But he was old-fashioned enough to eschew the indiscriminate compassion which was Roland Cleghorn's stock-in-trade. And among average, well-adjusted people such as himself, the lingering, painful death of Ronald Carpenter could not be viewed with anything short of exultation.

Arthur was masterful. Arthur was mighty, handsome and wise. "I hope you didn't feel that party was too much for you," he said.

"Not at all. I enjoyed it very much. Such a lot of nice people." The only thing girls need and expect from a man is mastery. As the taxi drew up outside Albany Chambers, Arthur struck. He lunged at the soft and fragrant thing in the corner, and wrapped it in his arms. Having got so far, he was not sure what to do next. His face appeared to be buried somewhere in Elizabeth's neck. Limpet-like, he clung.

Elizabeth was surprised. At twenty-two, she was quite accustomed to the importunities of men, and had vaguely supposed that Arthur's attentions were not entirely disinterested. But when he had left her completely unmolested for so long, she had gratefully put the matter out of her mind. Then, like a thunderbolt, he fell.

She became frightened; there had seemed something peculiar about Arthur all along. Perhaps he was a maniac, who murdered girls in the back of taxis. In any event her present position was appallingly uncomfortable and embarassing.

"Please, Arthur," she said faintly.

He clung to her harder. She struggled. The grip tightened. Then she became conscious of a blunt instrument pressing into her back. It was Arthur's chin.

"Let go, help, someone. Get off. Help. HELP!"

The taxi driver waited patiently for his customers to sort out their problems. Elsewhere a window opened, a door slammed. Ferdie and Gray bounded along the pavement.

"Help, get off me. What are you *doing?*" Liz cried.

Arthur was dragged, still clinging, out of the taxi. Elizabeth, shivering tearfully with fright, was folded in the arms of her lover. Ferdie found himself manhandling Arthur on the pavement. There was something disgustingly soft and squelchy about Arthur's face. Ferdie punched it hard.

The blow was cowardly and unkind. It was also extremely painful. Arthur sat on the pavement, nursing his face in his hands. He detested pain.

"Get off the pavement and pay for your taxi," said Ferdie.

"Twelve and sixpence, sir," said the taxi driver.

Numb with pain and humiliation, Arthur took out his little leather purse and counted twelve and sixpence. The taxi driver waited. Arthur gave him another sixpence.

"Cor, thank you," said the taxi driver sarcastically, and drove away. It was too much. Arthur sat on the pavement and wept.

"He's half drunk," said Ferdie.

"I'm not surprised," said Gray. He regarded Arthur with contempt. "Now look here, Mr Friendship. I am going to take Elizabeth back to the Hilton, then I am coming round here for you. I can see you're crying now, but you have received nothing to what's coming. If I don't come myself, I shall send my friends round. We know where to find you. One of these days, you're going to learn respect for your fellow human beings. I wouldn't like to see your face when we've finished with you. Now, come on Elizabeth." Gently, protectively, he led Elizabeth to his huge white Cadillac.

Arthur moaned. As Gray drove off, he glanced contemptuously back at the abject figure on the pavement.

"Come on Arthur, you can't sit around there all night," said Ferdie. He felt vaguely responsible.

"I think you've broken one of my teeth," said Arthur. "You

126

bloody fool." He was back at school, and Matron would hear about it in the morning.

Mrs Quorn was waiting for them inside. "Now perhaps you'll tell me what has been going on."

"There's been a fight," said Ferdie. "The trouble is, I think there may be another soon, unless we get Arthur out of the way."

"Not here, he's not going to hold any more fights," said Mrs Quorn. "I have had quite enough as it is."

Ferdie led Arthur upstairs. "You'll have to get out of here as quick as you can. Get some things packed. I'll look after the rest."

Arthur opened his little cardboard week-end case : pyjamas, tooth-brush, change of socks, smart new silver tie, bottle of Silvikrin, electrical shaving equipment, round leather collar-box which contained his studs.

"Will you look after my gramophone and records? You can play them occasionally, if you want, but remember to wipe them with a damp cloth first. And check the needle. A cracked needle can cause untold damage to records."

"Yes, yes," said Ferdie. "Do you want a change of underwear?"

Arthur looked at his only ornament, a photograph from Bloxham of his house's presentation of *The Rivals*. He could not leave that with Ferdie, who might guess the secret. Often it seemed to Arthur that the area of the photograph around where Lydia Languish sat in her gay summer bonnet must be worn down by the passage of his eyes. Certainly the face of Lydia, so round and innocent, scarcely fourteen years old, seemed to stand out from the rest of the photograph as if on a rubber stalk, to bob up and down and mock him. Mistress Languish was now thirty years old and worked as an accountant in Northampton with a wife and two children, if Old Boys news in *The Bloxhamian* was to be believed. Ferdie Jacques would never be allowed to gloat over the beauty of Alcock Two before thirty winters had besieged his brow and dug deep trenches in his beauty's field. He put the photograph in his suitcase, on top of the sponge-bag.

"Where shall I go?"

"Wherever you like. I should get out of this area altogether.

Try North London. Gray and his friends will be looking for you."

"What happens if they find me?"

"Well, honestly, old chap, you've only got yourself to blame. I warned you that these coloured people were jealous. What on earth were you doing to her in the taxi?"

A car drew up in the street.

"Hurry up, that may be them."

But it was only Mr Dent, returning to his well-earned rest. Arthur walked past him without a word, a lonely, hurt figure in a raincoat with his battered, cardboard suitcase.

"Elizabeth has just had a terrible experience," said Gray. "Would she like something to drink?" He often spoke to her in the third person. Perhaps it was a testimony to his sufferings in South Carolina.

"Yes, please," said Liz gratefully. "A Coca-Cola."

"Now I am going to sort out the worthless piece of trash who molested you."

"Please don't," said Liz. Gray had been rather hoping she would say that. "He didn't mean any harm."

"Young lady, it is not possible to allow anyone to behave like that, no matter his colour, creed or racial conviction."

"Please, Toe-mass. I just feel there's been enough trouble already."

"Elizabeth does not want me to harm him. She pleads for the life of her co-racialist. Very well, her wish shall be observed. But for no other reason."

"Thank you, Toe-mass."

He lent her a protective arm. Elizabeth clung to him. She had learned that in addition to being strong and foolish and conceited, he could be extremely kind.

Arthur cringed from the black ticket inspector in Victoria Underground station. His jaw still throbbed, and he had not the slightest idea where he was going. The whole of London's Underground system seemed infested with Africans. Some were inanely happy, chuckling to themselves at a private joke, others looked grim and dour, brooding over their wrongs. He bought a ticket for sixpence and changed to the Northern Line at Charing Cross. More Negroes. Arthur stared at his feet and tried to look natural. It was impossible that they should all belong to Thomas Gray's private army, dedicated to the revenge of Negro causes; in any case, his description was probably not yet known.

Yet Arthur was a superstitious person, and he had been brought up to believe that Negroes had some special means of communication unknown to the white man. Perhaps even now the tom-toms were throbbing from Shepherds Bush to Hackney Wick. Tall man in rain-coat. Thinning hair, distinguished appearance. Carries a suitcase. Likeable, kind face. Sentenced to instant execution.

He got out at Belsize Park. A black man was collecting the tickets. Arthur froze with horror, then, with the courage of desperation, walked past, staring at his feet.

"Hey, mister!"

Arthur looked round for a moment. It was a fatal mistake, as it allowed the ticket collector to see his face. The man was gabbling incoherently about his ticket. Arthur turned and ran into the cold, wet streets of North London.

The ticket collector followed him for a few paces, then returned, muttering imprecations.

"Room to let for careful lodger. Bed and breakfast £3 6s., payable in advance. Sorry, no coloureds!"

Arthur rang the bell of 128 Kitchener Drive. A woman's voice shouted through the letter box: "Who is it?"

"I am looking for a room."

"Oh, you are. Who are you from?"

"I have come from Victoria way."

The door was unlocked. A mean-faced woman in hair curlers looked out. With her, came a tremendous smell of frying.

129

"I believe you do not accept coloured guests," said Arthur.

Instantly, the woman became wary:

"Who told you that?"

"I read it on the notice."

"What is it to you?"

"Nothing at all. I just remarked on it."

The woman was now thoroughly suspicious. "I've had your sort round before," she said. "Are you one of those students trying to make trouble?"

"No, indeed not."

She did not like the look of him, nevertheless.

"Well, I'm sorry. We've no more rooms. And we don't take students, anyway."

"Oh dear. Where else can I go?"

"You could try Mrs Jacomb down the road. She isn't usually too choosy about the class of people she takes in."

A huge Negro was walking down Kitchener Drive, whistling nonchalantly – too nonchalantly, Arthur thought. Now, he was really frightened. There seemed nowhere he could escape from them.

Mrs Jacomb was a reasonable soul. She had watched too many television programmes to be healthy, Arthur decided.

"Well, it depends on the type of coloured person," she said. "If he was a respectable sort, I would probably say, 'All right, come on in'. On the other hand, if he looked dirty or underhand, I wouldn't let him in no matter what the colour was. It all depends on the individual case."

"I see," said Arthur.

"Personally, I don't approve of the colour bar," said Mrs Jacomb. "You should judge people by how they appear, not by the colour of their skin. Also, where would all of us be if we didn't have the blacks to work on the Underground, and do all the nastier jobs we don't fancy so much?"

"I see," said Arthur. "Funny thing is, I don't particularly like blacks. I'm trying to find a place where they don't have them. I don't know why it is."

"Probably you don't think they're very clean," suggested Mrs Jacomb.

"That may be it."

"Well, you can come in here. We certainly wouldn't have a black person unless he was properly clean."

"Do you know, I don't even like the clean ones, really? Perhaps you can tell me of a house where they don't have any blacks at all?"

"You get them everywhere, nowadays," said Mrs Jacomb. "It isn't like it was before the war. Still, they say you've got to move with the times."

"I know," said Arthur. "The trouble is, I've got to find somewhere to sleep, and I can't be anywhere near Africans. I have an allergy, you see."

"Ah," said Mrs Jacomb. "Have they tried treatment? I expect it is psycho-somatic."

"They have tried everything. My only hope is to avoid proximity."

"You had better go to Joanie Snow's at number 206. I wouldn't care to stay there myself, but if you've got an allergy, it might be better."

"Thank you so much."

"Not at all. My husband can't stand other people's socks. He even worries about his own, sometimes, when he gets confused and can't recognize them."

Number 206 Kitchener Drive smelled of disinfectant. Joanie turned out to be a wizened little creature of about forty-seven with brilliant red hair which even Arthur suspected of being dyed. She wore trousers of imitation leopardskin, but there was nothing flamboyant in her manner.

"No, I don't take coloureds of any sort," she said. "It's not that I've got anything against them. I just don't like their faces."

"Quite right," said Arthur. "Have you got a room for *me*?"

Joanie considered for a moment. "You wouldn't be a student?

No, I could see you weren't. It'll cost twenty five shillings a night, breakfast included."

"All right," said Arthur.

She led him into her sitting room. Disinfectant gave way to a strong smell of dogs, although there was none in evidence. A television set in the corner showed three intellectuals in earnest discussion, but the sound had been turned off.

"That's our Karen," said Joanie, pointing to the television set.

"Ah, yes," said Arthur.

"She's no trouble, really," said Joanie. "Of course, some men don't like children."

Arthur became aware of an object sitting in front of the television set. At first he had thought it was a bundle of dirty laundry. It was a girl of about four.

"How sweet," he said vaguely.

"Karen won't be any trouble at all," said Joanie. "She is quite happy watching television."

The room was as hot as an oven. Two electric fires burned on opposite walls. On the bed lay a pile of dirty laundry. Two other piles adorned a chest of drawers.

"I think it is very nice," said Arthur. He began to feel uneasy alone with the woman. Perhaps she was a prostitute.

"Yes, it is nice, really. It's what I call my little *pied à terre*."

Arthur became more uneasy.

"If you could show me my room, I shall unpack."

"There's only one other thing," said Joanie. "I take it you have no objection to cats."

"None at all," said Arthur. He particularly disliked cats.

"We've only got one," said Joanie. "But I couldn't allow anyone who was going to be unkind to her. If you like, I'll introduce you. Myrtle! Myrtle!"

Joanie opened the door and shrieked into the corridor. Karen looked round, removed her thumb from her mouth and started to cry.

"Our Karen has always been jealous of Myrtle," said Joanie.

"How sweet," said Arthur.

"Shut up your crying and our Joanie will give you a bottle," said Joanie.

She poured from a tin of condensed milk, added warm water from a tap in the kitchen, put on a rubber teat and handed it to Karen.

"Isn't she a bit old for a bottle?"

"She's four and a half."

"How sweet," said Arthur.

His bedroom was numbingly cold and smelled of cats. "It's a double bed," said Joanie. "I don't mind who you bring in here. One gets to know what men are like, and one has to be broad-minded. But I don't want any coloureds. They send the value of property down, and half of them aren't educated."

"That's right," said Arthur.

"You're the second person recently who has been round asking whether I take in coloureds. My answer is always the same. The first person must have been from the newspapers, I think, or from Welfare."

"No doubt," said Arthur. "Coloured people are extremely vin-dictive. If they imagine a wrong, they will never forget it. And nowadays they are organized."

"Really?" said Joanie.

"If we want to resist them, we must club together. You wouldn't like little Karen to marry a Negro, would you?"

"Of course not. She's much too young, already. Here's the bathroom."

The bath was surrounded by a plastic curtain. There were little notices all over the room.

"Very nice," said Arthur.

"Yes, it is very nice, really," said Joanie. "Of course, one gets used to it. If you need anything, I'll be in my *pied à terre*. If you want to use the gas fire, don't try gassing yourself. One man tried it, and I had to clean up afterwards. Apparently he went round everywhere trying to do himself in."

"Where can I get something to eat?"

"The Bonanza Café is the one used by the white people round

here. Past the church on your left. Say Joanie sent you, then they'll treat you all right. I've got a lot of friends. Well, I'll say goodnight. Breakfast commences after eight. Here's the front door key." Joanie always held a handkerchief to her face when she talked. Perhaps she doubted the purity of her breath. Arthur could have reassured her that among the multitude of unpleasant smells one more would have made no difference.

The Bonanza Café was full of people, all of whom stopped talking when Arthur entered. In the terrible silence which followed, Arthur said:

"Egg and chips, please."

He sat down, while everybody looked at him. Sheepishly, he lifted his fork to his mouth and smiled. Nobody spoke. His jaw still hurt. The proprietor said:

"The Rangers weren't on form last Saturday, were they?"

Arthur smiled. He supposed they were talking about football. For them, it was the basic currency of goodwill. He knew nothing about football. Slowly, conversation resumed, and Arthur was left to himself.

Earlier in the evening, Arthur had been exchanging jokes with members of the peerage. How amazed his grand friends would have been to see him now! But Arthur was not sorry. At last, he found himself among the true working class, the backbone of England and the salt of the earth. He could study them at leisure.

One day, Arthur Friendship was going to write a book.

On the way back to Joanie Snow's, Arthur passed the Church of the Sacred Heart and St Joseph. He went in. There was a familiar smell of incense and candle grease. An old woman knelt in the back of the church. In the front, Confessions were going on in a dark wooden box labelled: "Father Connolly".

"I have committed the sin of fornication," whispered Arthur.

"How many times?"

134

"Well, not even once, actually, Father." Too embarrassing to have to explain the details of his unsuccessful seduction of Elizabeth Pedal. "It was attempted fornication, really."

"That's just as bad. Try to avoid the temptation. Pray to Our Lady and she'll help you. Will you, then, now?"

"Yes."

"Say three Hail Marys and make a good act of contrition."

Arthur came out of the church with a lighter step. At least, he could face the Negroes with a clear conscience.

Chapter Eight

NO BIRDS SANG IN KITCHENER DRIVE. ARTHUR WOKE UP surrounded by unfamiliar smells. An ashtray beside his bed was made of pottery and designed to look like a shoe. It was full of ancient cigarette ends. The room was freezing cold.

Arthur went to the bathroom and cleaned his teeth. A notice above the mirror read:

LADIES!!!
Are requested to refrain from putting unmentionables
in the toilet but to use the receptacle provided.

THANK YOU!!!

JOANIE.

Arthur was so embarrassed that he could not meet his own eye in the mirror. He looked at the receptacle provided with horror. Another notice said:

GENTLEMEN!!!
Are requested to have due consideration to other
people requiring to use this bathroom. Please lift the
seat ! ! !

"At last," thought Arthur, "I know what it is to be a member of the working class."

Joanie served breakfast in a dressing-gown of floral design. Smells of toast and frying fat unsuccessfully competed against the prevailing smells of disinfectant, dogs and Joanie.

"Trevor will be down in a minute, but I haven't seen Myrtle anywhere."

Arthur wondered if perhaps the cat had died.

"You will like Trevor," said Joanie. "We're all very fond of him here. Of course, there is no need to take him too seriously."

"I have some work to do this morning. You see, I am a writer," he said.

"Of course you are," said Joanie. "There's some people don't hold with that sort of thing, but I like a good book occasionally myself."

"Do you ever read *Woman's Dream?*"

"No, I don't think I've ever read that one. Is it about love?"

"Frequently. And many other subjects – cooking, knitting, cancer, religion."

"I'm not sure I'd like that one. With so many books around, you can afford to be choosy."

"It is really very good," said Arthur. "Some of the book reviews in it are first class."

"Yes?" said Joanie. "Well, you never know."

Trevor came downstairs, also in his dressing-gown.

"Ho, ho! I spy strangers. What has the cat brought in this morning."

It was most amusing. Between chuckles, Arthur introduced himself.

"Well, Arthur Friendship, I hope you come in friendship. Woman, where's my tea? We are called Trevor. And we are a meat merchant. We welcome you to our humble abode. What brings thee hither, friend?"

"I am a writer," said Arthur.

Trevor leaned forward, suddenly grave. "If you're looking for material, you've come to the right place. We're going to see a lot of each other, you know. But I'll take a rake-off. It's only fair."

The doorbell rang.

"I expect that's more students doing social research into negroes," said Joanie. But it was two girls, looking for a room.

"Hello, hello, hello!" said Trevor. "What have we got here?"

"Don't you have to go to work?"

"The meat market is very slack on Thursdays. All those bloody R.C.'s. Mind you, I'm an R.C. myself, really."

"Do you mind if we join you?"

"Not at all, gracious ladies."

Beverley was large and dark. Lesley was dark and small. Both wore black jeans and jerseys. Neither was unattractive.

"Where have you come from?"

"We've been out all night. Started off as a party with some medical students, then a lot of Irish tried to break in so we all moved on to this warehouse place. But the police were there practically before we were. Somebody must have tipped them off."

"Welcome to our humble abode. This is me and my friend Arthur Friendship."

"Mutual, I'm sure," said Beverley.

"I like you," said Trevor. "Strictly speaking, you're my sort of girl."

"Well, you can take your dirty hands off me."

"She'll sock you in the balls," warned Lesley.

"Come, come," said Trevor. "I was only trying to be friendly. I didn't realize you were a couple of virgins."

"You're bloody well right I am," said Beverley.

"I don't think," said Lesley.

"Now, now, now," said Trevor, putting his hand inside Beverley's jersey. Arthur was slightly embarrassed, although interested.

"Look, Mister, just give us a chance, will you." Beverley had started talking with an American accent. She seemed ill at ease. "We haven't had any sleep for twenty-four hours. Give us a couple of hours off, and we'll see you at lunch time."

"All right," said Trevor. He was a reasonable man. "Arthur and I will prepare ourselves."

"Anything for some peace," said Beverley.

As Trevor was leaving the room to dress, he turned back. "By the way, I was forgetting. If either of you want a little kitten to take to bed with you, we've got Myrtle here."

From inside his dressing-gown he produced an enormous grey cat. He had kept it there all along. There could be no doubt about it, Trevor was a character.

"How cruel," said Lesley. She was genuinely shocked. "Come here pussy. Pussy. Myrtle puss. Come to Mummy."

Myrtle looked disgruntled. Her eyes were dull, and the manner in which she held her tail made her hind view most unsavoury. Her paunch almost touched the ground, and even from a safe distance it was plain that her pores commanded a battery of unpleasant odours. But still she was an animal.

"How sweet," said Arthur.

"Of course we are, aren't we, my little pussybell?" said Lesley.

"See you lunch-time, then," said Trevor.

In her new book, Teresa Thimble has chosen a much broader canvas than ever before, wrote Arthur. *The world is seen as a complex of personal relationships, from which certain are picked out under a spotlight. So ambitious, indeed, is the scope, that initially one trembled for her success. But our fears were groundless: with the deftness of an accomplished artist, Miss Thimble takes us effortlessly through that great and harmonious symphony of discordant sounds which is an individual life. The story is familiar to many Woman's Dream readers, who were privileged to a serialized preview of "Trenkettering Castle," probably the greatest female novel to come out since the war. But to comprehend the book as a whole, one must read it in its entirety. Of the three conflicts in the life of Sarah Trenkettering, the conflict between herself and her murderous stepmother, representing the old order against the new, is probably the most obvious. That between herself and her husband, Richard, who must choose between his love for her, and the claims of his great inheritance, is the most poignant. The third conflict is between Sarah Trenkettering AND HERSELF. It is in the unravelling of this thread that Miss Thimble reveals herself in her entirety, fit almost to stand beside the Jane Austens and Charlotte Brontës of the past.*

Yet Teresa Thimble is very much of the present. With her compassionate insight into the depths of human problems she is able to cut away the padding of artificial veneer and delve like a surgeon, straight to the very roots of human nature. A most salutary and exhilarating experience.

Arthur had never read *Trenkettering Castle*. He could tell at a glance it was not his sort of book, and in any case he had little time for reading. He had heard somewhere that the twentieth century was an age of indifferent writers but great critics. Like most literary people, he felt that criticism was more important, and looked forward to the day when it would be recognized as an abstract art form in its own right; without the necessity of referring to a particular book or author.

His own criticism approached the abstract ideal. A good book was described as compassionate and perceptive, a bad book as lacking in compassion and superficial. But he resented the oppressive discipline and of having to couple his beautiful formalized gems of criticism with anything so gross and old-fashioned as a book.

It was a cruel paradox that even the greatest critics such as himself stood no chance of recognition until they, too, had written a book. Arthur was resigned to the convention, although despising it, and accepted that one day he would have to write a book. Perhaps it would be in the form of the journal of a soul, calling for greater compassion in the world. Perhaps it would be a straight-forward satire on the folly of war. It might even be in the form of a novel, demanding the abolition of the gap between the rich and the poor. Whatever it was, it would be full of compassion and perception tinged with the melancholy of a genius condemned to live and work among the second-rate.

Wearily, he turned to the Reverend Cliff Roebuck:

If Christianity is to mean anything today, it must talk in a language which the people – ordinary people like you or I – can understand. Our grandfathers, of course, were different. In the Victorian age, spinsters used to cover even the legs of their pianos for fear of indelicate exposure! Nowadays, we are not at all like that . . .

"Give us a chance. We haven't even had anything to eat yet," said Lesley.

"Some men are just bloody disgusting," said Beverley.

"Mind, she'll kick you in the balls," said Lesley.

"Put your dirty great hands anywhere near me and I will too," said Beverley.

"Let's go and get some eats then," said Trevor. "Where to?"

"There's quite a good café down the road, called the Bonanza," said Arthur.

"That's funny," said Beverley. "Who do you think you are, Mr Rockefeller the Second?"

"There's a new Italian restaurant opened in Ypres Avenue – Cozeria Romana," said Trevor.

"What's wrong with the West End," said Beverley.

"No you don't," said Trevor. "Another day if you're lucky."

"It's you that will be lucky. All right, I suppose we shall have to come out to this Italian place."

"Wish I could come with you," said Joanie. "My life is dedicated to our Karen."

They were standing around in Joanie's *pied à terre*. Our Karen was still asleep, almost invisible in the huge double bed, surrounded by piles of dirty laundry.

"Well you can't," said Trevor. "Nobody's asked you."

"Our Karen has to have her bottle at one, or she doesn't get up all day," said Joanie. "The perfect life, really."

"I think it's simply disgusting, making a child of four feed itself out of a bottle," said Trevor. "You need a man in the house."

"I had a man once," said Joanie, becoming sentimental. "But he's dead."

"No he isn't," said Trevor. "He ran away." Everybody laughed at that.

"You men," said Joanie. "You're all the same. It was drink, if you must know."

"I'll drink your backside," said Trevor.

"What a lovely restaurant," said Lesley. "What are those bottles on the wall?"

"They're Chianti bottles," said Trevor. "Used by the Italian peasants to drink wine out of."

"Fancy that," said Lesley. "I wouldn't mind being an Italian peasant."

"You are a peasant," said Beverley. "May I see the wine waiter please? I want a bottle of Beaujolais."

"Listen to her," said Trevor.

"If you take us to a crummy hole like this, you might as well get the best service. What do you think, Les? A steak tartare or veal escalope aux champignons?"

"Have some caviare," said Trevor sarcastically.

"Very well, waiter, cancel that order. I want two helpings of caviare. Large, and lots of it."

"You're going to get into trouble one of these days," said Trevor.

"Call this caviare?" said Beverley. "I am afraid there has been a mistake, waiter. This must be for some other customer. I did not order cats' mess."

In spite of himself, Arthur could not help laughing. Undoubtedly, the younger sort of working-class person nowadays was quite unlike her Victorian grandmother.

Arthur's share of the bill came to eight pounds. It was too much. Trevor seemed upset by it too.

"Come on, then," he said to Beverley as soon as they were inside the door of 206 Kitchener Drive. "You come up to my room and I'll show you some interesting etchings I've got."

"Here, what do you think you're getting up to?" said Beverley. "Who said I wanted to look at your etchings?"

"You've had your lunch, and I am asking you to come up to my room."

"You are, are you? And suppose I don't want to come."

"You said it would be all right after lunch."

"But I didn't say *what* would be all right, did I?"

The joke was wearing thin.

"Go on, Bev," said Lesley. She looked up at Arthur with a friendly smile. "Bev's not usually like this. I don't know what's got over her. We'll go to your room, shall we?"

Arthur and Lesley climbed the stairs.

"Do you like it in the bed or on top? I think it's rather cold outside, don't you?"

"Oh yes, much too cold," said Arthur.

Afterwards she said: "Well, I'm glad somebody's happy."

Trevor said: "Couldn't think what all the fuss was about. She had the rags up."

"Oh, really?" said Arthur.

"What was the other one like?"

"All right," said Arthur, in a tone which suggested he didn't know what the meat merchant was talking about.

"Just my luck," said Trevor. "Another Thursday wasted."

"Bless me, Father, for I have sinned."

"How many weeks since your last confession?" said Father Connolly.

"Well, none, really. It is a day. Since then I have committed the sin of fornication."

"How many times?"

"Only once." Lesley had suggested that he should commit it again, but Arthur had not felt inclined to do so.

"For your penance say three Hail Marys. Now make a good act of contrition."

"O my God, I am sorry and beg pardon for all my sins and detest them above all things because they deserve Thy dreadful punishment, because they have crucified my loving Saviour Jesus Christ, but most of all because they offend Thy infinite goodness. . . ."

"Now go in peace and pray for me."

143

Arthur did not go in peace. The suggestion that he should pray for Father Connolly was never one which he felt obliged to take seriously, but he generally experienced a certain tranquillity of mind after going to confession which on this occasion was absent. Although formally absolved, Arthur knew that Lesley was still staying in 206 Kitchener Drive, and even if he did not have the immediate intention of sinning again, it would be unrealistic to close one's mind to the possibility of it. It had not been a good idea to go to Confession. He should have waited until the affair was unmistakably over.

Only Joanie was around when he returned.

"Have you got a newspaper?" he asked. He had not seen one for two days.

"There was one somewhere," said Joanie. "Here we are." It was a copy of the *Daily Sketch* three weeks old. "I expect you want to hear more about the war."

"What war? Is there a war?"

"I thought I saw something about a war," said Joanie. "It might have been on television though."

"For Heaven's sake, who's involved."

"I think it said something like us against the Russians. Or it may have been the Germans. I don't think it was the Americans. Pity, really. I wouldn't mind having them back here. I had a lot of friends among the Americans in the last war. Mrs Jacomb down the road says it's a great mistake to have a war nowadays, and we'll none of us be better off, but I'm not so sure. You meet a lot of interesting people and make new friends. Now I must get our Karen her bottle. She'll eat us out of house and home, that girl, war or no war. And there's something else in the papers, too, I heard someone say. They've invented a new drug which stops anyone getting any older. High time too, if you ask me. But it's quite interesting what you see in the papers, if you read them closely. I never have the time, of course."

Arthur felt that he had heard of the wonder-drug before. He walked to buy a newspaper at the Tube station, shrinking from a Pakistani ticket collector in case he turned out to be a Negro in disguise. There was no mention of any war in the *Evening Standard*. Just to be on the safe side, he bought the *Evening News*, too. Nor was there any mention of a wonder-drug. A mysterious fire in Brixton had incinerated a landlady and two lodgers. A police dog had been awarded the George Medal. Surely that was wrong? No, it was perfectly true. Rex, a four-year-old police dog, had been awarded the George Medal for conspicuous gallantry in tackling a gunman while simultaneously saving two children from drowning.

What was the world coming to, when dogs were awarded the highest medal for gallantry in the land? Greatly perturbed, Arthur retraced his footsteps to Kitchener Drive, shielding his face behind the *Evening News*.

Animals would soon rule the world. There was no place left for human beings, let alone intelligent, sensitive human beings like Arthur. Geniuses would have to be drowned at birth, like kittens in a bucket. Various animal welfare societies would hold Britain in a grip of iron, like the Communist Party in Russia. Top jobs would be available only to card-bearing members of the RSPCA. Expressions of dislike for animals would soon be illegal; even the hardened criminals in Pentonville or Wormwood Scrubs would refuse to talk to a prisoner condemned of such a crime.

Arthur loathed and detested the entire animal creation. He hated its smells, its lack of subtlety, its sub-human stupidity, but above all he hated its effect on his fellow human beings. In his more intellectual moments, he saw the patronizing benevolence which the Western world extended to animals as a sinister form of neo-colonialism. At other times, he reflected on the enormous fund of goodwill and kindliness which the English expended on their animals, thus enabling them to harden their hearts against their fellow-creatures, the starving millions of Asia. But, by and large, he just did not happen to like animals.

It was as much as his job was worth to say so, and Arthur was not cast in a heroic mould. If one was to be a leader of thought or fashion – in short, an artist – one must reflect the spirit of the times in which one lived. Novels of the last decade were quite properly expected to deal with the various problems and attitudes peculiar to the working class. They were no more than the artistic expression of that great upheaval in thought known as the working-class movement. Then, for a brief period, there had been a time when the only novels taken seriously dealt with the problem of having been born a Negro in the modern world. Arthur had felt himself excluded from both these trends, since his background was anything but working-class, nor could he feel himself entirely in sympathy with working-class aspirations; and he was handicapped by the historical accident of not having been born a Negro in the modern world. Obviously, animal novelists were the men of the future.

There had been a time when Arthur considered that Christianity might hold the key to the mystery of his own existence. By one remove from that, he thought that Peace might be the purpose in his life. But in such dismal moments as this, he began to question even the usefulness of Peace. Peace was already in existence, it was the status quo, the Establishment. Perhaps there was no threat to Peace at all outside his fevered imagination. Animals were the only thing that really mattered in the modern world.

There was no gramophone in Arthur's bedroom to assist his inspiration. A bed, a chair, two tables and Myrtle. Arthur placed Myrtle on the chair, and sat on the bed to study her. The first thing that struck him was her contemptuous indifference to his scrutiny. He had an uneasy impression that he was going to have to do most of the work.

There were three conflicts, he decided, in the life of Myrtle. That between herself and the jealous child Karen was the most obvious, and could only be solved by time, when Karen reached maturity of judgment. The second conflict, between Myrtle and the possessive, demanding love of Joanie Snow could only be solved by some violent catharsis on the part of Joanie. It was the third conflict which really interested Arthur, that between Myrtle and *herself*. He gazed at Myrtle hopefully, but she gave little clue to the inner struggle.

It was much easier, he decided, to write a criticism of his novel than it was actually to write the novel. This was an age of indifferent novelists but great critics, and Arthur undoubtedly belonged to the latter school. Criticism needed no apprenticeship, and it was an intolerable imposition, a denial of everything he believed in, to appease the convention whereby critics must first write a novel. Perhaps its purpose was to thin down the field of potential critics, thus preserving exclusiveness. Qualifications could equally well be quite different – red hair, or a name beginning with Z. But hair could be dyed, and names changed. Since nobody ever read novels anyway, there was no reason why Arthur should not pretend to write a novel. Then all the critics could exercise their ingenuity in reviewing it, and Arthur's name would be made. But no critic would co-operate in welcoming an outsider. The profession was a closed shop, like the tallymen in London docks, and Arthur felt the injustice bitterly.

He practised the television interview he would give when his novel appeared.

"No, I don't feel that animals are necessarily more intelligent than human beings. I have nothing against humans whatsoever. Some of my best friends, of course, ha ha. But I do feel that inside the personality – she would be insulted by the expression, I should say *animality*, for it is essentially that – of this one cat – er – Myrtle, there is much of the human predicament in microcosm."

"Do you feel there is a great future for the animal novel?"

"Oh, I think there must be. All the arts are moving in that direction – towards simplicity of form. The only criticism I can accept is that I might be a little ahead of my time. But this is an obstacle which has confronted every artist and writer from Leonardo da Vinci to the present day. Somebody has got to blaze

147

the path and take all the knocks from entrenched opinion."

"Thank you very much, Mr Friendship."

Arthur had been walking up and down the room in his excitement, watched contemptuously by Myrtle. At the end of the interview, Arthur's excitement subsided. It was much easier to give a television interview about his novel than it was actually to write the bugger.

He felt cold, and climbed into bed. Often the best ideas came to him in bed. At least in bed, he was safe from Negroes. Myrtle scratched her chair, emitted a new odour, curled up and slept.

The eldest of three sisters, Myrtle came from a typically working-class background. Much of her childhood was spent helping her mother about the house, and she had no time for the high life of some of her contemporaries. These were the days of the depression, before cat-owners were made aware of their responsibilities. Dead kittens were thrown into dustbins, and others, still alive, were made over to the vivisection hospitals for medical experiments.

So she grew up the hard way. She was a loyal and affectionate cat. When her master, the unknown Mr Snow, lay drunk in the gutters of Kitchener Drive, deserted by his friends, he could be sure of her wet nose pushing affectionately into his hand.

She was a military cat carrying messages unmolested through the enemy lines, stepping delicately over the minefields, and shell-holes and decay which was the abomination of desolation on the South East Asian Front.

She was the humane cat whose excited barks brought rescuers hurrying to the side of the Regent's Canal in time to save two twins, a boy and a girl, from drowning. Later, the twins brought her home.

It was she who was chosen to be the first British cat in space, whose pitiful mews, relayed on the wireless, caused the West to be ashamed, renounce the space race and dedicate itself anew to peace.

She was the noble cat whose canonisation in the Vatican

marked one of the major breakthroughs in dogmatic thought. It was she, the George Medallist, Life Peeress and Nobel Prize-winner, who plunged through the holocaust, with atom bombs exploding all around and her tail on fire, to rescue the Queen from Buckingham Palace. Cantering down the Mall, she observed that the Palace was no more than a pile of smoking rubble. From deep inside the wilderness of scorched masonry, plaintive cries could be heard. Heedless of personal safety, Myrtle set to work digging . . .

Arthur became aware of a burning sensation in his throat and a violent smell of petrol. He rubbed his eyes. The room was full of smoke, and he could hear crackling noises coming from the stairs. He opened the window. The drop was not more than eight feet, and he prepared to climb out. Myrtle was ahead of him.

Reflecting that he had some obligations to his other lodgers, he shouted "Fire!" and opened his bedroom door to shout it louder. A great balloon of flame struck him in the face, and he staggered back, with smarting cheeks and scorched eyelashes. As he climbed on the windowsill, he noticed his singed hair and a moistness on his scalp, but it was only when he landed on the concrete outside that he realized he was in great pain.

At the front of the house a small group of people had already gathered. Joanie was there, with Myrtle cradled in her arms. Beverley and Lesley were shivering in white nylon nightdresses. Trevor wore a huge dark overcoat, with nothing underneath. A few neighbours arrived and stood watching. Mrs Jacomb had telephoned for the Fire Brigade.

There was a small explosion, and flames gushed out of one of the downstairs windows.

"Our Karen is still in there," said Joanie, in a pathetic little voice. She was watching the front door, as if expecting her daughter to walk out. Trevor pretended not to have heard.

"Good God, where?" said Arthur.

"In my bedroom."

149

Without pausing to think, Arthur rushed up to the house. When he opened the door, it created a draught and the flames seemed to withdraw from him. Through the smoke he saw into Joanie's *pied à terre*. The smell of petrol was still around, but it had given way in part to the choking fumes of burnt cotton.

Arthur forced himself to advance through the heat which scorched his face and closed his eyes. If he put his hand over his mouth, the pain caused him to withdraw it. The bedroom was dark, but dimly he perceived a pathetic defenceless bundle on the bed. Seizing it to his chest, he fought his way out through the corridor, past the telephone and into the street.

With agonising gasps for air, Arthur collapsed into the arms of a fireman. There was a moment's silence.

"Poor man, he's in a bad way," said the fireman, as Arthur was lifted into an ambulance. Mutely, they agreed. With a final explosion, fire burst through the roof and illumined all their faces as they stood in a group looking at the small pile of dirty laundry on the ground.

PART TWO

November 1963

Chapter Nine

"HAVE WE OPENED OUR BOWELS THIS MORNING?"

Arthur woke from a nightmare of unspeakable horror and smiled fatuously around him. Friendly faces looked down on every side. There was a smell of flowers, and a particularly delicious brand of antiseptic called Domitol. It was better than being chased down the alleys of his unconscious mind by ferocious Negroes, and cancer-ridden members of the working class who wished to discuss their symptoms with him.

"I think there was a fire," he explained amiably.

"Have we opened our bowels this morning?"

"No, Sister, we haven't," said a pretty young nurse, standing by Arthur's head. "We seem to be having a certain amount of difficulty."

"Have we tried Chocolax?" said Sister.

"No, Sister. We have been a tiny bit sleepy for the last few days."

"Put him on senna tea," said Sister. "And I want to see his dressings when they are changed. Bring them to me in the office, Golightly, before mid-morning break."

"Yes, Sister," said Nurse Golightly.

Arthur drifted off, and dreamed that he was picking primroses in a wood.

"Would you like cocoa, Horlicks, Bovril, or Ovaltine?"

"What?"

"Would you like cocoa, Horlicks, Bovril or Ovaltine?"

"Yes, please."

"I said would you like cocoa, Horlicks, Bovril or Ovaltine? You can't have them all."

"Of course," said Arthur. He was feeling particularly benign, and could not become involved in the dispute.

"Have some cocoa, then," said the nurse, and left a thick cup of brown liquid beside his bed, where it grew cold and grey until she removed it an hour later.

"You haven't drunk much of your cocoa," she said.

"Ah, no," said Arthur, smiling.

"Dressings," said Nurse Golightly. She pulled the curtain around his bed, and pushed in a trolley. In the intimacy thus afforded, Arthur reflected on the extreme attractiveness of a nurse's uniform. The modern generation of beatniks, with its trousers and jerseys and long hair would never understand. There was nothing in the world so becoming to woman as a starched white apron and frilly cap.

He submitted to her ministrations in a humble spirit.

"Dear, oh dear, we are in a bad way," said Nurse Golightly, when she had removed the bandages from his head and face. Arthur's only sensation was of dampness. "We must have been to the wars."

"I think there was a fire," said Arthur.

"I'll say there was," said Nurse Golightly.

"Do you know if the little girl was all right?"

"I expect she was. There aren't any little girls in the Casualty Department with burns. There's little June Piccarda, who poured a kettle over herself, but she's been here three weeks."

"Not Karen Snow?"

"No Karen Snow."

Arthur relaxed.

"Are we comfortable?" asked Nurse Golightly, when a new bandage had been secured. Arthur supposed she was talking about the lavatory, and looked coy. "I think we might need a blanket-bath. Wait here, and I'll get some water."

Arthur waited in eager anticipation, but the blanket-bath never materialized. Instead, he was informed of a visitor, Miss

Chinette Codell, from the *North London Herald and Mercury*. Arthur regarded her with loathing.

"I have nothing to say to the Press." It was too tiresome, the way they pestered one. Many people sought personal publicity, but Arthur thought it vulgar. Besides, somebody as close to the Royal Family as himself had to be very careful what they said in public.

"Is this the first time you have been involved in any heroic action?"

"I shouldn't describe it as heroic. Anybody else would have done the same."

"Ah, but they didn't," said Miss Codell. "Of course, you were too badly burned to do anything. There's some talk of Trevor being awarded a medal by the Animals League of Mercy."

"I don't understand," said Arthur.

"For saving the cat."

"Trevor did not save the cat. It jumped out of the window on its own."

"I think you must have become muddled after your injuries. The cat was saved."

"It jumped out of the window."

"Oh dear. I really should have left you a bit longer. It is well known that cats never jump out of windows."

"This one did. I saw it. That was before I went in and rescued the child."

"I am afraid you are making a mistake," said Miss Codell quietly. "Nobody rescued the child."

Arthur felt disposed to be lenient. She was obviously a young reporter out on her first assignment. "You've got the whole story wrong. Strictly speaking I've got nothing to say to the Press, but you might as well have your facts right. Nobody saved the cat. It saved itself by jumping out of my bedroom window. It happened to be in my bedroom at the time. I saved the little girl Karen, which is why I am here now. Not that there was anything particularly heroic about it."

155

Miss Codell sighed. The man obviously had a fixation. She decided to be tactful.

"There is some talk that the fire may have been due to arson. Have you any idea how it started?"

"Well, you do get a lot of doubtful people in that part of London. Some of them are coloured. I'm not saying they all are, but it would be unrealistic to suppose that none of them is, just as it would be unrealistic to say that all Americans are warmongers. And, of course, you do get a housing problem."

"I see," said Miss Codell, who had taken down none of this racist harangue. "To return to the pussy cat, which is the only bright spot in the tragedy of Kitchener Drive, um." Miss Codell had lost the track of her question. She could see that her journey was abortive. There was no human interest story to be extracted from this source. Hospitals made her feel ill. "That is to say, are you fond of animals?"

Arthur saw the trap, and avoided it craftily. "It depends on what you mean by animals," he said. "If you are talking about snakes and lizards, that is something different. Perhaps you mean mammals, but where does one draw the line? Whales are technically mammals, you know." He warmed to his work. She might as well ask him whether he liked human beings. *Some* human beings were extremely agreeable. About others, the only compassionate thing to say was that they came from an unhappy background. Possibly through no fault of their own, they were a product of the society in which they lived.

"I mean Myrtle," said Chinette Codell.

"Myrtle is an extraordinarily interesting cat," said Arthur. He paused. Would he explain about the three conflicts in Myrtle's life, the humble background and unexpected depths of her character? He decided against. He disapproved of people talking to the Press, and instinct told him never to trust a fellow-writer. Not even the paper-back market would be able to support two biographies of the same cat. "There is more to Myrtle than meets the eye."

"Oh, really? In what sort of way?"

Arthur grew alarmed. The woman was asking too many questions. "Nothing, really. I suppose she's just an average sort of cat. I just happen to be quite interested in ordinary sort of cats."

"I see." Chinette Codell looked bored. "Well, it's very kind of you to see me."

"Not at all," said Arthur. "I wish I could have been more helpful. Obviously, you realize that people in my sort of position can't go round talking to the Press."

"No, I suppose not," said Chinette. "By the way, how do you like to be described?"

"I am a writer and literary critic," said Arthur. "I suppose you would say I am best known for my literary criticism."

"Of course. Now let me see. Where does that appear?"

"In *Woman's Dream*," said Arthur, with quiet dignity.

"Gosh, lucky old you," said Chinette, with the first sign of animation. "How did you get there? I suppose you must have had a scholarship."

"Not exactly," said Arthur. It was hard to explain to one so artless that there were things which counted more than academic distinction – one's friendship with circles close to Royalty, one's ability to mingle effortlessly with the mighty and the humble alike. In fact, his introduction to the gilded world of *Woman's Dream* had been entirely due to his acquaintance with Ronald Carpenter, but Arthur chose to forget this.

"I have been waiting six years for an opening like that," said Chinette bitterly.

Arthur looked at her compassionately. What could one say? Some people had got what it takes, others had not. There was no room for egalitarianism inside the highly competitive world of top journalists. No doubt, she would find her level.

"Never despair," he said brightly.

In the evening, Arthur developed a temperature and lay alone with his thoughts, sweating. They brought him some senna tea, which he drank gratefully. In Sister's room, they discussed the new development without much alarm.

"They always show a touch of toxaemia before it begins to clear up," said Sister. "If that senna tea doesn't do anything, I'll wash him out with a syringe myself. But it's very seldom that senna tea doesn't do the trick. How many pods did you put in, Golightly?"

"Twelve, Sister."

"Not nearly enough. Twelve is what you use for a child."

"I thought that as he had ten per cent burns, more than that might cause him some discomfort."

"You're too soft-hearted, Golightly, to make a good nurse. Ask Staff Nurse Bluebell to give him another dose. That'll fix him."

At about eleven o'clock that night, Arthur became convinced that his death was imminent.

"Nurse, nurse."

"Sh. What is it?"

"I think I may be a little unwell. Does there happen to be a Catholic priest around?"

"I will make a note for Father Connolly to come to you in the morning." The nurse was Irish, but she came from Belfast and did not approve of that sort of thing.

"Nurse, I think it may be too late in the morning."

"Why would that be, then?"

"I think I may be going to die," said Arthur in the small voice of a child announcing that he's going to be sick.

"Can't you wait until the morning? There's no reason for why anybody should wish to go dying at this time of night. You look perfectly all right to me. You've had one sleeping pill already, but if you're still feeling poorly in an hour's time I can give you another."

"Thank you, nurse."

"See if you can get some sleep now. And let the other poor souls get some sleep, too."

Arthur was convinced that if he allowed himself to go to sleep, he would never wake up. All the idealism and vigour of his nature was concentrated on the single task of keeping alive. Nothing in the world – the established fact that nine-tenths of the earth's population were starving, the dangers of nuclear holocaust – nothing was more tragic than the death of a single man. It was unimportant whether two hundred million people were dying simultaneously. The sum of two hundred million individual tragedies was no greater, for each participant, than his own death. Death was the ultimate disaster, and it was a terrifyingly lonely prospect. It could well be that the Christian religion was right, in which case he desperately supposed that he was laughing. But, on the other hand, it could so easily be wrong, or he might even have miscalculated his chances inside the Christian framework. It was fashionable nowadays to disbelieve in Hell, but at death's door one did not feel like chancing it. Alternatively, he might face total extinction, as the modern rationalists claimed, but he did not find the prospect comforting. Nobody could conceivably be of any comfort to him, as he was the only person who was dying.

He tried to be humble, but from a purely objective viewpoint he could see neither what he had to be humble about nor what possible advantage might accrue from his humility. Perhaps the whole Christian religion was devised to prevent people from making a scene on their death-beds. If so, it was intolerable.

"Nurse, nurse. I don't think it is going to be long now. Please can I have the light on?"

"You certainly cannot. I shall get you another pill. Sister will hear of this in the morning."

With all the miracles of modern science at her disposal, this fiendish woman proposed to take no steps at all to prevent Arthur passing away into the lonely, twilit world of death.

"Sacrilegious bitch," he whispered at Staff Nurse Bluebell, as she gave him an amytal tablet. They were the first words of abuse which came to mind.

"What's that?"

"Nothing."

"You try and get some sleep."

Arthur in excelsis. He was loved and respected. The greatest literary critic, statesman and world leader of all time. They were waiting for him to say something, give a ruling on the one issue of burning importance in all their lives. He would be compassionate, and yet firm. His would be the right decision. The world was waiting.

"Nurse, nurse! Can I have a bedpan, quickly please?"

There is no situation so abject that a resilient spirit cannot turn it to his advantage. After the bedpan had been removed, Arthur, pleased to have attracted some attention, commended his soul to its Creator and slipped into a dreamless sleep.

"Congratulations, Mr Friendship. I hear we opened our bowels last night. Open your mouth and I'll put the thermometer in."

Arthur awoke in considerable discomfort. His face was throbbing and his right hand, strapped in plaster, ached. But he was alive, and in his exhilaration he nearly swallowed the thermometer.

"We're quite famous this morning, Mr Friendship. Have you seen the *Daily Mail*?"

The blanket bath was performed by a coloured nurse who was known to the other patients as Princess Monolulu. Arthur trembled as she massaged his pressure points with soapy water, remembering the terrible vendetta. Could he be assassinated by the application of some revolting African poison to his pressure points? The Princess was cheerful to the point of imbecility, but Arthur resolved to take no medicine from her.

Arthur's first visitor was Father Connolly, who had been summoned by Staff Nurse Bluebell. Finding himself alive, Arthur had nothing to say. They discussed photography, and the price of second-hand motor cars.

"We have Communion in the Wolfson Ward on Sunday morning," said Father Connolly.

"Oh, really?" said Arthur.

On Arthur's right lay Winston Coggins, who had ruptured

himself at work. He groaned frequently and swore. On the other side, the bed was empty, but it was filled at midday by a small man with a moustache. He was covered in bandages.

"What happened to you?" said Arthur.

"Difference of opinion with the wife."

"Did she do that?"

"Would have killed me if the people in the flat below hadn't heard something. They had to lay her out with a milk bottle then put the divan on top of her to prevent her getting up."

"Heavens, how awful. What was it about?"

"Money. She gets like that. Likes to have a bit of money of her own, but I happen to believe that the man should be absolute master of the household. I've got no time for all this stuff about the equality of the sexes. She's different."

"I see," said Arthur.

"Mind you, when she gets into a rage, she doesn't know what she's doing half the time. Once it was over the postman's strike. She says they have no right to go on strike, as they're providing a service, and I incline to the more liberal viewpoint, saying as anyone can go on strike that needs the money, so the wife picks up the saucepan and tries to pour the boiling water and peas over me, but I get out of the way, not being a fool, and she pours them over herself. Then she stands there screaming with peas sticking all over her, and I laugh myself into the toilet. It's like I say, they aren't our equals, because they haven't got the brains."

"No, I suppose not," said Arthur.

"And it's detrimental to marriage."

"Of course it is."

"That's what's wrong with all these teenagers. They've been brought up to think they've got nothing but rights, and no obligations like we was taught is an essential concomitant to our rights. They think nothing of bashing an old lady over the head."

"I don't think they do," said Arthur, becoming wary. "But I believe in Youth, of course. I think it has an essential part to play."

"They never stand up and have a fight, like me and my missus. They run away."

"You have got to have new ideas," said Arthur. "I think in many ways they're less hypocritical than our generation was."

"I agree there. I've got nothing against sex at all. But I wouldn't like to be married to one of them."

"No, I suppose not," said Arthur. "I hadn't thought of that." Was this what the working classes were thinking? Of course, they were absolutely right. It was quite surprising how intelligent some of them were.

"They have no respect. And if you have no respect for other people, you can't have any self-respect either."

Seldom had Arthur heard his own opinions expressed so concisely. It was most heartening to hear a member of the working classes talk in this way. Teenagers missed a lot of the things which life had to offer by denying that respect which was due to their betters. Of course Arthur would be at the summit of any pyramid of respect. At the top was a plateau where those people lived who, by virtue of being recognizably superior to everybody else, mixed on terms of absolute equality. But the respect of others was essential to Arthur's self-respect, and no doubt the working classes felt the same.

"What's your name?"

"Paul Potts," said his friend, quite simply.

"Mr Friendship has a visitor. Are we clean and tidy?" said Princess Monolulu arranging his bed with unnecessary roughness. She has no respect, thought Arthur.

"Now, let's try and smile," said Princess Monolulu. "The world's not as black as all that. I'se white inside. Ha, ha, ha." She stood at the end of his bed, hand on hips, rocking with laughter.

Arthur allowed himself a bleak smile. He supposed that she was referring to Kipling's description of Gunga Din:

> "An' for all 'is dirty 'ide
> 'E was white, clear white inside."

162

That had been the beginning of the rot. From it followed the automatic identification of a black, or coloured, exterior with a heart of pure gold, which was surely mistaken. Many coloured people were cruel, avaricious and conceited.

"Ha, ha, ha, ha," said the nurse known as Princess Monolulu. Even if she was not cruel, avaricious or conceited, she was surely unintelligent. Fifteen years ago she would have had a ring in her nose and would have worn nothing but tribal scars. She would have dined quite happily off water rats and mangoes. He resolved to discuss the colour problem with Paul Potts at his earliest opportunity.

"My dear Mr Friendship. Thank the Lord you are looking so well." Mr Besant smiled benignly at Princess Monolulu, who walked away, still chuckling. "I read all about you in the *Daily Mail*. You will not believe it, but amid all the world crises of the moment, I found time to weep at my desk when I read of your terrible misfortune. Ask my secretary if it is not true."

Arthur had no doubt that there would be a neat entry in his secretary's diary, "0930–0932 hours. Weeping for Mr Friendship, organizer, Victoria Branch". But he was touched that Mr Besant should have found time to come and see him. It all went to prove what Mr Potts had been saying about respect.

"How nice to see you, Mr Besant. I hope that things are going all right in the world."

They were not. Without Arthur's presence, the various world crises under his direction had gone from bad to worse. China had declared that any infringement by America of the territorial integrity of the North Vietnam would be treated as an attack on the mainland of China. America had replied by reinforcing the puppet government in Saigon. Vast troop movements were reported on the border between China and North Vietnam. China threatened to invade Formosa. Mr Besant was leading a procession to complain about it all outside the American Embassy that evening. Russia had closed the Berlin motorway to all except civilian traffic. The world waited in hourly dread of provocative action by either side. Mr Besant had sent telegrams to the Prime Minister and Foreign Secretary, protesting against British involvement in Berlin.

"Everything is terrible. One begins to wonder if one's life work has not been in vain," said Mr Besant, his eyes shining. "We cannot wait for you to return to work."

Arthur suddenly remembered something.

"Oh my God. There is the outing to Slough tomorrow, to the Egg Marketing Board's warehouse."

"Everything has been looked after. Young Ferdie Jacques is to be the expedition leader. The char-a-bancs will be waiting. He is a most efficient group commander. You need not worry."

"I am sorry to miss it."

"Alas, I shall not be there either. Egg distribution and supply is just another facet of the great Peace movement which I have to neglect. Often, I think there is too much work for one man – I shall have to appoint a deputy one day. It will have to be someone in whom I have complete confidence, Mr Friendship."

"Oh, but Sir," said Arthur in a deprecatory manner. He was overwhelmed.

"Nothing has been decided yet. Now, I shall leave you with the newspaper. Do not read the front pages in your present delicate state. The reference to your accident is on the fifth page. But remember what has been said between us and give it some thought. I only wish it had come at a less anxious time for us all. Things are moving too quickly and we need a breathing space. If only we could all retire to hospital for a week or so and cover all our faces with bandages. But perhaps that would be too drastic."

"Ha, ha, ha," said Arthur, showing respect.

"All I want to know is why you are allowed visitors at any hour, and the rest of us has to wait until visiting time at seven o'clock," said Mr Winston Coggins.

"I'm afraid I can't tell you," said Arthur. How could he explain the reason? It would be obvious to anyone of intelligence like Pau Potts, but most unfortunately he had fallen asleep and was snoring loudly.

"Good. That's all I wanted to know," said Mr Coggins. "I take it you will have no objection if I bring the matter up with Sister."

"No, of course not," said Arthur, wondering how Sister would handle the thorny topic.

"Another visitor for Mr Friendship," said Nurse Golightly.

"Crikey, this is getting beyond a joke," said Mr Coggins. He was a most ignorant and disagreeable man. If he were more pleasant, thought Arthur, he would have less injustice to contend with. When Arthur came to write about him, he would have to be compassionate and decide that the most mature thing was to pity him, but now they were living side by side, it was obvious that Mr Coggins represented the great army of boors and louts who should be kept down. Without vigorous action by someone somewhere along the line, the world would never be a fit place for people of delicate sensibility such as himself, Mr Besant and Paul Potts to inhabit. About two-thirds of the human race were probably as nasty as Mr Coggins. It was the duty of the remaining third to remain on top.

The visitor was Elizabeth Pedal, looking extremely nervous and carrying an enormous bunch of chrysanthemums. She could not identify Arthur through his bandages, and was most affected by the sight when it was pointed out to her.

"Poor Arthur. How perfectly terrible," she said with a giggle. "These flowers are from Ferdie."

"Hullo, Liz," said Arthur. "How's things?" He could not help remembering the circumstances of their last meeting. Perhaps she had forgotten them. She must be so used to people making a pass at her in the back of taxis.

"We all wondered what had happened to you. I am terribly sorry I was so silly that night. I think I must have been tired."

Unless Arthur's ears were playing tricks, the lovely Miss Pedal seemed to be inviting him to try again. Unfortunately, the suggestion was impracticable.

"What has happened to – um – Toemass then?"

Elizabeth looked tragic. She must have been conscious of her beauty at that moment. Certainly everyone else in the ward was, and a terrible hush fell as everyone strained to listen.

"Toe-mass was only here for a few weeks. He has gone to Harvard, where they have made him Professor of Humanity or something like that."

Probably the best place for him, thought Arthur. But he said: "Oh dear, I'm so sorry. It must be very sad for you."

"He was such a wonderful person," said Liz. "After that quarrel he had with you – I can't remember what it was about – he forgot the whole thing and said he would like to meet you again. I think he hoped you could take me off his hands. He was so sweet. There will never be another man like him."

"Oh, I don't know," said Arthur.

Liz smiled. Such a beautiful, sad smile. Arthur marvelled that her slender shoulders could carry the burden of such beauty. Protected by his bandages, where no blush would betray itself, he felt curiously calm.

"We must have that dinner we arranged when I get out," he said.

"Poor Arthur, I can't bear to see you all wrapped up in bandages like an Egyptian mummy," said Liz.

"What about that dinner?" said Arthur.

"Yes, of course we must," said Liz. "Ferdie might come too. He sent his regards and said your gramophone was keeping fine."

"Oh good. I don't mind if he plays it occasionally, so long as he wipes the records with a damp cloth."

"I am sure he does."

"You would be surprised how much damage one cracked needle can do."

"I know. It's dreadful. Well, I'm glad to have seen you. Get better soon, Arthur."

166

The sweetest and gentlest girl in England left the ward. Arthur basked in the nurses' admiration. He reflected that in the tragedy of Kitchener Drive, he had lost his photograph of the Bloxham school play of *The Rivals*, but its loss seemed somehow less important, now. No doubt he could order another copy from the School secretary.

Chapter Ten

IN EVEN THE MOST ILL-FAVOURED LIVES THERE ARE incidents which must be recognized as turning-points: expulsion from school; failing an Army Medical Test; the first bounced cheque. One of these occurred to Ferdie when Mr Isinglass returned early from lunch and discovered him making love to Nina Cattermole on the deep pile carpet in the Director's Office.

"It isn't a question of discipline or morals," said Mr Isinglass. "We can get along quite nicely in this office without any of that sort of thing. It is a question of image."

Ferdie, after a moment of retirement, had returned to his employer's office spitting with rage. Most of it was directed against Nina. Ferdie had not wanted her in the first place. She was insatiably demanding, and there was nothing so unattractive as nymphomania. Girls ought to be taught that at school. As it was, they seemed to imagine that men respected them more if they made complete fools of themselves.

"Luckily it was I who walked through that door," continued Mr Isinglass. "But it might quite as easily have been one of our biggest clients, Mr Dresden Shoemaker or Sir Hanbury Ketchup. For all I know, they are devotees of moral rearmament."

"Hardly," said Ferdie. "Not Mr Shoemaker nor Sir Hanbury Ketchup."

"Even if they are not, there is a recognizable pattern of behaviour whereby employers expect a higher moral standard among their employees than they feel the need to set for themselves."

"Hypocrisy," explained Ferdie.

"And this is not, of course, the sort of incident which we can risk to see repeated. It is all a question of image."

"It depends what sort of image you want. Of course, you may prefer to cultivate the old-fashioned atmosphere. Americans are said to like that. Perhaps we should all sit on high stools and write with quill pens. You could call me Pecksniff. I mean there are lots of people who like that sort of thing. The only question I wonder about is would it be viable? Would *all* our customers like it? Of course, you could always have a Pickwick Department, where the executives wear frock coats and take snuff. Then we could have the rest of the office devoted to normal, non-kinky customers, where people behave naturally, like me and Nina, without upsetting the abnormals. All I mean to say is that there are lots of solutions to this sort of problem which may need a fresh reappraisal, particularly from the viewpoint of what might be called – you know – the younger sort of person."

Ferdie was being extremely reasonable. He could have put his point much more strongly, had he wished. But he had no desire to hurt Mr Isinglass's feelings at this stage. He was being patient and logical. It was an awkward situation, brought about by the anomaly of their relative positions. Ferdie could quite easily give Mr Isinglass a three-hour lecture on how to run an advertising office, but it was difficult at such a moment when he might be accused of self-interest.

"I am very sorry, Ferdie. I know you have your own ideas, and I have mine, you see. If it was known that I had kept you on the payroll after this little incident, I should be the laughing-stock of the Athenaeum. I am afraid it is all a question of image. Advertisers do not like to think that their accounts are being handled in a Caracas brothel, even if they spend most of their own time, as you say, inside a similar sort of brothel on their expense accounts."

"Who said this was a brothel?" said Ferdie. On reflection, he became rather indignant. "You have no right to describe Miss Cattermole as a brothel. What you have just said is slanderous and personally offensive. No doubt you cannot understand the difference between a tart you pick up in the streets and a meaningful relationship with a member of the opposite sex. None of your

169

generation can. The younger generation just happen to be different. We have not been brought up to believe that hypocrisy is the supreme virtue. I shall demand an apology for Miss Cattermole. You have no right to sack a girl and then insult her behind her back."

"I have not sacked Miss Cattermole, and I am not sure that I have any intention of doing so."

That silenced Ferdie. It would be ungallant to point out the injustice of retaining Nina, but Ferdie felt it keenly. There was one law for men and another for women. If only Mr Isinglass knew the proportion of blame which rightly attached to Nina, he would sack her instead. But it would be too undignified to explain.

"Very well, I shall go. I don't mind, but it seems a shame for the poor firm. You become quite fond of the place, with all its faults. My crime, I suppose, is that I tried to be too modern."

The bitter sarcasm was lost on Mr Isinglass, who scrutinized a folder on his desk.

"Collect your Insurance cards from Miss Rhapsome. The accountant will forward your P.45 when he has brought it up to date."

The main office seemed curiously preoccupied when Ferdie walked through it. Even Nina was intent on a folder of dual purpose cat and dog foods.

"Well, goodbye, everybody," said Ferdie. "I'm off."

"Are you going?" said a silly little secretary with buck teeth. "Why is that?"

Everybody else looked embarrassed. They avoided Ferdie's eye, as if he had let the side down.

"Goodbye, Nina. You had better take over the folder for Kat-O-Sand. I thought of two lines to develop: 'It's the Best, It's Odourless', or more simply, 'The deodorant litter which makes the best toilet for cats'."

"Goodbye, Ferdie. What about improving on the tag which

170

was turned out for Katmeat Jelly Balls, "The Best Toilet for Kittens of All Ages'."

"Yes, that's very good. It might even be better than my one. But just you try and get it past Mr Itching Arse."

"Goodbye, then, Ferdie. I expect I'll be seeing you."

"Yes, around the place."

Both suspected that they would never meet again. They had never met outside office hours. Nina had a permanent lover of Polish extraction who shared her flat. Ferdie's life was rich and varied, but at present he was seeing rather a lot of Liz Pedal.

Nobody would have guessed, as they watched Ferdie saunter nonchalantly from the building into the great, unexplored world of Berkeley Street that he had left a bit of his heart behind him, among the Jelly-meat Cat Balls and the Best Toilet for Kittens of All Ages.

"The only thing which upsets me about the whole episode is that you should choose to use the floor of my study. There must be more comfortable places than that. I've got a flat in Eaton Square, but it would never occur to me to use the floor."

"I'm very sorry, Mr Isinglass. It will not happen again," said Nina.

"Of course it won't because I've asked Mr Jacques to resign and had to accept his resignation. The only question is what I should do with you."

"Yes, Mr Isinglass."

"I don't think you could very well stay in the main office, after what has happened. You can't trust girls not to gossip. The only possible thing would be if you came in here and worked with me. I don't know if you'd like that."

"Yes, please, Mr Isinglass."

"You could have a small office in my flat, too. It would mean

more irregular hours, of course, but I hope there would be con-
solations. You could have a bedroom there to yourself, if you
wanted one."

Nina paused. Then she made up her mind, looked straight
into her employer's eyes, exuding the mysterious flattery of
her sex.

"I think I will like that very much, Mr Isinglass."

"Good," said Mr Isinglass. "And for Heaven's sake call me
Roderick!"

With Ferdie's talent and knowledge he did not suppose it would
be very difficult to find another job. His newspaper told him every
morning that the country was crying out for young men with new
ideas. Ferdie was young, and all his ideas were those which are
generally accepted as being new. He approved warmly of abortion,
homosexuality and divorce. He was prepared to countenance the
idea of Communism being given a try in England, provided he
was awarded a suitably important rank in the Party hierarchy to
which his youth and the novelty of his ideas entitled him. He
felt that the starving masses of Asia and Africa were somehow a
product of the English class system. *Apartheid* was the most extreme
expression of the public school ideal. When America threw its
weight around among the under-developed nations of South East
Asia, it was the old story repeating itself of the nouveau-riche
parvenu who did not know how to treat his servants properly.
England, with its long history of obsequiousness to the lower
classes, was far better equipped to give the world a moral lead.
The English working classes were too materialistic, but they
had learned it from the Americans, and inwardly craved for a
return to the pre-socialist days of the industrial revolution when
socialism was something you could really believe in. It was time
for a general world shake-up to get the public schoolboys like
Salazar and Chiang Kai Shek out of high positions and make way
for a world government based on youth and new ideas.

Who would not want to employ such a person? And Ferdie had

many influential friends. Len Drewsome was senior creative director of an enormous firm specializing in weedkillers, agricultural machinery, plastic flooring and ready-cooked pies.

"I can't tell you how much I envy you. I would give my right hand to be out of the whole business," said Len. "You know how it is. Advertising gets a grip on you, and you can't struggle free. I swear, I would give my eyes to be out of the whole sordid business."

"Yes, it is a relief," said Ferdie. "And I certainly needed a change. But I wondered if there were any vacancies in your firm – for really senior positions, I mean. After all, I don't think I should leave the trade yet."

"The senior positions are a bit difficult. We usually take in people who have been Cabinet Ministers, or ex-ambassadors. Of course, there are always a few jobs for people who have worked their way up from inside the firm."

"Or even a junior post," said Ferdie. "It would be quite amusing to be junior again, for a while. I am beginning to forget what it was like. And then, of course, as soon as I had proved myself to their satisfaction, they could give me a proper place."

"Quite honestly, you know, Ferdie, I should take this opportunity to try something else. You will probably never get another chance. At last, you are out of the rat race, and you want to get back in it again. Frankly, I can't understand you."

Ferdie was not prepared to admit the real reason – that he needed the money. Len spoke as if a dozen jobs were his for the choosing. So they were, no doubt, but people had yet to learn that he was available, and there was no question of being given credit by Mrs Quorn, the fiendish white supremacist landlady. It was very difficult to explain.

"Yes, I see all that, but honestly it's my own affair, and I wouldn't mind another post in advertising. Do you know of any in your firm?"

"Become a theatre reviewer or something. Do you know how much Ken Tynan is paid?"

"No."

His friend named an enormous figure. "Or go into industry.

That's where all the money is. No sane person wants to stay in advertising nowadays."

"Please, Len, do you think you can get me a job in your firm."

"It's not as easy as that. There aren't any jobs available just at the moment. We have a waiting list for the next 25 years. Sorry, Ferdie. No can do. I would try something else."

"Perhaps I shall," said Ferdie.

"We take in a few recruits outside the normal channels," said Captain Starter. "You can apply for a junior clerkship with the acting-rank of Lance Corporal, but you generally need to have a Certificate in Russian, German or some Far Eastern language."

"I haven't got that," said Ferdie.

"No, I was afraid you might not," said Captain Starter.

"How on earth did you get into the Intelligence Corps?" asked Ferdie. He had often wondered.

"Fellow came round just before I passed out of Sandhurst asking if anyone would like to join."

"Oh, I see," said Ferdie.

"I think they judge candidates on previous sales experience, maturity, trustworthiness, charm and turn-out," said Mr Dent. "You probably wouldn't stand much chance because, of course, you're far too young. You could always go to a sales representatives' college, you know. The courses take nine weeks, and at the end you're given a diploma, which some people say might help you get a job, but I don't know."

"How did you get taken on?"

"I learned the hard way, in the army," said Mr Dent.

Ferdie wrote letters in reply to three advertisements in *The Times*, and two in the *Daily Telegraph*. Most of the advertisements seemed to require skilled computer operators or engineers, but

Ferdie thought he would try his hand at being a draughtsman, because he did not know what it was, and applied to another advertiser who required an unspecified type of executive who was not dismayed by the thought of earning £12,000 a year. None of his letters was ever answered, except one, which applied for a post in advanced computer research. The reply was an incomprehensible mimeographed form which Ferdie took to be a studied insult, and threw away.

"No wonder we're governed by morons," said Ferdie, bitterly. "They have what must be the most elaborate system in the world to prevent anyone of intelligence or originality getting in. A candidate who cannot convince them of his utter mediocrity at the first interview might as well resign himself to a life on the dole. Talent is anathema to them. What they require is proof of imbecility in the form of qualifications which have taken five years of abject servitude to acquire."

"Poor Ferdie," said Liz. "Have you tried the National Assistance?" She was finding it a bit expensive to support him in the manner of life to which he was accustomed.

"National Assistance," said Ferdie, in tones of the greatest contempt. In fact, he had already applied. When they asked him if he was registered at the Ministry of Labour, how many children he supported, and hundreds of other impertinent questions, Ferdie had walked out in a huff.

"Why did you leave Polden and Catchlaus?"

"I've told you, Liz, I wanted to get out of the rat-race. There is a certain point beyond which one is no longer prepared to prostitute oneself."

The spaghetti lay glazed and untasted on their plates. Ferdie spoke earnestly, as if he were terrified of being misunderstood. Liz wished she could be more helpful.

"What about the BBC?"

"Ha, the BBC," said Ferdie sarcastically. In fact, he had not thought of it. "You may have something there." It was the natural home, after all, for everything young and bearded and slightly Left of Centre. "It would be rather a laugh if one day I turned up and joined Dave and Nick and Reg and Julian Coddlecock and Bunny and Tim on the Foreign broadcasts. Or I could try Alex Simperatz on the Home Political. They might even give me a place on the Critics' Panel along with Professor Elwood, Lady Birdbath and the Bishop of Hungerford."

"I am sure they would."

"Of course Nick and Reg and all that crowd would be terribly jealous. Better not tell them I'm applying." Ferdie by now had an uneasy awareness that his contemporaries and friends were not the likeliest source of advancement.

"No, better keep it quiet for the moment."

The prospect of dignified employment made Ferdie livelier. "Let's have another glass of red wine each."

"All right," said Liz, who was paying.

"Make it a bottle," said Ferdie to the waiter, in a fit of reckless generosity.

"Twenty-five shillings," said the waiter menacingly. Liz paid.

"Shall we take it back to your flat and drink it there?" Ferdie began to feel the Italian restaurant oppressive.

"I was thinking of an early night, actually." Elizabeth Pedal was far too sweet a person to refuse any man what she considered to be his right, but she felt she had seen enough of Ferdie for the evening.

"I'll just come in for a short time, then."

They mounted Arthur's scooter, which Ferdie was looking after for him while he was away, and drove to Iverna Terraces where Liz shared a flat with a girl who smelled like a horse and took jazz seriously. Probably she was unhappy.

"I'm not saying I'm more intelligent or talented than anyone else."

"Of course you are, Ferdie."

"If I am, that's my own funeral. All I am saying, is that suppose just for a moment I *was* more intelligent and talented than other people."

"That's right."

"Suppose I was the most intelligent and talented person of my generation in the world."

"Of course there are a lot of talented people around nowadays."

"They *still* wouldn't know what they were missing. I might be Einstein himself, or Bertrand Russell, for all they care."

"I think they're being stupid," said Liz.

Ferdie walked over to where she sprawled by the gas fire, put his hand inside her skirt and kissed her passionately on the mouth.

Ferdie drove back to Ebury Street in a tumult of self-satisfaction. Strictly speaking, Liz was his type of girl. He was not going to say she was better at it than some of his girls had been, but she was certainly not worse than others. And it was good for prestige to be seen around with her. Personally, he preferred them plumper and darker, with slightly more vitality, but he was prepared to concede that Elizabeth Pedal's type of looks were the more fashionable. She was a bit too humorous about the whole thing, and he was going to have to knock some of that out of her. But, on the whole, he was pleased with himself, and was even prepared to countenance the idea of a long affair, much as he disliked being tied down.

A week after Arthur was admitted to the casualty ward of the North London Hospital, Paul Potts received a visit from his wife. They did not discuss the principle of collective bargaining inside a free economy or any of the other burning topics on which they were liable to disagree. Mrs Potts was an enormous woman with a double chin and more than a suggestion of a moustache. Arthur admired his friend tremendously for the way he handled her. He always called her "my good woman" or just "woman", except when he was feeling sentimental. Then it was "lass" or "lassie". Since Mr Potts was not a North Countryman, it must have been something he learned on television. Arthur resolved to call his own wife "lass", if ever he abandoned the ascetic discipline of celibacy for the carnal indulgence of the married state. Mrs Potts had brought her husband a bottle of Lucozade, which he drank resentfully under her gaze.

Mr Coggins was visited by a niece, to whom he complained loudly of his difficulty in passing urine.

Arthur had no visitors for the first half-hour. Mrs Potts took pity on him.

"Would you like some Lucozade?"

"No, thank you. I have just finished my tea."

"Yes he would. You go on, Art. Give him some, Marigold." Paul Potts was clearly anxious to share his good fortune.

"No, really, I don't even like it much."

"You go on and drink it up," said Mrs Potts, in a mock-bossy voice which nevertheless carried a distinct threat.

Arthur was cowed into accepting a glass of fizzy yellow liquid which tasted sweet.

"Just like champagne," said Mr Potts encouragingly.

"It's better than champagne. It does you good," explained Mrs Potts.

"I'm not saying it's better. Just that it's similar," said Mr Potts, asserting himself.

"I certainly think it's as good," said Arthur.

"Look, he's drinking it," said Mrs Potts.

All the visitors from neighbouring beds crowded round to watch the apparition of drink poured into a totally bandaged face.

"Oo, look, Uncle Winnie. He's drinking something."

"It's not drinking that's difficult. It's when the drink tries to come out the other end."

"What a marvellous man. He must be very brave."

Surrounded by admiring glances, Arthur sat in bed and drank Lucozade.

"Visitor for you, Mr Friendship."

His admirers dispersed, with the fickleness of a crowd, and resumed their admiration of husbands, uncles and fathers. Arthur was left alone with a glow of self-satisfaction.

"You don't know me, Mr Friendship, I'm the new Deputy Features Editor of *Woman's Dream*."

"How do you do," said Arthur. He was among his own people, where he was admired, and resented this intrusion from the cruel world of Ronald Carpenter.

"Mr Carpenter sent me along to give you the good wishes of the staff."

"How kind."

"He also sent these flowers. There was a collection among the staff, and as it was not quite enough Mr Carpenter said we could make it up out of the entertainments account."

"How thoughtful."

"And all the staff send their best wishes for a quick recovery."

"Oh, good."

"Is there anything you want?"

"No, thank you."

"Well, then, I had better be going. You're sure there's nothing else?"

"Quite sure."

"While I'm here, there's a tiny bit of business. Do you know how long it will be before you can resume your column?"

"I'm afraid I don't know. With luck, I should be out of here in a week or two. It's a matter of how long is needed for the skin to take."

"Oh yes, of course. You don't know how long that will be?"

"Probably in a week or two."

"Good. Then I'll tell our contributions departments to suspend payments until then."

"Thank you so much."

"I know it sounds a bit ungenerous, but it is not as if you were on the regular staff. We're having to get someone else to do Dr Dorkins, and we've said the Rev. Cliff Roebuck is on holiday."

"He may remain on holiday longer than you think," said Arthur grimly. He was by no means sure that he was going to return to *Woman's Dream*. Personal assistant to the Director of

Peace Education seemed a much more dignified employment.

"I hope not."

"He may never come back."

"Come now, Mr Friendship." The Deputy Features Editor assumed that Arthur was suffering from some male equivalent of post-natal depression. "The magazine isn't the same without you."

"Of course it isn't," said Arthur. His book reviews were easily the best feature; indeed the only one which redeemed it. But he had an uneasy feeling that *Woman's Dream* was something bigger than himself. If the entire staff died, from the buxom girl at the reception desk to Roger Barracks, Cleghorn and the Editor himself, *Woman's Dream* would continue to appear week after week without any noticeable difference. It had a life and soul of its own nothing could change its knitting pull-outs and summer cookery hints. If it appeared with totally blank pages, its two million readers would not notice the difference, turning the pages happily as they dreamed of mansions in Cornwall, marriages unconsummated until the last chapter, men called Richard dressed in cardigans, girls called Sarah dressed in red, hints for redecorating their homes in the Scandinavian manner, the problems of imaginary teenage daughters.

"By the way, I bought some books," said the Deputy Features Editor. After one glance, Arthur knew them all. *Jacquetta and I, Trenkettering Castle, Childbirth and After Care, Some Common Diseases, from Colds and 'Flu, to Arterial Sclerosis, Illustrated, Beekeeping as a Hobby, Collecting Antiques, Away from it All,* a new novel by Priscilla Page, *What every Teenage Girl Ought to Know, Cowslip Cottage,* another new novel by Priscilla Page, *The Walled Garden,* yet another, *A Sparkle among the Fern,* her autobiography.

Arthur knew them all terribly well because he had written reviews of them all. Reviewers were not allowed to keep their copies from *Woman's Dream* – a pointless meanness of Carpenter's, who said it was his duty to safeguard the company's property. Consequently, they lay around in the office until they were thrown away.

"By the way, when you have finished with them, I should be

grateful if you would let me have them back, as they belong to the company."

"Take them back with you now, then."

"There's no hurry. Just so long as I know where they are."

When the Deputy Features Editor had gone, Arthur stared at the pile of books. He could remember every word of his reviews. His criticism of Miss Page's autobiography – Arthur preferred to think of it as a tribute to a wonderful old lady – had been particularly ingenious. He recalled Tennyson's poem, from which Miss Page drew her title:

> "I come from haunts of coot and hern
> I make a sudden sally
> And sparkle out among the Fern
> To bicker down the valley.

An exact description, he had said, of the wit and sparkling vivacity of Miss Page, enjoyed by her countless millions of readers for the last sixty-five years. He had capped it by quoting the poem's punch line:

> "For men may come and men may go
> But I go on for ever."

A sub-editor in Doncaster, where *Woman's Dream* was printed, had cut out the last reference. Perhaps it hinted that Miss Page was, or had been, a prostitute. Women's magazines were so sensitive about that kind of thing. Nearly every review of Arthur's seemed to hint that someone was a prostitute. It was one of the hazards of life in the post-sexual age.

Three hours after his visitor left Arthur realized that he had not the slightest idea whether he had been talking to a male Deputy Features Editor or a female Deputy Features Editor.

Chapter Eleven

THE NATIONALITY OF FERDIE'S MOTHER WAS WELSH. HE had been connected with too many political organizations to list, but he chose the Education for Peace Movement and the Keele (Staffs) Committee of 100 as representative. He had been born in the United Kingdom, and his father, so far as he knew, was Edward William Le Cock Jacques, Lecturer in Chemistry at the University of Brisbane. His interests or hobbies were politics, foreign affairs, jazz and modern subjects. He had no wife, nor was he engaged to be married, so discussion of his wife's nationality and political affiliations was fruitless. His educational qualifications included a Higher Certificate of Education in biology, an Ordinary Certificate in biology, chemistry, elementary mathematics and French, written and oral. He had no relatives or dependants who lived behind the Iron Curtain. His medical history included no fatal or recurring diseases. All in all, he was a thoroughly suitable candidate for the BBC.

But even as he signed his name with a flourish at the end of the four-page inquisition, he knew that he had not done himself justice. It was clearly of interest to the Personnel Officer that he had never suffered from tuberculosis, malaria, diabetes or malignant anaemia, but it was only part of his strength, and rather a negative part.

There was no probing of his inner self, no curiosity as to what it was that made him tick, for Ferdie had no doubt whatever that he did tick. Was it genuine radical zeal, or lust for power? Did he hope to improve the world, or merely to influence it? Did he have the over-all vision and ruthlessness required for such a task? Was he a genius, and, if so, was he benevolent or evil? Would he revolutionize the BBC, or be content to take the pickings? These were the questions which exercised Ferdie in his more introspective moments. In all honesty and humility, he was not sure that he knew the answer to any of them; they were more topics for discussion than questions for catechism. But the BBC should at least enquire.

Before calling on Mr Iltyd Llew-Williams, in Bush House, Ferdie trimmed his beard and cleaned his fingernails.

"Ay, we received your form, lad, and we've filed it," said Mr Llew-Williams. "What sort of a job is it you're looking for?"

Wherever his talents would be most useful. A position of responsibility, of course. He had been thinking about Critics' Panel.

"We're a wee bit full up on Critics' Panel just now. But we have a Junior Leaders' Course which starts in May. They pay you ten pounds a week while you're on the course, then fifteen hundred a year if you pass."

Ferdie was looking for something a little more definite than the vague hope of employment in five months' time.

"The only other way into the Corporation is to answer the advertisements as they appear in the *Daily Telegraph*."

"The *Daily Telegraph*," said Ferdie sarcastically. It was his nearest approach to expressing something of himself.

"Ay, the *Daily Telegraph*," said Mr Llew-Williams. "All the posts available are advertised in that organ." It was his nearest approach to expressing approval of everything that Ferdie stood for. "Each candidate is considered strictly on his merits. The only thing is to apply."

In Albany Chambers, Ferdie sat down to read back-numbers of the *Daily Telegraph*. Mr Dent allowed Mrs Quorn to take his copy every evening. There were only two posts advertised – for a deputy head of educational series in the West Region and for someone fluent in the Albanian language to monitor broadcasts from that country.

Ferdie threw down the newspapers in disgust. Once again, he had come against the unspoken Freemasonry by which men of mediocre abilities the world over conspired to exclude the talented few from gainful employment. People wrote about the disadvantages of being born a Jew, a Negro, an atheist, a member of the working class, but the greatest handicap of all was to be born a genius in the modern world.

"Mr Friendship, you have a visitor."

It had passed. Arthur awoke, soaking.

"A visitor," explained Nurse Golightly, "who has come to see you."

"Hi, Arthur. I didn't expect to see you here. You look as if you've had an accident." Ferdie was clicking his fingers in a way which meant that he was embarrassed.

"Hello," said Arthur.

"I've come to see you," said Ferdie.

Arthur waited.

"I wondered if there was anything you wanted."

"No thank you." He waited again.

"Actually, I rather wanted a little talk with you."

"What about?"

"Is it all right if I talk to you?"

"I suppose so."

Ferdie settled himself down in a chair and blew on his fingers. "Are we allowed to smoke in here?"

"No." In fact, everybody was allowed to smoke except the nurses, but Arthur decided it would be good for Ferdie to exercise a little self-restraint.

"Christ, no wonder the National Health Service is so unpopular. You must be having a terrible time."

"On the contrary, I find it very pleasant."

"Have it your own way. What I wanted to talk about was something personal. I am thinking of giving up my job in advertising."

"Oh really," said Arthur. "Why?"

"They're too hidebound. It's like working in a monastery during the Middle Ages. Reality means nothing."

"No, I suppose not."

"I am thinking of going into journalism."

Arthur had been waiting for this and was prepared. "I certainly shouldn't do that, you know. People are far better off in advertising, and journalism isn't even a very easy profession to get into nowadays."

"You must have a lot of high-up friends in journalism."

Arthur supposed that he had, but he was certainly not going to betray his friendship by recommending Ferdie Jacques to any of them.

"Journalism is no place for a creative young man, Ferdie. Why don't you strike out on your own?"

"I was wondering if you knew of any jobs in your sort of journalism."

"As a matter of fact, I do, but it would not be suitable for you. Not your cup of tea at all."

"Tell me, then, Arthur please." Ferdie abandoned any pretence of dignity. "After all, we have been quite good friends. It is not much fun being out of a job."

"Ferdie, I would help you if I could, but this isn't the sort of job you would like. As a matter of fact, it is my own job on *Woman's Dream*. There is some talk of a new post for me, which I obviously cannot talk about, as nothing has been decided yet. It appears that Mr Besant is looking for an executive director to co-ordinate work in the major departments. He has asked me, and I am considering his offer at the moment."

"Please, Arthur, do you think you could put me up for your old job on *Woman's Dream?*"

"But you wouldn't like it at all, Ferdie. It is much too old-fashioned for you – to do with literature, and that sort of thing."

"Please, Arthur."

"Quite frankly, Ferdie, I am not sure that you're the sort of person they are looking for. It is an extremely responsible position, and they expect someone a bit older and with more experience. If you went and worked for some sound provincial newspaper and then came back in ten years' time, they would be delighted to have you, of course. If I were Editor, I would certainly hire you, but you know how sticky these people are. If you really want to be a journalist, I should go out into the provinces."

"Thank you very much," said Ferdie. "I don't happen to like the provinces."

"You could try setting up as a free-lance reviewer. They are the ones who make the really big money. Write a specimen review and take it to an Editor."

"Yes, I might do that," said Ferdie miserably, agreeing only because he wanted to end the conversation. He had never been so humiliated before. To have asked for a job writing about feminine subjects on *Woman's Dream* was bad enough. To have been refused it was the final degradation. Never had Michelangelo or Beethoven been required to suffer so much.

"You can borrow these books, if you like," said the obscene bandaged Thing in the bed.

"Thank you very much," Ferdie picked up the pile.

"They present quite a challenge to the inexperienced reviewer. Write a good criticism of them, and you will be able to do anything."

After Ferdie departed, Arthur was left to his dreams and his solitary discomfort. There would not be another blanket bath until seven o'clock in the evening.

War seemed inevitable on every front. In Berlin the crisis grew. In Asia, the Americans had been bombing successive swamps and resumed discussion of defoliating the entire South East with low yield atomic weapons. Mr Besant became terribly over-excited. The non-aligned nations were appalled. But Mr Besant's lovely Sinhalese secretary was bored. She had not heard from her hatchet-faced lover for three days. He said he was going abroad on a mission, and April was left with the sexless urbanity of Mr Besant and the perpetual buzzing of her telephone, like a colony of bumble bees the day before independence.

"Hello, Mr Besant's office," she whispered silkily.

"This is Ferdie Jacques, Victoria branch. I hear that Mr Besant has a new post to be filled. Would he be able to see me about it first?" Ferdie was going to tell him on no account to employ Arthur in a position of responsibility. He had reason to believe that Arthur was a double-agent, working for the white racialists. He had been found at two lodging-houses where white racialism was practised, and Ferdie had other evidence.

"Wait a minute, please." All the hope and tenderness of a young bride were in April's voice. It was something they taught at the Colombo finishing school she had attended. "Unfortunately, Mr Besant has not a free moment until midnight tomorrow. Would that be too late for you?"

No, it would not be too late.

"Very well, then. Come to the Hilton Hotel. Suite 2013. Thank you."

"Can I take your coat, Sir?"

Members of the Horseferry Road Tenants' Association were most unwilling to part with their coats. Ferdie scowled and ground his teeth. The Victoria Assembly Rooms, scene of so many dialectical battles, were much less exciting from the cloak-room attendant's enclosed quarters. So far, Ferdie had collected only five coats, which would probably mean less than half-a-crown in tips. With his ten shillings stipend for enforcing propriety in the mixed toilets, and the threepence which a member of the Tenants' Association had been foolish enough to leave in his overcoat pocket, it brought his night's earnings to twelve shillings and ninepence.

"I am surprised I take the trouble," thought Ferdie bitterly.

Three coats arrived in quick succession. One in herring-bone tweed, contained a paper bag with some boiled sweets stuck together. Ferdie disengaged one, sucked it and spat it out. The other was a long black riding cloak such as Count Dracula might wear in a village hall production. It had no pockets. The third, worn by a diffident, bald man about four feet high, contained a letter which was more or less unreadable. It dealt in the main with the writer's privations, and appeared to start "Dear Tiddly Winks."

With a sigh, Ferdie turned to his other work. After a glance through the books he had borrowed from Arthur, he decided that "Jacquetta and I" by Elsie Peartree was probably the one which offered most scope for his talents. So anxious was he to start his criticism, that he omitted even to read the dust-cover. But a glance at two or three pages inside, and a scrutiny of the chapter-headings told him all he really wanted to know:

ESCAPE FROM REALITY

Escapism runs through art like a silver thread. Just as Nero fiddled while Rome burned, Michelangelo, who lived in the time of some of the greatest social injustice in the history of man, contented himself with painting pictures of angels and madonnas. Beethoven is another case in point. This trend probably reached its apogee at the time when baroque, and later rococo, overwhelmed Southern Germany in the seicento.

Miss Peartree, in her latest autobiographical excursion, deals with the interplay of characters and events through the eyes of one person – in this case a middle-aged English spinster literateuse – in terms of her relationship with a character symbolized in the hyperphallic imagery of a wild animal domesticated, a female kangaroo.

The choice of kangaroo is significant. Just as the bull has been accepted as the symbol of heterosexual fulfilment, as in the Palace of Minos at Knossos, and the goat is traditionally the symbol of masculine virility, so Miss Peartree offers us the kangaroo as a symbol of another form of relationship.

"Excuse me."

"Yes, what is it?" Olympian, disdainful cloakroom attendant.

"Can you tell me where the Gents is?" It was Tiddly Winks who spoke, so small that his little shiny head hardly appeared above the cloakroom counter. He seemed agitated.

Ferdie yawned. "I expect so." He produced a saucer which he had filled with florins and half-crowns.

"How much is it?"

"As much or as little as you please."

"Have you any change for a florin?"

"No, I am terribly sorry, but I do not appear to."

Ferdie showed him the lavatory and resumed his meditations. Had anybody ever given serious consideration to the potentiality of the male kangaroo? Of course not. Kangaroos were things which carried their young in a pouch, quintessentially female. What part did the male kangaroo play in this scheme of things? Indeed, how did he set about it? Perhaps they were auto-reproductive, like the worm.

Terrible noises rose from the cubicle where Tiddly Winks was confined. Ferdie closed his mind to them.

Thus the book may be considered on several levels, but consideration of even the first, which is a straightforward account, in the most compassionate terms, of the neo-lesbian dilemma, leads us straight away to the second. How far are we to accept that Jacquetta represents another entity, in the conventional girl-meets-girl situation, and how far are we to suppose that Jacquetta is in fact no more than a projection of Miss Peartree's own mind, what used to be described (in the 'thirties) as her alter ego? Acceptance of the last synthesis in its entirety would lead us still further down the slippery slope of existential speculation, until we are left with only the bare bones of a kangaroo in which, as an objective proposition, no reader could possibly be expected to believe. What, then, is Miss Peartree's purpose? Conventional nihilism needs no such elaborate dressing; indeed is denied by it. For the answer, we will probably have to wait for Miss Peartree's succeeding volumes in the trilogy which she has promised us.

"Thank you very much," said Tiddly Winks.

"Not at all," said Ferdie. He was already bored by his work. Elsie Peartree was clearly a liar, but he dared not go further in exposing her without risking the libel laws. It was inconceivable, as she claimed, that a kangaroo could be trained to eat Irish stew. Everybody knew that they were vegetarian. Even if she had lived with a kangaroo for a short time, it could only have been as a publicity stunt. There was no reason why he should help a fellow-writer to attract publicity.

In fact, this book fails in almost everything it attempts. I very much doubt whether the kangaroo will ever be adopted, like the bull in the Palace of Minos, as the brand-symbol of any type of human relationship.

There may be a justification for escapism as a means of confronting reality by diagonal approach, that is to say by reducing unreality to an absurdity, which leads the writer, through his hero, from a vicarious rejection of the world of make-believe to a more whole-hearted involvement in the world as it is. But this has yet to be achieved successfully. As it is, Miss Peartree has supplied us with a sugar-coated pill safe to leave around for the children, because inside that coating of sugar they will find nothing but more and more layers of sugar.

A lean-faced Tenant demanded to know the way to the urinals. Ferdie showed him without demur, judging that there was no largesse in his soul.

"Is the meeting nearly over?" Ferdie had an appointment at midnight, and he had eaten nothing.

"Ar."

"Have you sorted out those landlords yet?"

"Ar."

"I think the Government ought to act on landlords. Prison sentences quite frankly aren't enough. It doesn't deter them at all. First of all, we should protect tenants' rights. No eviction under any circumstances. All properties from which tenants are to be evicted should, *ipso facto*, be nationalized without compensation and the tenant reinstated. Then the landlord should be forced to pay an agreed sum to the tenant by way of recompense for his previous exploitation, and a further sum to the State to cover costs and maintenance."

Ferdie supposed that it was indelicate to continue talking to the lean-faced man's back, and wandered into the Assembly Hall.

A grey-headed woman spoke in an expressionless monotone. "Resolution before the Tenants' Association, that while we have no prejudice of any sort ourselves and are prepared to accept neighbours of any class, creed or colour strictly on their own merits, we would nevertheless draw the attention of the Housing Committee of the London County Council to the grave undesirability of establishing a hostel for immigrant and other unmarried mothers in the neighbourhood of Horseferry Road, having regard to the health hazards that such a proposal might create, and our very real concern for the morals of our children, many of whom are still in the early teens, and the character and amenities of the neighbourhood."

Nobody dissented.

A man stood up and said: "We don't want the coloureds."

There was a general murmur of agreement.

"Of course we don't," said the grey-headed woman, "we've said that already. But you've got to be careful nowadays, or you'll end up in prison. It will be against the law to say you don't like coloured people soon. Well, I take it we're unanimous."

Ferdie felt inclined to barrack, but he knew it was as much as his job was worth. If they really did not like coloured people, there was little he could do to persuade them otherwise. In a sort of way, he agreed with them. It was the public expression of such likes and dislikes which was morally repugnant.

"Copies of our resolution will be sent to the people concerned," said the grey-haired woman, and the meeting broke up. Ferdie realized that he had left the lean-faced man alone in the lavatory, and hurried back. There was no sign of the lean-faced man, nor of the money which Ferdie had left in the saucer. It amounted to twelve and sixpence, plus the two shillings gratuity from Tiddly Winks. He swore loathsomely.

It was a bad night for tips. Perhaps the fury in the cloakroom attendant's eyes or the empty saucer put people off. When the last coat was gone, Ferdie had only collected sevenpence. With the threepence which he had stolen from someone's pocket, he possessed tenpence in the world.

He telephoned Elizabeth Pedal:

"Can I come round and get something to eat?"

"Oh Ferdie, darling, I'm so sorry. We've just finished our dinner."

"You and who?"

"Didn't I tell you I was going out this evening with your friend Martin Starter? We had such a lovely time. He took me to the Crazy Elephant. We've only just got back." Her voice was innocent of guile. A more sensitive person would have been enraptured by the musical lilt of it.

Ferdie, thinking only of the hunger he carried like a struggling infant in his belly, decided she was drunk, and rang off in disgust. The telephone call had cost him fourpence. No bus went from Victoria to Park Lane, and the Underground involved two changes, costing more than sixpence. He would have to walk.

A cursory examination of the lavatories – he had been told to leave them as clean and orderly as he found them – revealed that the compartment occupied by Tiddly Winks had been violated in the most offensive way.

A man and woman were waiting outside the Assembly Rooms.

"He left threepence in his coat pocket when it was hung up. I know he did. He told me he had," said the woman.

"Here you are," said Ferdie. "It fell on the floor, and I didn't know from which coat it had fallen."

He plodded heavily towards Hyde Park Corner, reflecting that he had had nothing to eat since lunch, starving amidst plenty. He gave a bitter laugh.

"My dear Ferdinand, I am so sorry to have kept you waiting so long before you could see me." Mr Besant was in his shirtsleeves.

His head, above a spotlessly white nylon shirt, was framed in a circle of light.

Ferdie sat in an armchair beside him, with a tumbler of Campari soda, ice, lemon and gin. He tried to reach a bowl of outsize olives.

"My poor young man, you are starving." Mr Besant must have seen the naked hunger in his eyes. He telephoned room service and spoke fluently in Italian.

"You have come to talk to me about the state of the world," said Mr Besant. His face was tired and infinitely lovable, with a strange exhilaration about it. "Things are terrible, terrible, terrible. So much is happening at once. I should not be at all surprised if this was the last night of peace upon the earth. Already, the bombers are flying overhead, waiting to go off on their ghastly missions. The rockets are poised, with warheads fitted. It needs just a word, a sudden movement, a sigh, and we are all plunged into destruction. Civilization as we know it will be at an end. All that remains will be a few scattered pockets of small intelligence and uncouth ways. We are all waiting, waiting for the touch of a button. At times such as this, it is good to have a friend at one's side."

"Yes," said Ferdie. "The world situation looks pretty bad. But it wasn't exactly that I wanted to talk about."

"I am reliably informed that the order has gone out to scatter all our nuclear weapons and keep those planes which are not airborne on a three-minute alert. Only twice before has this happened, over Suez and Cuba. The Americans, of course, are always having alarms, but the English, the stolid, phlegmatic English – are you not a little perturbed, Ferdinand? Think of seventy million people being killed in the first exchange, lasting less than seventeen minutes."

"Yes, terrible," said Ferdie, sipping his drink. "All those people. But what I really wanted to see you about was a job." He had been thinking, as he trudged against the traffic up the slippery pavement of Park Lane. If he had it in his power to exclude Arthur from the post of Deputy Director of Peace Education, why should he not intrude himself? "I hear there may be quite an important job going begging in the Movement. Arthur Friendship was talking about it."

"He should not have done," said Mr Besant thoughtfully.

"Poor old Arthur. I like him a lot, but I'm afraid he's not a very trustworthy sort of person."

"You may be right. I often wonder if he has enough . . ."

"I don't think he has," said Ferdie.

They sat for a moment in silence. Food was brought in a metal dish – mushrooms, bacon, eggs, a lamb chop, two kidneys and raw ham. Ferdie ate ravenously without removing his eyes from his plate. He was going to let nothing stand in the way between himself and this new job.

"Of course, it may already be too late," said Mr Besant. "After my life of work." He sipped a brimming tumbler of whisky, and put it down again. "Tonight we will drink a liqueur which I keep for special occasions. It is a trifle rough, not unlike the *grappa* of Italy, the *marc de Bourgogne* of France or the *bogasi* of Portugal. I have kept it a long time, and it has travelled far."

Ferdie wiped his mouth with his wrist and smiled intelligently. "I am sorry to have come hungry. I was robbed by a gang of white racialists at a meeting down in Victoria."

"Ah yes," said Mr Besant, who obviously did not believe him. "It is extraordinary what these people will do."

"Cleared me of every penny I possess, except fourpence."

"You have no other money?"

"None at all."

"And you are out of a job."

"Yes."

"Then you must be desperate, my poor boy. Have you contemplated suicide?"

"Yes, I am ashamed to say I have, Sir." Ferdie had not so much as given a thought to it, but he produced the answer which was expected of him.

"I think we all do, at times," said Mr Besant cosily. "There are so many disappointments in life. But do you come to me because you are desperate?"

"I thought I might be useful to you."

"What I need is a personal assistant in whom I can have absolute confidence. He must be loyal to the point of imbecility. For instance, if I were to ask you to do something for me which at first glance might seem to be contrary to your moral code, would you do it?"

"Without hesitation," said Ferdie, wondering what sort of sneer was intended by this reference to his moral code. "I have the utmost trust in you."

"Good man," said Mr Besant, filling both glasses with a white liquid. "Do you know, I have never had a personal assistant all these years? From Switzerland, where I tried unsuccessfully to collect a few possessions from the ruins of a shattered world, to New York, Buenos Aires, Leopoldville, Paris and London, I have always been a lone wolf. But you impressed me by the way you handled the group's expedition to Slough."

It was in Slough that Ferdie had set about the seduction of Elizabeth Pedal. His glamour as Group Leader no doubt helped. After the last member of the expedition had climbed down from the char-a-banc and disappeared into the night, Ferdie and Liz were found by the driver locked in a close embrace. After that it had been easy.

"It was nothing," said Ferdie.

"My only difficulty is that I cannot be sure how far you would be in sympathy with my purpose."

"Totally," said Ferdie.

"You know only one side of me, the busy-body do-gooder, rushing around to organize little committees of nit-wits, making silly little speeches down microphones, flattering the vanity of gross and over-privileged Negroes."

"Yes, I have often rather wondered about the coloured races," said Ferdie. "I mean, are they quite all they're cracked up to be?"

"Cretins," said Mr Besant. "But my dear boy, your glass is empty. No man of intelligence could possibly take them seriously for a moment. I have nothing against them – indeed, I quite like their silly, fuzzy little heads. But as a force in the world, black nationalism means nothing. The people who count are white Negroes, those people of intelligence and power on both sides of the Iron Curtain who identify themselves, for some reason best known to themselves, with the inarticulate and feckless masses of the African continent."

"You're not a white Negro?"

"Of course not," Mr Besant threw his arms open in an expansive gesture. "Do I look like one? But we can use these people, because they really are a force in the world."

"You mean, we can use them for our own purposes."

"Exactly."

"For peace, and all that sort of thing?"

"Yes." Mr Besant looked thoughtful. "Of course, there can be no peace in this world until conditions are perfect. I sometimes think that other people do not grasp my concept of ideal peace."

"Something as tangible as a piece of cheese," suggested Ferdie.

"Exactly," said Mr Besant. "You know, I really do believe we are going to see eye to eye. But one has to keep one's true meaning to oneself. There are so very few people who are prepared for the sort of ideas we share. It would not do to shout around what our plans are." Mr Besant was sweating under his nylon shirt.

"Never," said Ferdie, "people are so suspicious."

"There can be no peace when the world is divided."

"Of course not."

"When I look around me at the decadence on every side – popular music, which is in reality the screaming of over-sexed adolescents, so-called modern art – the daubings of a chimpanzee would be more interesting – complacent materialism taken for social progress, I see nothing, nothing in which I can believe."

"Some modern pictures, actually, aren't too bad."

"What is that? You talk to me of those insults to human intelligence, the product of demented apes?"

"Well, Annigoni," said Ferdie. He had not bargained for this.

196

"Peradventure there be one just man. But there isn't. The decadence of our society is absolute. Who believes in anything any more? Do you? Of course you don't. Do I? That is a question to which I have never found the answer. At one time, I used to believe very strongly. Now, I am not so sure. One suffers for one's beliefs, and in the course of suffering the beliefs undergo a sea change." Mr Besant relapsed into silence, cradling his glass, a misty, faraway look in his eye.

It was very late, and clearly he was tired, but Ferdie always recoiled from sentimentality.

"That's rather the way I feel about my experience this evening."

"What was that?"

"The racialists who stole all my money."

"Ah, yes, to be sure. Please fill up your glass, my dear boy. Don't wait for me to do it." Mr Besant clearly regarded Ferdie's presence as a minor irritant.

"Nothing can be done, unless we do it. Everybody is so timid. But there can be no true peace until all this is swept away." A wave indicated the entire Hilton Hotel.

Ferdie had an uneasy suspicion that it included himself. He had always suspected that Mr Besant was a Communist. Now, he thought his suspicions were confirmed. Most people among Ferdie's acquaintance would confess, if not to Communist sympathies, at least to a preference for Communism as against capitalism, if you scratched them hard enough. The thought of working consciously for a Foreign Power rather excited him, but there were risks.

"I think I begin to understand the sort of job I'll be doing," he said. "But would you mind telling me the details – the salary etc."

"Basically, you will be paid at the standard rate for UNESCO Clerks grade three, that is to say £2,500 a year with expenses and foreign allowance. But we receive money from all over the place, including the most unlikely sources, and part of these sums will be used to supplement your basic income, which is, of course, derisory."

"Thank you. When can I start?"

"It sounds to me as if you are short of money. Let me see." Mr Besant looked into his note-case. He took out three £10 notes. "Will that tide you over?"

"I expect so," said Ferdie, taking pains not to appear impressed. "My duties, presumably, will be to – er – collect information. Then you will pass it to those who will put it to a more peaceful use."

"Exactly. Peace in the fullest sense of the word."

Ferdie had once read that there were more than twelve thousand Communist spies working in London, and had vaguely wondered how he could get into the racket. It seemed both dignified and idealistic.

With the happy certainty of employment, he paid less attention to his host and more to his drink.

"What is this?"

"Schnapps. It is a form of aquavite."

"German," said Ferdie, finishing his fourth glass.

"Not necessarily. In fact it *is* German."

"Best thing the Krauts ever produced."

"Ah, yes, it is very special. But do you see what I mean? We must be completely on the same wavelength. We both believe in Peace, is that right?"

"Oh, ur."

"Has there ever been Peace on this earth? Have there not always been warring factions?"

"I suppose there have."

"There can never be Peace while there is life. But, to me, Peace has always been a secondary consideration. Peace, universal Peace in the world, is only a by-product of our efforts. There is the decadence, the putrid smell of decay about the world. Do you follow me?"

"Oh, yes."

"The world has come to the end of its long life. What remains is an affront to intelligence. There are only two active forces left on the planet, Communism and terror of Communism, but both are

198

nearly spent. Before it is too late, the confrontation must be made to occur. I often think I am the only person who realizes that the confrontation must be made to occur."

"I'm with you," said Ferdie drowsily. He could not even summon the energy to appear intelligent. Mr Besant continued to talk to himself, sometimes growing excited, for a long time. Ferdie picked up snatches and nodded his head wisely.

"No selection . . . detestable creed of Communism . . . a negation of human dignity . . . indifference of the West . . . effete . . . decadent . . . belief . . . destiny betrayed . . . gross materialism . . . sloth . . . debilitating effects of socialism . . . dice loaded against us . . . the death force of pacifism . . . bring about a realization . . . confrontation . . . manoeuvre . . . take advantage of universal stupidity . . . confrontation . . . total, utter . . . Peace."

At the end of his speech, Mr Besant stood up, his eyes shining. It was nearly four o'clock.

"My dear Ferdinand, I am so delighted to have found you. Come and see me tomorrow and we shall work out the details. To think, I nearly employed that ridiculous Arthur Friendship."

"Great mistake."

"What interested me was when I discovered he had seen through the half-hearted black racialism we have to teach now. All the time, he was working hand in glove with the white activists, arranging incidents. Pathetic, of course, but any striving after a realization is interesting."

"Ah, yes," said Ferdie.

"It may be too late," said Mr Besant. "If the moment of realization occurs tonight, if the bombs and rockets shower down upon us like locusts, then our partnership is at an end. But if nothing should happen tonight, at least we shall have hope for the future."

As he descended to the ground floor, Ferdie speculated on how many nights of the week his employer went to bed confidently expecting Armageddon by the morning. Mr Besant was clearly an emotional man. Ferdie thought that he was on a good thing.

Chapter Twelve

WAR WAS NOT DECLARED THAT NIGHT. ARTHUR SUCKED his thermometer and waited patiently while Princess Monolulu counted his pulse.

"Another eight-year-old girl has been strangled," said Paul Potts. "It always seems to be about that age." He rather fancied himself as a detective. "I shouldn't be surprised if it was all done by the same person – someone with what might be called a *penchant* for eight-year-olds."

Arthur could not reply without upsetting the mechanism of his thermometer. Potts needed constant reassurance, and became most upset if Arthur did not interject a grunt from time to time by way of approval.

"Almost certainly the man is a pervert. He's probably got something terribly wrong with him, like a deformed hand or a hideous scar on his face. It's that sort of thing which turns a man peculiar. They feel they have no sense of belonging. Best possible thing for that sort of person is hanging."

Arthur supposed he might be right, but it was the sort of remark with which he was liable to disagree, simply because he knew so many cogent arguments against hanging. He found himself increasingly in disagreement with his neighbour, ever since Potts had revealed that he was a life-long member of the North London Communist Party. This admission seemed to invalidate his other judgments, on such matters as the best way to grow marrows, the advantages and disadvantages of travel by bus, as against the underground railway, and the colour question.

"I don't mind people bumping each other off in the normal way, like between husband and wife in a fair fight," said Potts. "But not the indiscriminate murder of teenagers and small children. No, that's perverted. You have to draw the line some-where. If I was in charge of this country, I would say: 'All right, go on and murder anybody you like, bank managers, coppers, the lot, BUT LEAVE THE CHILDREN ALONE. Otherwise, my man, it's the gallows.' It's the only way. There wouldn't be any incentive to kill defenceless children, then."

Princess Monolulu took the thermometer.

"That's right, Mr Friendship. We're removing the dressing today."

"What about the real perverts who enjoy being hanged?" said Arthur.

"I wouldn't hang them," said Mr Potts. "I would hold them up to public ridicule and contempt. That would be a much more effective deterrent. Perverts hate being laughed at. In any case, I'm not so sure these people exist, who really like being hanged. It's just a piece of propaganda used by the anti-hangers. I mean, how can they *know* whether someone's enjoyed being hanged or not?"

"They think they're going to," said Arthur.

"That's what people say. But you're not pretending we should refuse to hang anyone just on the off-chance he's going to enjoy it."

"I can't go into all the arguments against hanging," said Arthur airily. He was becoming bored with his friend. Paul Potts was an extremist, which put him beyond the pale of rational discussion; furthermore he was uneducated, which made it impossible to use rational arguments against him. There was no common ground for discussion. Either one approved of hanging, or one didn't. For his own part, Arthur did not approve of it. He thought it was uncompassionate and retrogressive. Scientists had proved that it was no deterrent to the potential murderer, and Arthur would be extremely pleased when it was abolished. But there was nothing to be gained by further discussion with Mr Potts, because he was uneducated. "Few people of education and intelligence who have studied all the facts are any longer in favour of hanging," said Arthur.

Mr Potts sensed that he was being rebuffed, and became quite nasty.

"All your fine ideas haven't done much to save poor little Cindie Sweetman, have they? Her poor little body's still lying on its cold marble slab in the mortuary, while the man guilty of the crime walks around free. I often think that people like you who are so keen on letting criminals go free are really thinking the whole time how much you might like to knock somebody off, only you don't dare at present."

"Not at all," said Arthur.

"Well, *do* you dare? You only think of the criminal. You never spare a thought for his victim. You don't care how many small children are murdered. You don't like them, anyway."

"Yes, I do."

"Eight-year-olds?"

"Yes."

"All right, so you've got what might be called a *penchant* for eight-year-olds."

"I didn't say that."

"I never said you did. It is what I deduce. Now if I was in charge of enquiries into Cindie's murder, my reasoning would go something like this: look for a man who is single and un-attached. One who probably does not have much success with women. He might well have some sort of deformity – a speech impediment, a withered hand, a terrible scar. And find out if he's got what might be called a *penchant* for eight-year-olds."

"That's absurd," said Arthur.

"Why is it absurd?"

"Well, I haven't got a withered hand." No sooner were the words out of his mouth, than he realized he had damned himself.

"It's extraordinary how people jump to conclusions. Nobody mentioned you. Your name hadn't come into our consideration at all. The first and only time anyone mentioned your name was just now."

Arthur became flustered. "Don't be silly, Paulie. You know it couldn't have been me. The girl was only murdered yesterday, and I was here in bed all day."

"*I* may know that, but then I've only got my own word to go by," said Potts. "I might very well be lying to protect you. After all, we are what might be described as friends. The police aren't much interested in what friends say. I might be prejudiced."

It was an extremely uncomfortable moment. Mr Potts had raised his voice so that the rest of the ward could hear. Arthur could tell by the way they pretended not to be listening, that everybody present believed he was guilty of the murder of Cindie Sweetman. He had knowledge of his own innocence to sustain him, but even certainty of his righteousness was no comfort when twenty-eight others present were convinced of his guilt. Luckily, he was saved from further speeches in his own defence by the arrival of a procession at his bedside.

Princess Monolulu led the way, followed by the white-coated figure of the houseman, Dr Freelove. Behind him came the Registrar, Mr Atcherly, followed by Sister and the consultant surgeon, Mr Arnold Dimsdaile Egerton-Upcock. Mr Upcock was what passed for a Prince in the egalitarian world of North London surgery. Finally, Staff Nurse Bluebell arrived, masked and robed as if in anticipation of a poisonous gas attack. They surrounded Arthur's bed and looked down at him with expressions varying between gloomy malice and fatuous benevolence.

"We've come to remove your dressings," said Mr Upcock. "Now then, Sister, if everything is ready."

"Is everything ready, Bluebell?" said Sister.

"There's just the blue liniment sterilizing lotion," said Bluebell. Princess Monolulu was sent to fetch it.

When the dressings were removed, Mr Upcock said:

"Ah yes. Well, um. Of course, not too much was to be hoped for, but the graft has not taken too badly, really, all things considered. What do you think, Atcherly?"

Mr Atcherly scrutinized Arthur's face carefully. "The edges

are all right. There's a bit in the centre I'm not too happy about. Most unusual, really."

"Is it better?" asked Arthur, delighted that he should be unusual. There was an awkward silence.

"Of course, it will grow much less livid with time," said Sister. "When it settles down."

"I don't think there is any need for a re-graft," said Mr Upcock.

Everyone agreed to that.

"Can I have a look," said Arthur.

There was another awkward silence.

"It isn't quite ready for you to see yet," said Sister. "Just let Nurse Bluebell clean it up a bit first."

The caravan moved away. Left to himself, Arthur looked around, enjoying the air upon his face, and the freedom from confinement. He smiled at Paul Potts.

"Christ!" said Mr Potts.

"What's the matter, Paulie?"

Potts said nothing. Soon, Nurse Bluebell came back. She started swabbing Arthur's face with a roughness which seemed to indicate dislike.

"Ow!" said Arthur.

"You've got nothing to be sorry for yourself about," said Nurse Bluebell. "There are many much worse off than you are."

"Can I have a look?"

"There's no hurry. You'll have the rest of your life to look at yourself in."

Sister came back. "Now, Mr Friendship, you mustn't be alarmed at what you see. It always takes a bit of getting used to, when you've burned yourself. You're a lot better than some other people I've seen come in here. Remember that where the patches show a vivid red, that will probably tone down a bit in time. All in all, it's quite a nice new face we've given you."

Nurse Bluebell smiled sourly. "Very nice indeed."

"Will you get the mirror from next door, Bluebell? Now, don't be worried, Mr Friendship. It's a miracle we've got you as nice as you are. All the skin had to be grafted from your bottom, you know. Wonderful new machine we've got, removes the skin by vibrations. Even if you'd been awake, you wouldn't have felt anything. And it's lucky we've got such a brilliant team of surgeons. Mr Upcock is one of the best men there are at this kind of thing. Now here we are. Are you ready? Smile please."

Arthur could only gasp at the spectacle of horror which greeted him from the mirror. First, he noticed his eyes, which had become a yellowy-pink colour. His eyebrows were a dirty line, and he had no eyelashes. From the middle of his cheek, on the left side, a livid scar stretched over his temples to the forehead. But worse than any disfigurement was the look which met him from his own eyes. He was a repulsive, slightly hostile stranger.

Then he started noticing greater detail. A burn above his lip, on the left, made him look as if he was pursing half his mouth. His left ear was a large yellow-painted scab. There was more yellow paint on his neck and down the bridge of his nose.

"It's not as bad as all that, is it?" said Sister.

Arthur started crying to himself. Salt tears smarted on the raw wound where his eyelashes had been.

"You don't want to cry," said Sister.

"My eyes," said Arthur.

"Your eyelashes and eyebrows will grow again," said Sister. "It will only look funny for a week or so." She turned to Nurse Bluebell. "I think we had better give Mr Friendship a mild sedative. He seems rather upset."

Ferdie reported for work dutifully at half-past eleven. Mr Besant was already seated at his desk, shaved and fragrant of tropical herbage after a rainstorm.

"You will take my secretary's desk. I am very pleased to have got rid of her. There is something shifty about those Asiatics, and work is entering an important phase now – too important to be seen by anyone in whom one has not complete confidence." Mr Besant smiled conspiratorially.

Ferdie felt uneasy. He knew that he had heard many confidences on the night before, but he could not remember what they had been about. He remembered that Mr Besant had been vaguely anti-Negro, and had not taken his work for Peace as seriously as might be imagined, but that was all. He was not sure whether he had decided that Mr Besant was a Communist, a Fascist or a middle-of-the-road extremist. In fact, he did not care much either way, so long as he could fit in. Neither mentioned the fact that Armageddon had unaccountably failed to occur during the night.

The newspapers were full of Cindie Sweetman's murder. Ferdie yawned. There was also talk of a housewives' strike in Southend against proposals to put their men on 24-hour shift work. On the front page of the more responsible journals was a passing reference to the world situation. It appeared that on the evening of the day before the Prime Minister of England had sent a dynamic telegram to U Thant, Secretary General of the United Nations, in which he expressed hope of peaceful solutions to all outstanding world problems.

On inside pages, it was announced that bombing of Viet Cong positions continued. Cambodia protested against infringement of flying space. A dim American diplomat had denounced the East Germans for their behaviour on the Berlin autobahn.

"Those Americans," said Ferdie.

"Warmongers," said Mr Besant roguishly.

About half-way through the morning, the telephone buzzed. A thick, foreign voice spoke after there had been a jangle of coins.

"April, my darling, I am back."

"I beg your pardon," said Ferdie.

"May I speak to Miss April Kalugalla?"

"Miss Kalugalla has left," said Ferdie.

There was a pause.

"Is that Mr Besant?"

"No, it is Mr Ferdinand Jacques. I am Mr Besant's personal assistant. Can I take a message?"

But the caller rung off without a word. Otherwise, nobody seemed to want to talk to Mr Besant.

At lunch time, Mr Besant came into Ferdie's office in his shirt sleeves.

"I suppose I should try and take a few minutes off for a bite of lunch."

"Yes, you go on, Sir. You've earned it."

"Thank Heavens I have got someone I can trust to hold the fort for me when I am gone. Can you wait half an hour for your lunch? Or would you like it sent up here?"

"Send it up here," said Ferdie. He was enjoying his new job.

"Let me see, I *think* it is safe to go out for half an hour. So much is happening. It may be too late."

As Ferdie tucked into an enormous porterhouse steak, he wondered at his employer's ability to sustain himself in the belief that the world was about to be blown up.

"It's all he lives for," he thought charitably to himself. Everyone needed a little eiderdown to protect themselves from the cold world. To take away that eiderdown would have been the cruellest thing imaginable.

Ferdie had finished his lunch and was playing with some eyeshadow which the former occupant had left when a soft knock on the door revealed a hatchet-faced visitor.

"Hello, Johnnie. Come in and have some coffee."

"You remember me. I have come to ask some questions about Mr Besant."

Ferdie supposed that part of his job was to conciliate Mr Besant's fan club.

"What can I do for you? I haven't any photographs of my employer, I am afraid."

"Thank you very much. I already have many. I wish to know about Mr Besant's plans for the future."

"Much the same as before, I think. You know, campaigning on for Peace and all that sort of thing. Would you like to know what he had for breakfast? Grapefruit juice, followed by corn-flakes, then choice of kipper or grilled gammon rasher, tea or coffee. It doesn't say which he chose."

"Ah yes," said Mr Milchiger. "But has he any immediate plans? Is he going to any parties?"

"To tell you the truth, I'm not sure. But I could easily find out for you."

"That is very kind. We will pay handsomely, you know. But it is most important that Mr Besant should know nothing."

"Might embarrass you, eh?" Ferdie detested homosexuals, but he saw no reason why they should not pay for their predilections like everyone else. If all the spaghetti he had bought for his girl-friends were put end to end it would stretch to Peking. "Well, if I get to know anything, I shall let you know."

"Here is my telephone number. Ask for Johnny the Milkman. They will understand. We will pay twenty pounds for each piece of information. Here is an advance payment." Mr Milchiger produced two five-pound notes. Ferdie wondered why he had ever agreed to be an advertising executive, when his talents were so much in demand.

"Thank you very much, Johnny. We always try to be helpful."

Mr Milchiger relaxed. In repose, his face bore less resemblance to a hatchet, more to a wooden mallet.

"So you have joined Mr Besant. Has he told you anything?"

"Oh yes, I think I am pretty well in his confidence. He is a very wonderful man, of course."

Mr Milchiger stiffened. "I must go. Remember, not a word. Tell nobody, and whatever happens, do not reveal that telephone number. If you are tortured, you must eat it. If you let me down, I will come after you."

Soon after he had gone, April Kalugalla telephoned. Her voice was as soft as a kitten's paw.

"Someone may call who wishes to speak to me."

"Nobody has done so yet."

"It will be a man – tall and slim and athletic looking. He is called Johnny."

"You mean Johnny the Milkman? He was just in here, but he did not ask after you."

"He is back in London?" The voice became breathless with excitement. "Can you tell me where?"

"I am afraid that is not possible."

"Please, Mr Jacques. It is most important. Unless you tell me, I may not be able to find him. It is worth anything to me."

Ferdie played with the idea of suggesting they should meet, but remembered Mr Milchiger's warning. In any case, he had been told that ninety-eight per cent of Sinhalese girls suffered from venereal disease.

"I am sorry, Miss Kalugalla. If you like, I shall tell him you rang."

"Oh yes, please do. I shall ring again tomorrow."

Mr Besant returned in a state of high excitement.

"There is talk of wonderful news."

"War in Berlin?" said Ferdie hopefully.

"Not quite," said Mr Besant with a chuckle. "I lunched with a member of the British Foreign Office. He was trying to find out if it was true that America and Russia had concluded a secret agreement. He always comes to me, because he thinks I have influence with the Russians."

"Would you like me to organize a demonstration?"

"It is hard to know exactly what we would demonstrate about."

"American warmongering in South East Asia. British involvement in Berlin. Or just a moral protest about the world situation."

"I think we should leave the world situation alone at the moment. We might try to rattle the Government in other ways. What about these housewives on strike in Southend?"

"What's the point? They're only a crowd of over-excited women."

"Of course, you may be right. I have been working at the business for so long, that I sometimes lose touch with what is important and what is not. I thought that if perhaps we could create a worrying home situation, the Government might be forced to take drastic action abroad, but perhaps you are right. Nothing we do will ever make much difference. There are so many people working against us. The instinct for survival is stronger than any idealism. That is why I send people to see eggs being packed in Slough. It is important to keep busy, or we should all go mad. Perhaps we are the only people in the world working for a confrontation. Five years ago, there were people who advocated war. Now, the only force in the world is this dreadful instinct for survival. If we cannot harness it to our purpose of destruction, there is nothing left. There will be no limit to the decadence. The world should have been brought to an end in 1945."

"Of course it should," said Ferdie soothingly. "I was too young, then, to do much about it. But I'm sure that between us we will manage something." This pessimism was not good for future prospects. "By the way, I have brought my National Insurance cards. They are up to date."

"I used to think that if we could convince the Russians by our pacifist demonstrations that we had no will to fight, we might tempt them to some rash act which would summon all the terrible retribution which has been prepared."

"That's right," said Ferdie.

"But after Cuba, even the Russians seem to have lost their heart."

"Oh, I don't know," said Ferdie. "There's always the Chinese."

"You don't think they are a paper tiger?"

"Oh no," said Ferdie warmly. "They certainly mean business. I am sure they feel just as strongly about all this decadence as we do."

"Whatever happens, we will have had no influence."

"You never know."

"You are right. It is the principle that matters. Human intelligence has not become so universally vitiated that there is nobody left who can see the right path. We may only be stumbling along it, but at least there is a conscious force, however small, working in that direction."

"That's right," said Ferdie. It was hard to say at what moment in time he decided that Mr Besant was mad, but the increasing certainty brought him tranquillity.

"For the last twenty years I have been alone," said Mr Besant. "Never breathing a word to anyone, always acting a multitude of parts. It becomes very lonely. I often think that the greatest actors must be terribly lonely people."

"Oh certainly," said Ferdie. "Sir Laurence Olivier."

"If I did not have confidence in my idçals, I should have given up the struggle years ago."

"Of course you would," said Ferdie.

Arthur was discharged from hospital three days after his dressings were removed. He was not sorry to leave. An awkward atmosphere pervaded the place since his estrangement from Paul Potts. Even though few of the patients believed that he was a murderer, some of the mud was still sticking; the livid scar on his left cheek appeared proof of an irregularity.

"Goodbye, Mr Coggins. I hope your hernia doesn't last long."

"Well, it won't if I stay here much longer. I shall be bloody dead. I can't pass urine at all now, except in small quantities. There's the National Health for you."

Why on earth should Winston Coggins ever pass urine? Did he imagine he had some divine right? The English were becoming spoon-fed.

"Goodbye, Paulie. Don't get into any more fights with the wife."

"On that score, I shall follow the dictates of my own inclinations," said Paulie disagreeably. "I happen to have certain principles." The inference was that one of these principles, however controversial, precluded the murder of small children for sexual purposes.

"Well, goodbye then."

"Goodbye. I am most interested to have met you. I shall follow your subsequent career, no doubt, in the papers."

Arthur made a sort of grin, as if they both realized he was joking. Paulie did not return it. Arthur began to wonder if the working classes really added up to much.

"Goodbye, Nurse. Goodbye, Sister."

Nurse Golightly accompanied him to the door. Arthur had arrived with nothing, and he left with nothing. His clothes were those he had worn on the night of the fire, and they still had a charred smell about them.

"Here are your papers. Have you got a doctor of your own?"

"Not really."

"Never mind. If you want to apply for sick benefit, write to the Almoner and she'll send you the papers. It's only a couple of pounds, but better than nothing. I should take it easy for a day or two. Have you anywhere to go?"

Arthur was going back to his bed-sitting room in Ebury Street. He would be able to play his gramophone records again. Soon, he would be talking on equal terms with members of the peerage and circles close to the Royal Family.

"I would like to say how very much I appreciate all you have done for me."

"Not at all," said Nurse Golightly, embarrassed.

"Hello, Arthur. Fancy seeing you back. Quite a stranger." There was a suspicious bounciness about the odious, blue-haired editor.

"Thought I'd look in and tell you that I'll be able to resume work for next week."

"Well, that's good news, I'm sure. What on earth have you got on your face? Oh, I'm sorry. It must have been very painful."

"It was."

"There have been a few changes on the magazine since you were away, which I think I should tell you about. By the way

212

Tristram Catchesyde, who saw you in hospital, says you were thinking of leaving us. I hope that isn't true?"

Changes in *Woman's Dream*? It was inconceivable. Arthur suspected a plot against him.

"No, I don't think so." Arthur had heard nothing from Mr Besant about the new post. He always thought it was too good to be true. Although he yearned to be free of the undignified obligations involved in working for Ronald Carpenter, the thin voice of common sense whispered that the job was his lifeline, and even with his qualifications he could not be sure of another job in the tough, competitive world of journalism.

"Good. We hoped there was nothing in it, but of course we had to be prepared for the worst. Consequently there has been a certain amount of reorganization. As you know, for a long time the Chairman has not been too happy about the idea of having a clergyman on the magazine. In an age when only one in eight people ever go to Church, it seemed a bit out of date."

"He was a very modern clergyman," said Arthur mournfully. "The idea was to bring Christianity to the people in present-day terms."

"Yes, I know all about that," said Carpenter. "But people don't pay any attention to clergymen nowadays, however modern they are. So we decided to have a woman's column, giving a woman's point of view."

"I suppose I could do that," said Arthur reluctantly. He had rather liked the personality of the Rev. Cliff Roebuck.

"I have no doubt you could," said Carpenter. "But we decided that as it was to be a woman's column giving a woman's point of view, we might as well have it written by a woman. It's going to be called Frankly Yours by Ursula Sparrow."

"Who is Ursula Sparrow?"

"Rodge Barracks is going to be in charge. She will write it herself for the first few weeks, just to show everyone what is wanted, then she may take contributions and suggestions from any members of the staff."

"What sort of suggestions?"

"From female members of the staff," said Carpenter. "We are also looking for a young gynaecologist to take over from Doc Dorkins, although, of course, you can go on with him until we find one."

"Thank you very much. What am I supposed to do afterwards?"

"Well, there is always *Pets' Corner*. We need someone dynamic there. You wouldn't care to take that over, would you? This is a serious offer."

"No," said Arthur. "I'm not interested in *Pets' Corner*. What about my book reviews?"

Ronald Carpenter had obviously forgotten about the book reviews. He looked annoyed.

"Well, I don't suppose there's any harm in your continuing with them, if we can find room. Of course, generally speaking, we haven't much time for book reviews in a woman's magazine."

"I've noticed that," said Arthur. He was smarting under the injustice. It was absurd to pretend that Miss Roger Barracks was any more of a woman than he. Everywhere, Arthur found himself disqualified by reason of birth. He had been handicapped by not having been born a member of the working classes or a Negro, now he was expected to be a woman.

He knew exactly what he was going to do. He was going to go straight to Mr Besant and tell him that he accepted the post of Personal Assistant. This was no time to prevaricate. There was an open conspiracy against him inside *Woman's Dream*.

As Arthur was leaving, there was a faint cry. He returned to the aroma of gentian violets.

"One other thing I forgot to tell you." Carpenter was now smirking maniacally. "Bad news about your special number, I'm afraid. At an editorial conference, we decided it would be against the public interest to give too much publicity to cancer. Mr Condiment has agreed to hold it over."

"I'm not surprised. It was much too good for your magazine.

I don't suppose you've ever heard of realism." Even as he left after this bitter retort, Arthur felt that he had not done himself justice. The pretty receptionist had been replaced by a hideous one with spots. Symbolic, thought Arthur, as he stumbled into the cold, competitive world of Holborn.

Chapter Thirteen

MANY PEOPLE RECALL THE LATER DAYS OF NOVEMBER 1963 as the time when international affairs suddenly became interesting again. It would be inaccurate to say that the world held its breath. The casualty ward of at least one major London hospital was still preoccupied with the murder of Cindy Sweetman, eight, of Hackney. Suspicion had now shifted to Dr Freelove, the unpopular young houseman, who bungled the collection of a blood specimen from Mr Winstone Coggins so badly that the ward decided he must have been prompted by malice, concealing homicidal tendencies.

Mrs Jacomb, of Kitchener Drive, who always took a keen interest in current affairs, tried to start a discussion in the Bonanza Café, with no success. A few of the windows in the American Embassy, Grosvenor Square, were broken by London University Students displeased with the American conduct of affairs in foreign parts. The Prime Minister agreed to set up an inquiry into allegations of brutality by the police in restraining them.

Berlin was scarcely noticed, except by a small collection of Communists, hooligans and Liberal Members of Parliament who presented an incomprehensible letter to the German ambassador in London.

Arthur felt that he could not have returned to the political scene at a more opportune time. Mrs Quorn welcomed him sourly and demanded nine pounds arrears of rent which she reduced to eight pounds after a certain amount of haggling about uneaten breakfasts. Ferdie lent him the money with uncharacteristic readiness.

"What are you doing here?" asked Arthur, holding a hand

over the left side of his face. It was a nervous habit he had adopted. "Shouldn't you be at work by now?"

"I seldom go to work nowadays before ten-thirty," said Ferdie airily. "Now you come to mention it, I might be strolling along."

A letter from Arthur's bank informed him that he possessed thirty-eight pounds nineteen shillings, a small fortune by any standards. On the strength of it, Arthur delayed telephoning Mr Besant until he had read the newspapers and edited his opinions on the world situation. Clearly everything was in a terrible mess. It had been most irresponsible to turn his back for so long.

"Hello. Mr Besant's office."

"Can I speak to Mr Besant please?"

"I am sorry, Mr Besant is not available. Can I help you?"

Arthur thought he recognized a nasal twang in the voice at the other end of the line, but paid no attention to it.

"I am afraid it is rather a personal matter. Do you know when he will be in?"

"Unfortunately, he left no message. This is his personal assistant, Mr Ferdinand Jacques here. Are you sure I can't help you?"

Swifter than the flick of a serpent's tongue, Arthur perceived the full treachery of what had happened. His responses were slower than his brain. In a broken voice, he said: "Oh, Ferdie." Soon afterwards he realized that he had rung off.

There must be some mistake. Mr Besant was incapable of injustice or meanness. Perhaps Ferdie was occupying the job on a temporary basis until Arthur came out of hospital. No doubt the unscrupulous villain had omitted to tell Mr Besant that this had happened. It was most important that he should see the Director of Peace Studies without delay.

"Oh, by the way," said Ferdie. "Arthur Friendship rang up. He wanted to see you. It is rather embarrassing, really. Shall I tell him you are tied up for the next month?"

"Ask him to the reception," said Mr Besant.

"That's two hundred and thirty-two people," said Ferdie.

"Never mind. The news, if true, is too wonderful for words. It may easily be the last party we shall ever attend."

"You mean this peace pact," said Ferdie. "I thought it might be what you would call a trifle retrogressive."

"Ah yes, the peace pact," said Mr Besant vaguely. "But there is other, even more exciting news to follow it. News which cannot be announced, or even guessed at, because it has not yet happened. By English time, it should occur at about seven-thirty tomorrow evening."

"During the party," said Ferdie. "But shall I say we are celebrating this peace pact? It seems a bit doubtful to me, as nothing has been announced yet. And I can't see why you think it such a good thing."

Mr Besant smiled indulgently.

"It is the most wonderful thing. Can't you see, that if America and Russia sign a pact condemning the use of nuclear weapons, there is nothing to prevent a confrontation in Germany, and once that has started, nothing will prevent the use of nuclear weapons? Similarly, if, as is rumoured, there is a secret clause to the agreement, whereby Russia promises not to interfere in Asia if America promises not to interfere in Europe, then the confrontation is certain."

"Gosh," said Ferdie. "Then you mean there is going to be an end to all this decadence?"

"Exactly."

For the first time, Ferdie began to comprehend the implications of his work. He was by no means certain that he wanted the decadence to end.

"But, I mean, what will we do then?"

"That will be the end of our work. There will be nothing to do at all."

"A lifeless planet, spinning aimlessly in a cloud of radioactive dust around the sun."

"Imagine the peace."

"Are you sure that's what you want?"

Mr Besant looked wistful. "Is there any alternative? There is nothing we can do."

Ferdie busied himself with the invitations. It was as much as his job was worth to be too argumentative. He consoled himself with the reflection that there was no peace pact. He had watched his employer thinking it up one afternoon as they sat together after lunch. It was part of the elaborate dream-world in which Mr Besant lived. Often Ferdie felt sorry for him. Why couldn't they give him his little world war and keep him happy? At other times he resented the uselessness of his occupation. At least, in the advertising offices, he had company.

Later in the afternoon he telephoned Mr Milchiger.

"Mr Besant will be host at a reception tomorrow evening in the Princess Ida Room of the Savoy Hotel. Do you want an invitation?"

"No thank you. It will not be necessary. When will the party end?"

"At about eight o'clock, or quarter past. There was a girl who telephoned for you. Miss Kalugalla."

"Oh yes? Thank you very much, Mr Jacques. You will be adequately rewarded."

Arthur sat in Mrs Quorn's dining room and waited for Ferdie to come home from work. He wished to find out exactly where he stood.

"Hullo Arthur, old cock. What are you doing this evening?"

"I had given no thought to the matter. Will you tell me how you happen to have got the job Mr Besant offered to me?"

"Yes, I wondered if you were going to ask about that." Ferdie put his hand on Arthur's shoulder quite kindly. "I shouldn't take it to heart too much. Mr Besant just happened to prefer me."

"But I hadn't even given him my decision, yet."

"He seemed to think you had. Never mind, old chap. You'll get plenty of other opportunities. Let's spend a night out on the tiles at my expense just to show there are no hard feelings."

"But why did you accept the job, if you knew it had been offered to me?"

"Take it easy. Wouldn't you have?"

In honesty, Arthur had to admit that he would. But then he did not dissimulate to himself that he had any affection or respect for the beatnik. Ferdie's regard for Arthur was supposed to be warmer.

"Come on, let's have a night out together on me. When you're in the money and I'm skint, you can take me out one day."

"All right."

"What girls shall we have?"

Normally, Arthur would have been gravely embarrassed by this question. But he was a changed man.

"What about that girl – you know, what's she called?"

"Liz Pedal? We could ask her, but she's a bit elusive these days. Don't know what's come over her. Still, we could try."

Ferdie telephoned. Liz was terribly sorry, but she was engaged to go out with Martin Starter that evening.

"Well, bring him along, too. That'll make it six of us. It's the celebration for Arthur's escape. You know, Arthur Friendship. Yes, I am in the money these days. Crazy Elephant at eight, then. Long time no see. 'Bye." Ferdie rang off. "Damn. Now I've got to pay for that silly bugger Starter. And find two girls. You leave this to me."

A little while later he came back looking pleased with himself. "Margaret Holly and that girl Susan Tynan we met at the National Gallery. It appears she took a fancy to you, Arthur. It should be quite a party."

Arthur was extremely bad at dancing, and resented it. Both Ferdie and Captain Starter were bad, but they did not seem to mind. Everybody else in the Crazy Elephant danced with effortless and contemptuous ease. Beautiful, sun-tanned girls wriggled deliciously to themselves, yards away from their partners, united

only by the vague consciousness of a shared activity. In between
shuffled Arthur and Susie Tynan, clinging together like kittens in a
litter, through the difficult paces of a quickstep.

"Does it hurt?" said Susie Tynan.

"What?"

"Does it hurt?"

"What hurt?"

"Your face," she screamed.

Just then the music stopped and everybody turned to stare.

"I am sorry, I couldn't hear you," said Arthur embarrassed.

"I was wondering if your face hurt."

"I know, I heard you. Why should my face hurt? I mean, no it
doesn't."

"Oh good. That's all I wanted to know."

The music resumed. Everybody started wriggling again.

"Shall we continue?" said Arthur awkwardly.

"All right."

Arthur took her right hand in his left, held it at right angles to
her shoulders and led her into a foxtrot.

"Oh sorry," said Arthur, when they bumped into a tall, dark
young man in a white shirt.

"What did you say?" asked Susie.

"I was talking to that man over there."

"Oh, do you know him? He looks rather nice."

"No, I don't know him. I was just apologizing for bumping into
him."

"What?"

"Nothing."

They danced in silence for a time, puffing slightly. The lights
were low, and the music became softer. Over Susie's shoulder
Arthur saw that Captain Starter was standing stock still in the
middle of the floor with a pair of lily-slender arms locked around
his neck. Sometimes he thought that Elizabeth Pedal's immorality
went beyond a joke. Without saying a word, he drew Susie Tynan
closer until he could feel the hard lump of her brassiere against his
chest, and insinuated his cheek next to her own.

For a moment, Susie did not seem to realize that anything had happened. Then she remembered the livid malformity of his face and recoiled.

"Isn't it wonderful, here? Such a good band."

"What?"

"Nothing." Susie smiled, as if to indicate enjoyment.

Arthur did not try anything after that, but he allowed a touch of boredom to creep into the way in which he pumped her right hand up and down.

When the music stopped, Susie said: "You know, I think I could do with a coke."

"Yes, let's," said Arthur eagerly, and they returned to their table. Ferdie and Margaret Holly were already there in a tight embrace, lost to the world, and watched suspiciously by a waiter. They disentangled reluctantly.

"I've bought a bottle of Scotch," said Ferdie.

"Gosh, thanks," said Arthur, helping himself.

Arthur and Susie sat with an empty chair between them, contemplating the other two with an indulgent, sentimental regard. They were clearly so very much in love.

"Who was your handsome friend in the white shirt?"

"I don't know him," said Arthur. "I have never seen him before in my life."

"I thought you said 'Hello' to him."

"No."

"I must have been mistaken. I quite like the trumpeter in the blue blazer, don't you?"

"Yes," said Arthur. He could imagine that the trumpeter was probably quite nice.

"Where do you think he comes from?"

"The West Indies?"

"How wonderful. Have you ever been to the West Indies?"

"Do you know, I don't think I have actually."

"Neither have I. Think of all those wonderful people. I should love to go."

Liz Pedal and Martin Starter returned to the table.

"What was that?"

"We were talking about the West Indies, and how much we should love to go there, with all those wonderful people."

Liz met Arthur's eye, and they both coloured slightly in the golden gloom of the candlelight.

"Really?" said Captain Starter. "I used to know one of those coloured chaps at Sandhurst. First-class man at hockey, but, do you know, he could never tell his right foot from his left? Hopeless at drill, of course. That's why none of these African States ever has much of an army. We used to call him Fuzzy Wuzzy, but the staff there knew him as Bingo the Bongo, the big fat Dongo. He didn't mind. I remember one of the colour sergeants shouting right across the parade ground: 'Bongo, you great fat heathen bastard, if you can't start off on your left foot I'm going to cut off the damn black evil-smelling thing and send it to your parents.' The parade collapsed, of course."

Liz laughed extravagantly. Arthur disapproved.

"Was he very fat?"

"Not particularly." Captain Starter thought the question in bad taste. "Mind you, he never learned which foot was which. Must be quite a problem for these emergent nations."

Once Captain Starter had begun his Sandhurst stories, the party was never in danger of flagging. There was Ogilvy-Peacock who paid insufficient attention to personal hygiene, and had to be thrown naked into a cold bath-tub and scrubbed by his platoon-mates.

"That wouldn't be any relation to Angus Ogilvy, would it?" said Arthur.

"Who?"

"You know, Angus Ogilvy."

"I don't know. Might have been." There was Sandy Hargreaves who was a tremendous character and used to attend debutante dances in London every night.

"I wonder if he was any relation to old Don Hargreaves. You know, Lord Hargreaves of Chirtleside."

"Might easily have been." There was Spinky Loofman, a really nasty piece of work, who was suspected of lifting other chaps' valuables from their lockers. So one day all the other chaps got together and confronted him.

"I say, Liz, I wonder if you would like this dance?"

"Sh!"

Spinky could tell something was up as soon as he was summoned to the company mess. He started making excuses and looking shifty. Then, after fair trial, he was found guilty by unanimous verdict of the company and was sentenced to three strokes with a pace stick across the bare buttocks from everyone in the mess who had lost something.

"It was either that or being reported to the Commandant. Our junior under-officer offered him a fair choice. Of course, he chose the easier way out. We bent him across the lockers."

"How perfectly horrible," said Liz.

"Not at all. After that little incident, we didn't hear anything of valuables being lifted from other chaps' lockers," said Captain Starter.

"What happened to him in the end?"

"Oh, he was commissioned all right. I think he was taken by the Signals' Corps."

"Poor man."

"I say, Liz," said Arthur in a slightly louder voice. "I wonder if we could have this dance?"

"All right." Liz glanced at Captain Starter, who was absorbed in his reminiscences. He had greeted Ferdie's bottle of whisky with a cry: "Teacher's. Good-o." Now, he was lost to the world.

The band was playing a particularly hot number. The wrigglers threw each other over their shoulders and crawled underneath each other's legs. Arthur adjusted his foxtrot to the greater intensity of the music by wiggling his behind and doing clever things with his feet. To his gratification, he found that Liz put her arms around his neck. Perhaps she knew no other way of dancing.

"What a terrible story of Martin's about that poor man at Sandhurst."

"Wasn't it awful?" They had to shout to make themselves heard above the music. "I can't see Martin doing things like that, can you?"

"All men are the same when they get together," said Arthur gruffly. "We're all pretty awful swine when you get to know us."

"I'm sure you're not," said Elizabeth.

"Why do you say that? You'd be surprised."

"I'm sure you're not like that. You're much too gentle, Arthur."

Could there be a more obvious declaration of love than that? Elizabeth was looking unbelievably beautiful in the half-light. There was a light in her eyes, and her face shone with serene goodness. Her lovely, golden body was lithe and soft. Arthur wiggled his behind more energetically and twisted his feet around until drops of sweat appeared on his forehead and ran smarting down his face.

In the middle of the dance, he said "Darling Liz," and she laughed. Later he said, "Can I kiss you?"

"What?"

Arthur pushed his face closer, until he was practically touching her cheek. "Can I?" he said, and then his lips were so close that he found himself kissing her warm, fragrant neck.

Liz knew that she must not show revulsion from his terrible deformity. It would be the unkindest thing she could do. She was a brave girl, and a warm-hearted one.

"You are funny," she laughed. "You don't have to ask."

Arthur kissed her again, while the band reached a screeching crescendo and athletic striplings threw themselves all over the floor. As the music stopped, and they drew apart, Arthur felt her lips touch his left cheek, and his happiness knew no bounds.

"Darling Liz. Can I see you again? Tomorrow evening?"

"I'm going to a party organized by Education for Peace."

"So am I. After the party? We could have dinner."

"All right." Arthur never realized the extent to which Liz was consciously embarking on a charitable work. Half his mind thought he had captivated her, while the other half told himself he must be dreaming. "Now we must go back to the others, or they'll wonder what we're doing," she said.

Arthur laughed conspiratorially, and led her back to the table with his arm carelessly around her waist.

Ferdie was deep in conversation with Captain Starter. Margaret Holly and Susie Tynan looked disaffected.

"Don't you think it's getting rather hot in here?" said Holly.

"I think it's past my bed-time," said Tynan.

Arthur said nothing, but gazed at Liz with adoration in his pink-rimmed eyelids.

"Perhaps it is getting rather late," said Liz.

"I'll take you home in a minute," said Captain Starter. "I'm just having rather an interesting conversation with Ferdie."

"The whole idea behind this peace pact is to make it possible to have two world wars going on at once," explained Ferdie. "You see, the Russians want to have a war in Europe, so they can get us out of West Berlin, but they don't want the Americans to come along and blow them up. Similarly, the Americans want to have a war in Asia so that they can sort out the Chinese, but they don't want the Russians to come along and blow them up."

"What's to stop us – the English – dropping our bombs on the Russians."

"Well, we might, in which case everyone gets blown up. That would at least have the advantage of ending all this decadence." Ferdie's wave embraced Arthur, the band, Liz Pedal, the bottle of whisky. Clearly he was finding the evening more expensive than he had catered for. "But I don't think we would dare drop our bombs on Russia first, because they have got far more bombs to drop on us. Also, world opinion wouldn't stand for it. And Russia wouldn't drop its bombs on us first, because that would bring the whole peace pact to an end, and the Americans would be free to blow them up."

"I see," said Captain Starter intelligently. "But I haven't heard of any peace pact. Who says there is one?"

"It is an idea of Mr Besant's," said Ferdie. "We are giving this party to launch it."

"Well, don't expect me to come," said Captain Starter. "I don't like the smell of it at all. Sounds a bit unofficial to me."

Soon afterwards, the party broke up.

"Poor Liz, you look tired. I'll just run you back home," said Captain Starter. Arthur pretended not to notice.

"I'll take Margaret back to her place in a taxi," said Ferdie.

"Well, that leaves us," said Susie Tynan.

Arthur looked embarrassed. "If you would like a lift on the back of my scooter?"

"All right, come on. Pity about your friend. I would like to see more of him."

Arthur drove through the park, round Marble Arch and down the Edgware Road to the dilapidated building where Susie Tynan shared a flat with six other girls.

"Gosh, it's late," he said, as she climbed off the back.

"Well, goodnight," said Arthur.

Susie looked relieved. "You don't want to come in for some coffee or anything? You can if you really want to, but I must say it's very late."

"No thank you," said Arthur. Only as he drove away did he realize that he had just refused an invitation to sexual intercourse. But the reflection did not worry him. A much more important realization was that he was totally, utterly in love with Elizabeth Pedal.

Chapter Fourteen

OF ALL THE PARTIES BEING GIVEN AT THE SAVOY HOTEL ON the night of November 22nd, the one in the Princess Ida Room was easily the gayest. Ferdie had arranged for Mr Besant to be presented with a huge Cheddar cheese in recognition of his work for peace throughout the world. Mr Roland Cleghorn, a well-known literary figure, agreed to make the presentation.

"In presenting this Cheese of Peace, I should like to think that it will remain forever a symbol of mankind's striving against the horrors and cruelties of war. I should like to think of it standing as an eternal flame to remind us of the life's work of such people as Mr Besant and others who by their unselfish sacrifices have ensured that the hot air we breathe now is no longer poisoned by the nuclear gases in our babies' milk.

"My mother often used to say, and I think she was right, that if there were no men on this earth there would be no wars. It is only the men who quarrel and fight and resort to violence. This makes a humbling thought for us men, of course, but I think it is one we should all think of occasionally nevertheless. If we had listened to the women in our midst there would never have been a war in history, and if we listen to them now, there never will be again.

"Fortunately, with the relentless march of progress, women now have a bigger say in our affairs. Mr Besant has manged to rally thousands of people to his cause, many of them women. There are men who resent this state of affairs, saying that women should be kept out of politics, and that a woman's proper place is over the cooking pot. Well, there are two totally different schools of thought, and one should never underestimate the sincerity of either side. For my own part, I have no hesitation in saying where

I stand. It may tread on a lot of toes, and it will certainly make me a great many enemies, but I do not welcome a return to the Victorian era, with its terrible slums, where two out of every three children under the age of four died in childbirth, where the housewife spent all day at the sink and where even the legs of pianos had to be covered up in case they offended anyone's modesty."

Cleghorn's enemies were clearly under-represented that evening. A titter of merriment at this daring sally indicated general approval of the sentiments which had preceded it.

Arthur found himself standing next to Mr Condiment, the Chairman of so many lively magazines. He smiled coldly at the man who murdered the Rev. Cliff Roebuck. Mr Condiment greeted him warmly.

"Isn't it Dr Dorkins?"

"Friendship," said Arthur. "Arthur Friendship. I used to write 'Padre's Hour', also, under the name of Cliff Roebuck."

"Now I've got you," said Mr Condiment, not at all disconcerted by the withering scorn in Arthur's voice. "I've been meaning to have a word with you, Arthur. Could you come round and see me one of these days?"

"All right," said Arthur. He wanted to speak to Mr Besant much more urgently, confident that he could touch the strings of that good man's heart. Ferdie's new prosperity was utterly disgusting. There was even talk of his leaving the room in Ebury Street for a more elegant apartment elsewhere.

"Saturday morning, then. Make it twelve-thirty. I've got a proposition to put to you. I think you will be quite interested."

"All right."

Mr Besant stood up to reply. He had thought of keeping the Cheese of Peace as a memorial to himself, or presenting it to some national institution to preserve, but on second thoughts he had a better idea. Everybody present would be given a Cheese of Peace, he was sorry, he meant a piece of cheese, and what remained would be given to the under-developed nations. He thanked Mr Cleghorn most warmly from the bottom of his heart for the kind words he had uttered. What most struck people who had often watched Mr Cleghorn presenting things, was the sincerity with which he presented them. Insincerity was not something of which Mr Cleghorn could ever be accused, even by his detractors. For his own part, Mr Besant welcomed a fellow campaigner in the cause of Peace.

"One of the greatest dangers facing campaigners in the modern world is the danger of being misunderstood. There was a man once who turned to the other man travelling in the same train compartment and said: 'Do you love Jesus?' The other fellow smiled politely, and replied in excellent English, with only the trace of an accent: 'I *do not know* your English cheesus. But I *lov* our round, red Dutch cheeses!'"

An explosion of laughter greeted this joke. Arthur laughed immoderately, even with a touch of hysteria. As a Christian, he felt that all eyes were upon him to see if he was laughing properly. He did not let the side down. He was no prig. Tristram Catchesyde, the bright young Deputy Features' Editor of *Woman's Dream*, laughed so much that he had to take hold of the person next to him, who happened to be Liz Pedal. She was laughing, too, with happiness shining out of her lovely wide eyes.

Then somebody came in and said that President Kennedy had been assassinated.

"What's that?" said Arthur, madly gay.

"President Kennedy, he's been assassinated in Texas."

"Oh yes? Ha, ha." The person was joking, of course. Then it occurred to him that perhaps it was no joke. Unprepared to commit himself either way, he turned to an old lady who was laughing vacantly beside him.

"Did you hear that?"

"Dutch Jesus. Ha, ha. As if a Dutch Jesus was any different from an English Jesus."

Clearly she was a person of low intellect.

"That President Kennedy is dead. He has been murdered in Texas."

"Gracious me, who's that?"

230

"President Kennedy is the President of the United States."

"I know, but what did you say about his being murdered? Oh dear, poor man. How awful for him. How terrible."

The silly old woman found no difficulty in switching her emotions in an instant from fatuous merriment to sincere grief. Arthur decided that the news was probably true, and adjusted his countenance while his brain tried to work out the implications.

By now, everyone had heard.

"What a terrible act. Who can have done this atrocious thing? He was so young." Could there have been the tiniest hint of insincerity in Mr Besant's voice? Was his reaction just a trifle too glib?

"It has come over the teleprinter in the hotel lounge. They seem to think that it was a white racialist, protesting against Civil Rights."

"How frightful. I can't believe it." Liz was standing with her face in her hands, being comforted by Tristram Catchesyde.

A few people left to watch the tape machine. Mr Besant sat at the end of the room, waiting. Arthur judged that this was not a good moment to approach him about the job. There was a tenseness about the Director of Peace Studies which betrayed the turbulent emotions which must have been aroused.

"Kennedy was mad to go there. He knew that everyone in Dallas was after his blood. All those Americans are mad."

"Poor Jackie," moaned Mr Cleghorn. "How can she face life again? What a miserable thing to happen to a young girl like that." Then the idea came to him for an article. "I think they ought to make her President in his place. Honorary President for Life of the United States. It would go down terribly well with the American women."

Arthur looked at Cleghorn with distaste. It was a ghastly, tragic thing which had happened, and the columnist was trying to put it to his own advantage. If he had been completely honest with himself he would have had to admit that his first reaction on hearing the news was to compose a trenchant homily for the Reverend Cliff Roebuck to deliver on the transience of human existence, addressed to Mrs Kennedy and through her to all women similarly afflicted. Then he remembered that Roebuck was no more, and he was able to abandon himself wholeheartedly to the extravagance of genuine grief.

"That is most unlikely. Women are not allowed to be Presidents of the United States. It is written in the Constitution."

"They could pass an amendment. I think it would be a most touching gesture."

"She would have to be elected."

"Can you doubt that everyone would vote for her, after what has happened?"

"They might easily not. Look at Dallas. Not everyone in America was very keen even on her husband."

"Yes, but only *Honorary* President," pleaded Mr Cleghorn, as if Arthur somehow had the Presidency in his giving. "They couldn't object to that."

"Quiet, everyone, please," said Mr Besant, as if he were talking to two bickering children. "What is the news?"

"He was driving in a motorcade with the Governor of Texas and Jackie. They took him to hospital immediately, and surgeons operated. But there was nothing they could do."

"Yes, but the man. Have they caught the man?" Mr Besant leant forward, an almost hysterical note of anxiety in his voice.

"I don't think so yet. They are hunting for a white racialist with a gun."

"Damn," said Mr Besant. "All those southern policemen are such fools. Has nothing been announced yet about the sort of person they want?"

"Yes. The BBC has just announced that the murder was committed by a member of some right-wing splinter group which believes in segregation, that is to say the separate development of white and black in communities."

"It's not true," said Mr Besant. Rage and disappointment showed in his face. "Someone is suppressing the news. Kennedy was murdered by a Communist, a man just returned from Russia."

"Steady on," said someone. "That would mean world war."

"Of course there will be world war. It is inevitable. But some-one is suppressing the news."

After that, the party began to break up.

"World war? Oh dear, we'd better return and tidy the house."

"Should we get the children up, do you think?"

"No point, really. They wouldn't understand."

Tristram Catchesyde left, looking green and worried. Arthur found himself joined by Liz as he stood talking to Roland Cleghorn.

"The Presidency automatically passed to the Vice-President. That's what the Vice-President is for."

"Who is the Vice-President?" said Mr Cleghorn. "Do you think he will declare war?"

Nobody seemed to know who the Vice-President was.

"There's somebody called Nixon," said Arthur doubtfully.

"Isn't it Adlai Stevenson?" said Mr Cleghorn.

"No, it's Nixon," said Arthur, looking to Liz for support.

"I always thought he was called Nixon," said Liz.

Mr Besant sat alone, shuddering slightly. On the table in front of him loomed the Cheese of Peace, its rind uncut. Once again, Arthur did not judge it prudent to approach him about the job. Liz was standing by his elbow, patient, submissive Liz.

A waiter approached Mr Besant.

"There is a gentleman at the door for you, sir."

"Tell him I'm busy. Can't he see I'm occupied?"

Arthur took Liz by the hand.

"Come on," he said gently. "Let's go and get a bite to eat."

In the corridor outside, they saw a hatchet-faced man talking earnestly to a small group.

"Hello, Johnnie," said Arthur.

"Milchiger. Is the party nearly at an end?"

"Yes. Only a dozen or so people left."

"And Mr Besant will be out soon?"

"No doubt."

"These are my friends. Mr Abba Sapir, Mr Dov Allon, Mr Pinhas Barzilai, Mrs Golda Ben Almogi." Mr Milchiger's friends shook hands with energetic concentration, never allowing a smile to hinder their purpose.

"Terrible news about President Kennedy," said Arthur, by way of small talk.

"Ah, yes," said Mr Milchiger. His mind was on other things.

They dined at the Mirabelle. Over brandy, Arthur said: "Liz, I love you terribly. I have literally loved you from the moment I set eyes on you."

"How sweet," said Liz. It really was very sweet, however unattractive he was. Despite her radiant beauty, few people had ever told Liz they loved her. Perhaps the gaucheness of modern youth was responsible. Occasionally she worried about her state, but not often. No doubt she would marry one day, but nobody had ever asked her, and she was not particularly worried. Ferdie, in a sarcastic moment, had once summed up her philosophy: "Never put off until tomorrow what can reasonably be put off until the day after." She always took the line of least resistance, and so lived a charmed life.

"Darling Liz, I love you so much I can't bear to see you unhappy. Obviously you have been terribly upset by Kennedy's death."

"It was a bit sudden," said Liz. In fact, she had not been thinking of Kennedy at all, but she felt an unaccountable depression. Perhaps it was Arthur's earnestness, or his unattractiveness, or the excessively rich food he had forced down her throat.

"Did you know that I loved you?" said Arthur.

"Sh! You're shouting. All the other tables are listening."

"No they're not. I don't know if it's your beauty or the way you look."

"Sh! For Heaven's sake."

"Poor Liz. You're terribly upset about Kennedy. Would you like to come back to my flat and listen to some records?"

"It's terribly sweet of you, Arthur, but it's getting rather late."

"I'll drive you back."

Piccadilly was a silver cloud, and Arthur's Lambretta a magic carpet as Liz clung to his back. When they arrived at Iverna Terraces, Arthur said:

"Can I come in with you, just for tonight. Darling Liz, I love you."

"It's terribly sweet of you, Arthur, but it's terribly late. Don't you think we could leave it, just for this time? I mean, it does seem a bit callous, so soon after Kennedy's death, doesn't it?"

"All right, darling. But remember what I've said."

He kissed her on the cheek, and drove away with a devil-may-care swagger. Liz climbed the fourteen flights of steps to her flat, much relieved.

Mr Besant sat alone in the room called Princess Ida, his face buried in his hands. A waiter sympathetically removed the ash-tray.

"There's a gentleman waiting for you outside, sir."

"I will see him in a minute."

Even the greatest men suffer moments of total despair. If Mr Besant's had been a more resilient nature, he would have acknow-ledged a minor set-back and returned to the humble round of his life's work – organizing peaceful expeditions to the Egg Marketing Board's warehouses in Slough, demonstrations in Trafalgar Square, round-robins to *The Times*, meetings with important Negroes – but he was not such an one. When ascetism gives way to self-indulgence, it becomes a debauch. Mr Besant wallowed in his despair, just as he used to wallow in Sieglinde's predicament when, eloping with her brother in "The Valkyrie", she must watch him slain by her husband through Wotan's intervention. Never since the early days of the Bayreuth festival in his youth had Mr Besant felt such a turbulence of emotion. In a melodramatic gesture he raised his fist and brought it crashing down on the huge Cheddar cheese which loomed mockingly in front of him. But the Cheese of Peace was solidly constructed and did not yield a millimetre.

The pain and the futility of this dumb-show brought him

momentarily to his senses. It was still possible that when the identity of the assassin became known, public indignation would demand a reprisal. If not, there was always hope. Perhaps another crisis comparable to Cuba would so frighten America's European allies that they would withdraw from the alliance. Then retribution would follow as night follows day. For the rest, he must return to the humble line of duty which led, by inexorable processes, to the egg warehouses in Slough.

Standing up from his seat, Mr Besant shook off the egoistical pleasures of despair as a terrier shakes water from its coat. While there was a breath in his body he would never betray the master to whom he had pledged his loyalty nor the ideals by which he had lived through twenty years in the wilderness.

There were people to be seen, letters to be written. No doubt Arthur Friendship was waiting for him to discuss the next course of studies. With a benign smile to a waiter, and the affable stoop of a kindly, distinguished English gentlemen on his face, Mr Besant strode into the wide corridor which leads past the Princess Ida room to the Pirates of Penzance, the Gondoliers, Iolanthe, down some stairs to the Thames Embankment.

The story of what happened next has always been obscure. Besides the participants, the only witness was a Turkish Cypriot cloakroom attendant, whose account became more garbled with the re-telling. In fact, there was no confusion and every detail of the complicated operation proceeded without a hitch.

When Mr Besant appeared, a hatchet-faced man behind the door called a name softly.

"Baudenbach. Herr Baudenbach, there are some friends of yours waiting for you here."

Involuntarily, with the mention of that long-unremembered name, Mr Besant turned round. Immediately, the four members of Teyve Milchiger's squad sprang into action. Allon and Sapir pinioned his arms. While Mr Pinhas Barzilai drew back his head, Mrs Ben Almogi took from her handbag a wad of cotton wool which had been soaked in chloroform. Milchiger seized his legs. In under forty-five seconds he was carried down some stairs, through a revolving door, past a doorman who touched his hat, and into the cold, wet air of the Embankment. A taxi-cab was waiting which drove off as soon as they were inside it. Within two minutes they were across Blackfriars Bridge and lost in the gloomy maze of London South of the Thames.

No doubt it was the caustic action of chloroform, inexpertly applied against the skin, which accounted for the scar on the face of the prisoner when he appeared in Tel-Aviv under the name of Walther Baudenbach, shortly afterwards to answer charges of crimes against the Jewish people. Certainly, he had been intensively questioned, but it was no part of defence counsel's case that he had been maltreated in any way since his capture. And when the catalogue of his crimes against humanity became known, few people bothered to enquire further into the cause of a minor disfigurement.

The rest of his story belongs to history – how, after a trial lasting three months, the jury found him personally responsible for the murder of over eight hundred thousand Jews, gypsies and physically malformed people in Poland between April 1944 and February 1945; how he shared in guilt for the death of some sixty thousand others; how, after an unsuccessful appeal, he went to his death straight-backed and proud, shouting incomprehensible Nazi slogans.

But all this belonged to the future on the night of November 22nd 1963, when Arthur Friendship returned to his lodgings in Ebury Street radiant in the knowledge of love requited. At that moment, the monster Baudenbach was sitting trussed like a turkey in a bed-sitting room in South London, watched by a beautiful, sloe-eyed Sinhalese girl sadly combing her hair.

Arthur had no reason to doubt that his love was returned. His instinct told him so, and it was not in his nature to question the infallibility of his instinct. He only slightly regretted the clumsy attempt to seduce Elizabeth. She had shown that his regard was not entirely sentimental, and instinct suggested that this assurance might have been necessary. On the whole, he had behaved masterfully.

But it was undoubtedly a degradation of his love to imagine that he would behave to Elizabeth as he had to the girl Lesley in Kitchener Drive. The two things were entirely different. He began to wonder if his love for Elizabeth Pedal could only find true consummation inside the marriage bond. The notion sounded strait-laced and puritanical at first, but the more one considered it the more voluptuous it became. They would enjoy the freedom to make love whenever the spirit moved them at any hour of the day or night. There would be no need to buy cripplingly expensive meals before each furtive embrace on a narrow divan bed disguised to look like a sofa.

Weighing the Christian practice in sexual matters against the modern, Arthur decided that purely in terms of pleasure afforded, Christianity won hands down. It was true that the modern approach offered greater variety, but it was also much more expensive, and in his present state of infatuation Arthur could imagine no possible benefit to be derived from variety. It was then that he decided to marry Elizabeth Pedal.

The step was not without obvious difficulties. So far as wooing was concerned Arthur decided that to all intents and purposes she was already wooed and won, but there were grave practical problems. Since the death of 'Padre's Hour', Arthur could rely on a regular income of only fourteen pounds a week. Furthermore, there was a distinct threat to Dr Dorkins, which would reduce his income by a further eight pounds. The money he received from Peace Studies was scarcely enough for two people.

If only he could have spoken to Mr Besant. Arthur was confident in the justice of his Director, but he had an uneasy feeling that the longer he delayed, the less likely he was to be given Ferdie's job as Personal Assistant.

The only alternative was to write a book. He would dedicate it of course, to Elizabeth Pedal. The more he thought about the idea, the better it seemed. The dedication would read something like this:

The novel would centre around a beautiful girl with brilliant, laughing eyes and skin like that of a Madonna by the younger Lippi. She would be called Sarah Petal. There were three conflicts in the life of Sarah Petal – no, four. All four men were in love with her, according to their respective fashions. One of them, M'Bongo, was a Negro of African descent who wrote poetry. Sarah was sorry for him and anxious to improve race relations at a critical time. Another, called Captain Carruthers, was a young officer in the Intelligence Corps. Sarah admired him for his swagger and because she thought it might be rather manly to be in the Army. The third, Dickie Schulz, was more of a beatnik type, with vague artistic pretensions and a beard. He intrigued Sarah, who had never met his type before. Finally, there was Julian Dinsdale, a writer. Julian was a difficult chap to get to know – withdrawn, almost aloof. This was because he was a writer, and terribly sensitive.

M'Bongo is discredited when he tries to rape her. She soon sees through the pretensions of Dickie Schultz, when he reveals that he has no regular source of income and relies for his living on occasional presents from a rich, middle-aged woman whom he visits in the Ritz. Captain Carruthers is revealed to be a coward during an episode in a dance hall involving some Teddy boys, or Rockers.

So Sarah decides that all along she has much preferred the quiet, unpushing maturity of Julian Dinsdale, and they are married.

Alternatively, being more realistic, M'Bongo dies through being eaten by crocodiles during a swim in the Limpopo after a tribal dance; Captain Carruthers is squashed to death by a tank in particularly poignant circumstances; Dickie Schultz's death is too horrible to contemplate. His beard becomes entangled in some machinery, and he is dragged into the giant mixer of an ice-cream machine.

"But Mr Friendship," the television interviewer might reasonably say: "I notice you have a great many deaths in your book. Is this not a trifle uncompassionate?"

"Not at all," Arthur could reply. "Surely, death is one of the great things which is happening around us all the time. Even during this television programme, I dare say that two or three people have died while watching their sets. It must be a considerable responsibility for you television people to be present vicariously at so many deathbed scenes every evening."

After Julian and Sarah's wedding, the days of their honeymoon go by and nothing happens. Occasionally, perhaps, they feel that things are not complete, but their new-found happiness in each other's company is so great as to smooth over the worried cracks on the surface.

Then one day, walking by the sea-shore, Julian finds a baby drowning and rescues it. Afterwards, in their bedroom, Sarah says:

"That's a funny thing, you know, Julian. I never knew you liked children before."

"Oh, yes, I've always liked children. As a matter of fact, I was rather thinking of having a family of my own one day."

The words are said casually but their effect is instantaneous. With eyelids langorous of desire, Sarah falls into his arms.

The thought of Elizabeth Pedal falling into his arms under such circumstances was too delicious to be entertained without risk of sin, and Arthur hastened on.

Afterwards, when their love is at last complete, Sarah says with a light laugh:

"You silly gump. Why didn't you tell me earlier?"

Julian kisses her lightly on the brow. "Perhaps I was a bit silly. I didn't want to rush you."

Only when the excitement of creation had died down did Arthur reflect that it would take him at least four months to write the book. He could not propose marriage to Elizabeth on the prospects of an unwritten novel. Everything depended on his interview with Mr Condiment.

Chapter Fifteen

"HOW DID YOU JUSTIFY THE DEATH OF EIGHT HUNDRED thousand people, Herr Baudenbach?"

"I realized, possibly before others, that the greatest threat to world peace and living standards lay in what is now known as the population explosion. The world is simply producing more people than it can support. If we are to survive there must be drastic action. We believed – and this is really the only point on which we differed from modern thinkers – that such action should be selective."

"But why did you pick upon the Jews, Herr Baudenbach? What made them the particular objects of your hatred."

"I have never hated the Jews. Many of my best and closest friends were Jewish, and it was with the greatest sorrow that I saw them conveyed to the gas-chambers. The reason for the choice is obvious. It is no part of racial bigotry, which I detest, to state the historical fact that in Germany during the middle of this century, Jews were engaged in which might be called the middle-man trades to a very large extent. In other words, they were economic parasites. Even if one disregards the moral aspects of allowing an entire class of people to batten on the labours of the productive worker without adding one whit to the gross national product, we accepted that in terms of efficiency alone they were a drag on the national productive effort. Words like "gross national product" and "national productive effort" are cold ones, and unlikely to win sympathy for any cause, but if you translate them into terms of living standards, old age pensions and social security benefits, you will see that by extending the public sector to include the means of distribution and supply, we were, in fact, struggling towards the goal of all progressive politics, which is the greatest happiness for the greatest number of people."

"But Herr Baudenbach, it is surely not true that all Jews were employed unproductively? There were doctors, chemists, school-teachers, diamond cutters, men in all trades among your victims."

"I know, but you must remember that we were innovators. It was not realistically possible to separate all the wheat from the chaff, although we did our best. There were methods of selection all along the line, until finally in the camps themselves an attempt was made to preserve those still capable of productive labour. If we had been working under ideal conditions, and in peace time, we could have avoided these anomalies. But you cannot make a cake without breaking eggs."

"You claim that your purpose was not the extermination of a race?"

"Indeed I do. Of course, it was necessary to pay lip-service to crude emotions of anti-semitism. The people demanded it. But that was merely the package in which our scheme for the optimization of society was wrapped. It was an historical accident that the axe fell upon the Jews. Our real aim was to eliminate the work-shy, the incompetent, the unproductive elements in society and thus make the world a better place to live in."

"And there would have been room for the Jews inside this ideal society?"

"There would have been room for anybody who was not an enemy of the community."

In the air-conditioned long bar of the Dan Hotel, journalists crowded together between sessions to escape from the scorching, liquid Tel-Aviv sun.

"You must say this for him, he does speak up for himself."

"Hanging is much too soft for him. He should be tortured to death in public."

"Perhaps he should be put in a museum."

"There's not much point in keeping him in prison, as he'll never be able to get up to an more trouble."

"He could be a controversial sort of television personality. Every time he appeared on the box, some ordinary, intelligent type could stand up and put the opposite case, showing how wrong he was. Then people could make up their minds for themselves, and they wouldn't be tempted into his way of thinking."

The general opinion, however, was that he should be re-educated.

"That's the most humane solution, but what would we teach him to believe instead?"

.

"We always put social progress before any other considerations," said Baudenbach. "Our aim was to create a world without poverty, suffering or discomfort. Many people who approve of this aim are shy of the measures necessary to bring it about. They talk piously of voluntary contraception as a solution, but even if there was the remotest possibility of its making any contribution to the world population explosion in the next twenty years, it would not be desirable because it is unselective. Among the smaller numbers of children born you would have the same proportion of incompetents, people unable to take their place in the sophisticated industrial economy which is a pre-requisite for improvement. Furthermore, in the case of voluntary contraception, it is likely that those individuals most ready to accept it would be those most qualified by intelligence and education to breed children, and the total result would be a greater preponderance of incompetents producing more squalor, filth and misery than before. For a time, we imagined that selective sterilization could be introduced on a compulsory basis, but experience showed us that this produced discontent and inefficiency. When our purpose is to create a world of complete happiness, clearly any measure which makes for unhappiness is not to be countenanced. It would take an absurdly long time to re-educate all those individuals by whose sterilization the world family would benefit into a state of mind where they welcomed sterilization. Many are probably ineducable. No, the only solution to the problem of over-population must lie in selective thinning. If this thinning is undertaken humanely and efficiently, it will remove the root of all the misery in the world."

"Herr Baudenbach, does it never occur to you that many people might find such mass extermination immoral?"

"By what standards would it be immoral? No human suffering is involved. The transition from life to lifelessness would not even be noticed by those concerned. The world would be a far happier place to live in. There would be no poverty, no dishonesty, no squalor, no stupidity. By what standards do you call this immoral?"

"It was your intention to introduce this order of things when you supervised the killing of eight hundred thousand Jews?"

"They were not all Jews. There were gypsies, congenitally deformed and mentally retarded people, also. Yes, that was my intention twenty-one years ago, and when I worked for the National Socialist Government before the war. No human institutions are perfect, and there was much that was crude and repulsive in the methods we used. But at least I could feel that there was a purpose, that we were all working for an ideal. In time, perhaps, our methods would have improved, and our dynamic programme of social engineering could have proceeded in laboratory conditions. But in war-time, that was not possible. I apologize to you for that, gentlemen. Nobody regrets so much as myself the evidence which prosecuting counsel will show you in the form of photographs taken in the various camps under my direction. They illustrate cases of bungling and callousness which would be quite inexcusable outside the very special conditions of war-time."

"Have you made any attempts to proceed with this programme since the collapse of your Government in 1945?"

"No. When I saw that the cause was lost beyond any hope of redemption my first instinct, I am ashamed to say, was for survival. This was easier for me than for many of my colleagues. From Poland I was able to make my way into Switzerland even before the war was officially over. I had made a few arrangements there already, but I was fortunate in the good offices of an old friend from my student days who secured me a post on the League of Nations Committee for the suppression of the Slave Traffic. I have always felt extremely strongly against this appalling trade. It is the denial of everything I have ever believed in – human dignity, the right to happiness and social progress. As a humanist, I found my time profitably occupied. Then, as I realized increasingly the extent to which post-war events obviated any possibility of the eventual amelioration of mankind in which I had always believed, I determined on an entirely different course of action, and joined the newly-formed United Nations Organization."

"Would you like to describe this new course of action on which you decided, Herr Baudenbach?"

Here there was an interruption from defence counsel. Baudenbach had the good fortune to be represented by Dr Isidore Carpathius. Perhaps that wily old lawyer had an inkling from his conversations with the prisoner. As a result, the question was withdrawn as irrelevant, and nobody learned what Mr Baudenbach's intentions had been in the last twenty years of his life.

The only person in whom the prisoner had ever confided was called Ferdinand Jacques, an obscure out-of-work advertising executive who lived in London. Ferdie sometimes tried to remember conversations between himself and Mr Besant, but his memory was coloured by subsequent events to such an extent that his testimony would have been worthless even had it been coherent.

Mr Condiment kept Arthur waiting for three-quarters of an hour on the Saturday morning of their appointment, but Arthur never regretted his patience.

"Come on in, Arthur. Very good of you to come and see me. I've a little proposition to put to you. If you don't like it, tell me at once and I'll stop."

Arthur allowed him to continue.

246

"We've reached a position in *Woman's Dream* where one either has to stay stuck in the mud or move forward. As you may know, I've instituted a few editorial changes recently, and Mr Carpenter is co-operating with me in producing an entirely new format. Now what we want is bright and dynamic young blood with just enough experience for an entirely new position we're creating on the magazine. I was discussing the matter with Carpenter, without giving him any details of the job, of course, and as soon as he heard what it was about, he suggested your name. Now, the question is, are you interested?"

Arthur indicated that he was interested.

"Briefly the position is this. You will be in charge of an entirely new feature I've just thought up. Needless to say, the salary will be commensurate with the responsibility. It seems to me that a great many young housewives nowadays are taking an interest in things beyond the weekly wash and nappy returns. I may be wrong, but it is a hunch. Do you follow me?"

Yes, Arthur followed him.

"Now one of the things which interests them is how they can make their lives more interesting, exciting, alive. Right?"

"Yes."

"Of course this sort of thing needs pretty dynamic treatment if it's to cut much ice. That's why we brought you in, Arthur. We need someone with a new approach; compassionate without being sentimental. Above all, someone who can write English as women like to read it. See what I mean, Arthur?"

"Yes." Everything depended on this interview. If it meant a steady, well-paid job, he could marry Elizabeth Pedal and explore the unimaginable delights of her body whenever the inclination took him for the rest of their mortal lives. If no job was forthcoming, it meant the miserable, solitary existence of a bachelor in a bed-sitter for the rest of his life. It was even doubtful whether he would be able to stay in Ebury Street. "What sort of job did you have in mind?"

Mr Condiment paused. "Fifteen hundred a year. 'Pets' Corner'," he said.

With scarcely a moment's hesitation, Arthur's eyes lit up and he beamed.

"I think I could manage that, sir."

"Good. We'll start on Monday morning. Come round and see Mr Carpenter. He'll fix you up with an office and a telephone. You'll probably need a secretary too."

They shook hands, and Arthur bounded down the stairs like a schoolboy.

"Liz? It's me, Arthur. I've got something terribly important I want to talk to you about. Can I come round and see you?"

"Arthur? What on earth do you want to talk about?"

"I'll explain when I'm with you. I've just had the most wonderful news. Can I come round?"

"All right, I suppose so. You'd better not stay long though, as I've got to be somewhere else later this afternoon."

She wouldn't mind how long he stayed when she heard what he had to say. With a happy smile Arthur climbed on his motor scooter and set off down Holborn towards Iverna Terraces.

Chapter Sixteen

SATURDAY AFTERNOON WAS ALWAYS THE CLIMAX OF THE week for the Mlinoblecs. After Herbert had closed down the shutters of his small drapery shop in Hounslow, he returned to the bosom of his family for a light lunch in their flat in Gunnersbury before setting off on the afternoon's treat. This was the reward for his week of labour, and his wife's relaxation from all the trials of housework. For the two children, these weekly sorties were to be their most vivid memories of an idyllic childhood, prosperous, loved and secure.

"Is everything ready?" asked Herbert, when the plates had been cleared away.

"I have not yet got my fur, and Millicent seems to have lost one of her gloves. We shall not be a moment," said his devoted wife, Mary.

"Is the Zeph clean?"

Mrs Mlinoblec and her fourteen-year-old daughter Millicent spent the morning polishing Zeph until she shone like a Guardsman's boot. Nothing was ever allowed to disturb the tranquil passage of Saturday afternoon.

"Tunk, tunk" went the doors. Herbert's heart thrilled to the sound. A touch on the self-starter, and their Saturday afternoon had commenced.

Mary and Herbert sat in front, their backs as straight as Prussian cavalrymen. Charles, their only son, slouched behind, looking sarcastically out of the window. Next to him sat Millicent, extremely respectable in a blouse which served as the aggressive declaration of womanhood latent under her stout frame. She wore nothing on her head but the frizzy pale hair with which nature endowed her, and looked, as her father often remarked, as pretty as a picture. Her back was as straight as a plank, and her hands rested in a muff upon her homely lap.

"Mind the turning," said Mary. "Where are we going?"

There were four possible routes for their afternoon drive. Herbert always decided which they would take. Where Zeph was concerned, he was lord and master. Zeph was his especial toy, and the only rival to Mary for Mr Mlinoblec's affections. Throughout the week, she slept in a garage, lovingly wrapped in plastic. Then on Saturday morning she emerged, chariot fit for a sun god.

"West End," said Herbert.

"How lovely," said Mary. "I wonder if they'll have the Christmas decorations up in Regent Street. Mind that bicyclist, dear."

They drove for a time in silence. Zeph's mighty engine, capable of a hundred miles an hour, purred contentedly along at twenty. Mr Mlinoblec had never been known to drive faster than twenty-five.

"Oo, I think there's a zebra crossing," said Mary. She was absolutely right. After opening the window and performing complicated hand-signals, Mr Mlinoblec stopped. Nobody wanted to cross the road. They drove on.

"Lucky you spotted that one, Mary. You never know where they're going to put those crossings next. It's that madman at the Ministry of Transport. He'd make the whole of England a zebra crossing if he got his way."

Herbert's language was more violent than usual when he was at the wheel of Zeph. Mrs Mlinoblec, while always keeping a wary eye on the road, approved.

"I think there's a post van trying to pass you, Dad."

"Thanks, son." Herbert pulled into the side of the road. When the van had passed, he said: "Let him kill himself if he wants to."

As they proceeded down Chiswick High Road, Herbert became calmer.

"Which way are we going, then, Herbert? Kensington High Street or Cromwell Road?"

"Cromwell Road is quicker," said Charles.

"I shouldn't mind another look at the Albert Hall."

"Your mother used to play the 'cello, once, in the Albert Hall."

"The Cromwell Road is much quicker."

"Which is it to be, then, Herbert?"

"We shall manage to do both. Leave it to me."

"Mind this roundabout dear. You never know what they're going to do at Hammersmith next."

Mr Mlinoblec always minded the Hammersmith roundabout. He drove cautiously at five miles an hour, his face set in rigid disapproval.

A grey Ford Cortina drew past.

"Phew," said Millicent. "I thought that one was going to hit us."

Cromwell Road was only slightly less hazardous.

"Do you remember the war, Mary, when bombs were falling all around us? I often think these days are just as bad. Worse, really, because there's more bad manners."

"The West End," said Millicent rapturously as they passed the West London Air Terminal. It was moments such as this which made life worth living.

"We can't stay too long today," said her father. "You get all sorts coming up for the Christmas shopping. Many of them are from the country, and none of them can drive."

On the junction of Gloucester Road and Queen's Gate, Mr Mlinoblec's plan became clear.

"If I drive up here, we will all be able to see the Albert Hall on our right at the top as we drive past."

"I must say, it's lucky you know your way round London," said Mary. "Look where your Dad's taking us to."

With infinite caution, Zeph carried them safely past the Natural History Museum and the Imperial College of Science. It was just as they were drawing level with the Commonwealth Institute that the ghastly thing occurred which was completely to ruin their Saturday afternoon's excursion.

Herbert reckoned that his speed was between twelve and fifteen miles an hour when it happened. He was neither overtaking nor looking for a place to park. If there was any culpability for the tragedy, it must have rested on the party which suffered the worst consequences.

There was a shriek of brakes being applied; then a sickening, splintering crash which pushed Zeph forward with a jerk.

Herbert stopped his car and got out.

"Help. What has happened. Will somebody tell me what has happened?"

"I think there may have been a slight accident. Don't take on so, Mother. Dad's dealing with it."

"It's a motor cyclist," said Charles, peering out of the back window. "He's lying on the road and Dad's trying to talk to him."

Elizabeth Pedal waited until half-past three, wondering what Arthur wished to discuss. She was a kind girl and kindness did not allow her to snub anyone so pathetically vulnerable. It is possible that if his already unattractive features had not been further marred by a disfigurement, she would have warned him off in brusquer terms. As it was, she felt it her duty to talk to him, if he wanted. Misfortune placed an obligation on the fortunate.

When the telephone rang, she supposed that it would be Arthur putting her off. There were no other engagements – earlier, she had invented one as a defensive weapon – but it was most inconvenient being kept in all afternoon.

It was Tristram Catchesyde.

"Tristram, darling. How lovely to hear from you. Yes, I think I'm free this evening. Wait a minute, I'll check up. Ballet at Covent Garden? Of course I'd love to. No, I don't know *Marguerite and Armand*, I don't think. Nureyev? How super. And Fonteyn. I could come round straight away to your flat if you liked. Then you could tell me all about it. Yes, well I was waiting for someone actually, but he's obviously not going to turn up. I'll be straight round."

Nobody knows when Arthur Friendship died. The exact timing is of little historical importance. Certainly, he was pronounced dead on arrival at hospital.

He achieved a measure of immortality as a unit in the figure for road deaths produced annually by the office of the Registrar General. There he may still be found among the 6,921 other people who suffered a similar fate in 1963. No farther seek his merits to disclose or draw his frailties from their dread abode.

Within half an hour, the wreck of his motor-scooter was taken away. Broken glass was swept up. A small pool of blood on the hard, cold surface of Queen's Gate was covered with sand. Nobody passing the spot an hour later would have had any reason to suspect that a tragedy had occurred.

But nothing could alter the fact that the Mlinoblec's Saturday afternoon had been completely spoiled.

THE END

CHILTON FOLIAT, 1965